PRAISE FOR JOHNNY SHAW

PRAISE FOR *DOVE SEASON:* A JIMMY VEEDER FIASCO

Winner of the 2012 Spotted Owl Award for Debut Mystery

"[Johnny Shaw] is excellent at creating a sense of place with a few deft strokes . . . He moves effortlessly between dark comedy and moments that pack a real emotional punch, and he's got a knack for off-kilter characters who are completely at home in their own personal corners of oddballdom."

—Tana French, author of *The Trespasser*

"Johnny Shaw calls *Dove Season* a Jimmy Veeder Fiasco, but I call it a whole new ball game; I enjoyed this damn book more than anything else I read this year!"

—Craig Johnson, author of the Walt Longmire mystery series

"*Dove Season* is dark and funn
and a setting as vivid as a scorp
is a welcome new voice. I'm alr

—Sean Doolittle, Thrill

PRAISE FOR *BIG MARIA*

Winner of the 2013 Anthony Award for Best Paperback Original

"Comic thrillerdom has a new star."

—Starred Review, *Booklist Online*

"This is one you'll soon be recommending to your friends. It's lighthearted but not lightweight, funny as hell but never frivolous. Shaw writes like the bastard son of Donald Westlake and Richard Stark: There's crime, and criminals, but there's also a deep vein of good humor that makes Shaw's writing sparkle. Combine that with his talent for creating memorable characters (the supporting cast, including a mute, severed head, often threatens to steal the show), and you get one of the best reads in recent memory, an adventure story that might just make you mist up every once and awhile, especially during the book's moving finale."

—*Mystery Scene* Magazine

"Funny, fist-pumping, rockin, right-on, righteous fun."

—Barnes & Noble Mystery Blog

"Shaw has invented 'dust bowl' fiction for the twenty-first century. Funny, sad, madcap, compulsively readable, and ultimately, so very, very wise."

—Blake Crouch, author of the Wayward Pines Trilogy

"Johnny Shaw has an incredible talent for moving from darkness to hope, from heart-wrenching to humor, and from profane to sacred. His latest, Big Maria, is an adventure story that's equal parts Humphrey Bogart and Elmore Leonard, with just a little bit of the Hardy Boys thrown in. I loved every page."

—Hilary Davidson, author of *Evil in All Its Disguises*

"I loved every page of Big Maria. You don't often read a gutbustingly funny book that manages to maintain its fundamental seriousness and badass sense of plot. This proves what many of us suspected after Dove Season, that Johnny Shaw is one of the majors already."

—Scott Phillips, author of *The Ice Harvest*

IMPERIAL VALLEY

OTHER TITLES BY JOHNNY SHAW

The Jimmy Veeder Fiascos

Dove Season

Plaster City

Imperial Valley

Novels

Big Maria

Floodgate

JOHNNY SHAW

IMPERIAL VALLEY

A JIMMY VEEDER FIASCO

Published by Thomas & Mercer, Seattle

www.apub.com

ISBN-13: 9781503941298
ISBN-10: 1503941299

Cover design by Jason Blackburn

Printed in the United States of America

For Roxanne

I fucking love you.

The locations depicted in this novel combine both fictional and real places. While Holtville, El Centro, Calexico, Mexicali, and Mazatlán do exist, the real towns and cities bear little resemblance to the ones in this book, beyond shared locations on a map.

As I've stated in previous works, a hometown is like a younger brother. You can tease him, knock him around, and give him a hard time, but you'll always love him and stand up for him. I might take some liberties and do some name-calling, but this novel was written with the greatest respect and admiration for the people of Mexico and the Imperial Valley.

PART ONE

ONE

The last thing I saw before the onion sack went over my head was a purple velvet cummerbund that looked like someone had skinned the Grimace to make it.

Tuxedos Gutierrez in Mexicali might be a fine formal-wear establishment, but violent abductions usually have a negative effect on endorsements. I could already see my Yelp review. "Two stars. While I appreciated the bilingual clerks and the large selection of formal cowboy hats and nonruffled dress shirts, the transaction would have been more satisfactory without the grabbing-me-from-behind-and-taking-me-against-my-will monkey business. Ample parking."

When the burlap went over my head, it caught me completely off guard. The second that I froze was all my abductors needed to force my hands behind my back and zip-tie them. Efficient bastards.

I managed to say "Gwaa—?" Or "Fwaa—?" It's hard to be certain. Not that it mattered. I definitely didn't get a whole word out before a duct-tape gag was wrapped around my head from outside the bag. It forced the coarse material into my mouth, the taste of onions on my tongue.

I stomped my boot behind me, feeling my abductor's foot crunch under my heel. A muffled yell. The hands on my arms loosened. I kicked again, scraping shin and knee. Twisting my body, I wrenched myself free and blindly ran forward.

Vaguely remembering the layout of the store, I tried for the front door. Sleeves of jackets brushed against my bound arms as I weaved and ran past. I stumbled into a rack of clothes, flailing at the pants that surrounded me. I turned, braining myself on a metal rack and spilling onto the ground. I thought I heard someone laugh.

I gave up on running. Instead, I took a defensive position that I had called the "Turtle" in grade school. It consisted of spinning on my back and kicking my legs wildly. Kung fu by way of Curly from the Three Stooges. I probably looked like an uncoordinated breakdancer. Come at me and I'll Gymkata your shit.

Unfortunately, there are very good reasons why the Turtle isn't taught in reputable martial arts classes. It proved as ineffective as an adult as it had on the playground. I got beat up a lot when I was a kid.

Strong hands lifted me by the elbows and shoulders. Two people, one on each side. I kicked some more, but they leaned me back at a forty-five-degree angle and my legs couldn't bend in their direction. They dragged me across the floor and out the back door. We continued another twenty or thirty yards through the alley, my heels sliding in the gravel. A van door opened. They lifted me inside onto the cold metal of the van floor. Even past the odor of onions, the van smelled familiar, like a taco truck operated by gun-toting alcoholics. Cooked meat and stale beer and gun oil.

The van door closed, capping part one of my inaugural Mexican abduction.

Tuxedos Gutierrez had been my last errand of the day, my final stop in Mexicali before I headed home. I had been so focused on my shopping that I hadn't seen the signs of trouble. My spider-sense had tingled walking into the store, but I had ignored it. It wasn't a full duck-for-cover moment, but more of a hairs-on-the-back-of-my-neck feeling. I should have listened to my instincts.

In my defense, it wasn't rare for a couple of shady-looking Mexican guys to give me the hairy eyeball when I was in Mexicali. I was a gringo in Mexico. I figured that the two young guys across the street from the tux shop were garden-variety street toughs. The big guy at the wheel of the primer-gray pickup sat with his arm draped over the side mirror. A scar ran from the corner of his eye down to his cheek. His buddy leaned on the front fender with his arms across his chest. Tattoo sleeves on both arms, two teardrops on his face. Focused stares on me as I entered the store.

The thing was, Mexicali wasn't Ciudad Juarez or Tijuana or some of the more fucked-up places that have been turned upside down by the drug trade. Mexicali had grown more dangerous since the days of my youth, but not war-zone bad. For all the horror stories that came out of Mexico, it was mostly a place where regular people did regular things. Living lives, working jobs, and raising families.

I stupidly held on to the fallacy that if I wasn't looking for trouble, I wasn't going to find any. I was a farmer, after all.

Deep down, I knew that was bullshit. I had always been a shit-magnet. It was who I was. I should have expected the possibility of an abduction. Hell, I should have planned for it and brought my own, more comfortable restraints.

My captors didn't speak. Spanish play-by-play of a soccer game blasted through scratchy speakers. After twenty minutes of sliding around the back of the van, we came to a stop. When the van door opened, I felt the heat of the day but heard only quiet. We weren't in the city anymore. Which meant we were in the desert. Which was not good.

Nothing positive has ever happened when a person was bound and gagged in the middle of the desert.

I would only hurt myself if I attempted to fight or run. I let my body go slack. No reason to cooperate. They could carry my lazy ass. Maybe one of these assholes would throw out his back lifting me. That would show him.

They picked up my limp body, immediately dropping me on the ground, lifting me back up, and then dropping me again. Either I got the Mexican Jerry Lewises of kidnapping or they were violently protesting my nonviolent protest.

With my back held against what felt like a wooden post, the two men secured me at the chest, legs, and neck. I stood rigid and immobile. From behind, someone removed the gag and sack from my head.

Squinting into the bright sun, I saw no one. My abductors remained behind me and out of view. I didn't recognize the landscape. No visible landmarks. Only desert. Brown, flat, redundant desert. I guessed that I was still in Mexico, as US Immigration made everyone declare kidnap victims when crossing the border. Like fruits and vegetables.

I tried to remember who I had pissed off recently. There had been some shoving at Morales Bar a few weeks before. Some drunk who had gotten mouthy, but I doubted that he remembered it the next day. Had I insulted the tux guy when I had laughed at the cartoonishly large selection of formal bolo ties in stock? To be fair, there were at least one hundred, which was excessive by any standard.

As hard as I tried to lead a quiet life, in my short time back in the Imperial Valley I had attracted trouble with a capital Fuck You. Over the last five years, I had run afoul of a hit parade of shitkickers, desert bros, vatos, dangerous criminals, and random dickheads. I had also had more than the average amount of run-ins with Mexican gangsters—the average amount for most people being zero.

Then there were the really dangerous people in my life. My friends.

"Are you going to tell me what's going on?" I asked. "¿Qué sucede?"

No answer. Footsteps walked away behind me, followed by the van starting and the sound of tires. Dust billowed at my feet.

After the sound of the vehicle receded, I closed my eyes and listened. To nothing. To silence. Either I was alone or someone really quiet was standing right behind me. A mime, possibly. Which was a horrifying thought. Alone in the desert with a mime was the king of all nightmares.

"Is anyone there?" I yelled. "¿Hay alguien ahí?"

Nothing.

I screamed for help in two languages. I screamed until my throat hurt.

Nothing.

"What's the fucking point of this?"

Nothing.

"If you're looking for a ransom, I got two hundred and thirty dollars in my checking account and a jar of change on my nightstand. It's almost full, so you lucked out there. I already excavated the quarters. Maybe thirty bucks left, mostly nickels. It's yours."

Nothing.

"Does this have something to do with Tomás Morales? Is that it? Is this about Tomás? Sorry to disappoint you, but I haven't talked to that criminal in two years. Not a fucking word."

I knew I was talking to myself, but I had never let that stop me before.

"Who put this pole here, anyway? Is it for the occasion, or has it always been here? A standard Mexican kidnapping pole? The site of an ancient Mayan strip joint?"

A coyote howled in the distance.

"I fucking hate Mexico."

Fifteen minutes later, more than one vehicle arrived behind me. Different engines. Tires on gravel. Braking. Kicking up tons of dust. Multiple doors opened and closed. Footsteps in the hard-pack. Then nothing. Only the sense that there was a crowd of people standing behind me. The feeling that a monster was breathing hot air down the back of my neck.

I thought about my family. My fiancée, Angie, and my son, Juan. They were the only things that truly mattered in my life.

Whatever was going to happen was about to happen. The shit-quiet before the shitstorm. I was glad that the mystery of my abduction would soon be solved. But sure as Saint Lemmy, the patron saint of fuck, I wasn't looking forward to the answer.

Familiar voices blared from some serious speakers. "Dirty, rotten, filthy, stinkin'."

"Fuck me. I know that song," I said. It was the opening of Warrant's "Cherry Pie."

Then the air erupted with the sound of hair metal, the late Jani Lane's voice echoing through the vastness of the desert.

A small group of doves scattered, frightened by the rocking. Probably Dokken fans.

Six Mexican women in string bikinis pranced into my field of vision and formed a chorus line in front of me. They found their places and swayed to the music. One of the women approached, a crooked smile on her face. She started to undo my belt buckle.

"No, no, no," I said, attempting unsuccessfully to wiggle my hips away from her.

"Sí, sí, sí," she said.

"Bobby, you son of a bitch!" I yelled, trying to crane my immobilized neck. "I said no bachelor party. I meant no bachelor party. This is a fucking bachelor party."

The woman pulled my pants to my ankles, leaving only my boxers. I patted myself on the back for having done the laundry. Fifty-fifty on any given day that I was rolling commando. The woman returned to the row of dancers and found her groove. Their dance routine appeared choreographed, but horribly.

Bobby's laugh machine-gunned under the sound of the music. He appeared in my peripheral vision. "You knew I was going to throw you a bachelor party, dumbass."

"No, I didn't, fucker. I assumed that if I told you I didn't want one, that you wouldn't throw one."

"Well, there you go," Bobby said. "That's plain stupid. You can't blame me when you're the one that didn't think it through. Didn't realize who your bestest buddy is."

"An asshole?"

"Where's your esprit de corps?" Bobby said. "Would an asshole take weeks to plan the funnest night of your life?"

"Untie me from this post and I'll tell you."

Bobby shook his head. "Dig this. On top of these fine señoritas, I got a shit-ton of carne asada, a case of medium-shelf tequila, a couple kegs of Coors Light, illegal-even-in-Mexico fireworks, remote control helicopters, paintball gear, and a giant slingshot that can shoot a watermelon a hundred yards. And a van full of watermelons. I thought of everything."

"I brought Boggle!" a voice shouted.

"Why did you—?" Bobby turned his head. "Shut up, Snout. I told you we didn't need board games."

"Have you ever played?" Snout said. "It's really fun. You learn words and stuff."

"He's right." Another voice chimed in. It had to be Snout's brother, Buck Buck Buckley. "Did you know 'hubbub' is a real word and not just all made up?"

"Of course," Bobby said. "*The Apple Pie Hubbub.*"

"Hey. Assholes," I said. "I'm tied to a fucking pole in the middle of the fucking desert with my fucking dick in the fucking wind. Not my fucking idea of fucking fun."

"Such a potty mouth," Bobby said.

"Untie me!" I screamed.

"You're actually proving why tying you up was a necessary precaution," Bobby said. "When you told me you didn't want a bachelor party—which is like bullshit marrying horseshit to give birth to a new hybrid animal shit—you forced my hand. The only way to get you to have fun. Because you're like a grown-up or some shit now. Also, it gives you—what do lying politicians call it—plausible deniability. Angie can't say shit about shit. You were kidnapped. She might hate me for a year—if she finds out, which she won't—but totally worth it. I mentioned that this huge-ass slingshot fires melons like a half mile, right?"

"This is the stupidest thing you've ever done."

"Not even close. I've done tons of stupider things. Doubt this makes the top ten, to be honest. Remember that time I ran my truck into that house in high school?"

"You tried to back out like it was no big deal, peeling out on Mr. Doyle's living room carpet."

"The Christmas tree got caught in the wheel well," Bobby said. "And how about that time when Heavy Axler bet me I couldn't high-wire walk along that power line?"

"Point taken. You're an idiot," I said. "Are you going to untie me now?"

"These girls spent a week studying my choreography. I don't want all that rehearsal to go to waste."

As a distraction from their train wreck of a dance routine, the women all removed their bikini tops. There were breasts everywhere.

"This is crazy," I said. "I'm getting married. Tomorrow morning. Fucking tomorrow, Bobby."

"That's why we're starting early," Bobby said. "Don't worry."

"Did you say, 'Don't worry'? I'm not even in the right country, and I'm at the mercy of my human time bomb of a best friend and his topless army of hookers."

"They're dancers, not hookers. Show a little respect. These girls have strict orders not to touch your wang. We had a long sit-down about it. You aren't allowed to put any of your things in any of their things. You can touch their boobs. That's on the table. Which is a reasonable compromise."

I channeled the one yoga class I had taken seven years ago because I had a coupon and the teacher was foxy. Calm blue ocean.

"I will release you at the end of the song," Bobby said. "I'll warn you. This is the rare extended version. A Japanese EP I found on eBay."

"You're going to hell, Bobby. Not for this bullshit. And not for every other aspect of your degenerate life. But for being

Warrant's biggest fan. Even the devil is horrified by that level of depravity."

The version of the hair metal anthem was—no shit—nineteen minutes, with two drum solos. Two. Drum. Solos. The musical equivalent of watching someone unsuccessfully masturbate. Twice. The drummer enthusiastically pumping away while everyone smiles awkwardly, bored, annoyed, and a little sad for his desperate need for attention.

True to his word, Bobby untied me. I made some half-assed attempts to get a ride out of there, but nobody would give me their car keys. I resigned myself to the fact that I was trapped in the Mexican desert. No real choice but to try to enjoy myself.

A little craziness is good for the soul. It shakes the brain's snow globe. It's healthy to do one stupid thing every month. Not too stupid, but just stupid enough. And what better place than at a bachelor party. How else would I have good stories to tell my grandkids?

Bobby and I had slowed down over the last couple years. I was about to get married. I had a son. Bobby had raised Lety, a runaway teenager who was now attending her first year at UC Davis. His girlfriend, Griselda, had moved in with him. It would be their turn to get married soon. Considering that Griselda was a sheriff's deputy, that kept Bobby's actions—while not always smart—on the legalish side of things.

"I thought you said you quit drinking for good," I said.

"I did quit for good. Now I only drink for evil." Bobby winked. "I have strict rules about alcohol. I don't drink around Lety. I can if it's a social thing where everyone else is drinking, like a party. No more road beers, unless I'm irrigating, because that's boring as shit. I don't drink on weekdays, not including holiday weekdays. Or birthdays. Or special occasions. I wrote it all down. There's a chart. But we're in Mexico. None of those rules apply. Like international waters."

Bobby was my best friend and nobody made me laugh more. His ability to eventually pull me to the dark side was legendary. He was the human equivalent of Jägermeister. It started rough, became fun as hell, and I paid for it the next day. I started this particular adventure with an onion sack over my head. How much worse could things get from there?

The party took shape. Snout worked an oil drum barbecue, cooking carne asada, pollo asada, and pork tenderloin. Beer flowed through a homemade kegerator that our buddy Kirch had fashioned from salvaged refrigerator parts. Nobody really liked Kirch, but he knew how to keep beer cold. It wasn't a huge shindig. Aside from Bobby, Buck Buck, and Snout, the others were high school buddies and random cousins. And of course, the half dozen strippers.

Between playing with all our man toys, we sat in the dirt, drank beers, ate hot meat, and told our best lies. Buck Buck showed off his latest attempt at a jet pack made from eight leaf blowers and a fuckload of duct tape. It failed miserably, covering all of us with dust. The sight of Buck Buck jumping up and down screaming "How high am I?" might've been the funniest thing I'd ever seen. And I had recently watched a YouTube video of a goat kicking a clown in the nuts, so the bar was high.

I even played a couple rounds of Boggle with Snout. He was right. It was fun and I learned a new word: "bibble." Snout won every game. I didn't even know that the big baloney could read.

Bobby had really gone all out. We did all the things I love. We lit stuff on fire. Shot melons into the desert until they disappeared. Crashed remote control helicopters into each other. I'd say we played paintball, but we mostly just shot at Kirch.

Drinking and laughing with men I thought of as brothers. I was so touched that I drunk-cried and drunk-hugged everyone more than once. A lot of liquor was consumed.

The problem with free-falling is that landing is inevitable. I woke in a panic, covered in dirt, with a pounding headache and a half of a watermelon for a pillow. Bodies slept strewn across the desert floor. A dozen soon-to-be disappointed turkey vultures circled the scene.

"Wake up, you assholes!" I shouted. "I have to get married!"

TWO

Bobby and I got out of the limo in front of Saint Joseph's with fifteen minutes to spare. One of the guys I had been partying with the night before was the limo driver that Bobby had hired for our wedding day. Bobby told me that he had offered a discount if he got invited to the bachelor party. I found that strange and kind of creepy, but he had won the watermelon slingshot contest, so by my idiot standards, he had proven himself to be okay. I couldn't even see the watermelon when it landed.

Here's a fun fact that never would have occurred to me. When you're in a limousine, you get no hassle from the border authorities. Maybe for fear of insulting a foreign dignitary or someone with enough money to make their shit job worse. Although our limousine was painted desert camouflage, meaning the only possible VIP in the back was Ted Nugent or one of those *Duck Dynasty* spray-on rednecks.

Bobby might be a maniac, but he knew how to prepare a party from beginning to end. Still-warm menudo in a thermos waited for us in the back of the limo. The only effective hangover remedy I have ever known. We sweat out our bad judgment over the tripe and chunky vegetables, slurping the cure. Making a quick stop at my house, I got the watermelon out of my hair, dressed in my tux, and grabbed the rings and my vows. With no sleep, one cuff link, and a headache the size of your mom (assuming your mom is average-to-large-sized), I was ready to get hitched.

Mr. Morales and Father Joe were on us the moment we got out of the limousine. They both looked ready to fight. I held up my palms in defense. Bobby instinctively got in a boxer's stance. Father Joe might have been a priest, but that didn't mean he wouldn't punch a sermon into you. Father Joe fought welterweight as "Mexican Joe" Rios in his youth, and he still looked like he was at his fighting weight.

"Where the hell have you delinquents been?" Father Joe said. "You don't answer your phones anymore."

"Dead," I said. "Nowhere to charge it."

Father Joe lightly cuffed Bobby on the back of the head. "I know it was you, Robert. This has your stamp all over it."

"My hair, Padre," Bobby said, gently patting his bone-white pompadour. One of the reasons we were late was because Bobby spent twenty minutes to get his do just right. The procedure required a brush, a hair pick, a whole bottle of hairspray, and a dab of Bag Balm.

"I should've been there last night," Mr. Morales said, "to keep an eye on you two."

"You knew about last night? Why didn't you warn me?" I asked. "Did you think Bobby was going to throw a pinkies-out tea party? Brandy snifters and smoking jackets in the sitting room?"

"Don't blame Nestor," Father Joe said.

"Who?" Bobby asked.

It took me a second as well. I had known Mr. Morales my whole life, and I had never heard or known his first name. It felt like a secret revealed.

"Count your blessings that your lovely bride doesn't know how close you cut it," Father Joe said. "Get in the church and greet your guests this instant, or I swear I'll tell her and stretch out the Mass to a full hour. Latin, Spanish, and English. Really work your knees, and put the fear of God in you."

"Yes, sir," I said. "Sorry, Father Joe. Sorry, Nestor."

Mr. Morales gave me a look that told me that if I ever said his first name again that he would crush me with his bare hands until I was a basketball-sized person-wad, and then he would stomp on that me-lump until I was a human pancake. Mr. Morales had a very expressive face.

When I set foot in the church, it all became frighteningly real. Friendly faces smiled at me. Men I kind of knew shook my hand. Nicely dressed ladies gave me hugs. Congratulations came from cousins, aunts, uncles, old friends, and a girl I was in love with in the fourth grade. It felt like the whole Imperial Valley. My entire past was present.

Most of the folks wore short-sleeve shirts and church pants. A few ties. Formal means different things in different places. Your best clothes are sometimes just the cleanest ones. No one would look at you wrong for wearing a clean T-shirt to a wedding in the Imperial Valley if that's all you had. Not everyone can afford a suit. And in the desert, how often do you get the notion for tweed?

As the guests found their seats, I waited with Bobby, Buck Buck, and Snout. My best man and two groomsmen. Snout kept on his International Harvester ball cap. Even in a tuxedo, he would have looked weird without it. The three of them passed around a flask. When I got a light whiff of the alcohol, I resisted the urge to upchuck.

I watched my son, Juan, chat up the flower girl. He was a Veeder, after all. Natural ladies' men, the lot of us. It was going to break his heart when I told him that Kristi was his cousin. Looking adorable in his miniature tuxedo, he had taken his role as ring bearer very seriously, practicing around the house all week.

He looked over at me and smiled. I waved him over. He whispered something to Kristi, made her giggle. Veeders like to leave the ladies laughing.

"I need to tie the rings to the pillow thing," I said to him.

Juan handed me the square satin pillow. I found the rings in my pocket and tied them to the ribbons.

"How you doing?" I asked him. "You ready? You know what to do?"

He nodded seriously. "Do you know what to do?"

I laughed and handed the pillow back to him. He looked at the rings and gripped the pillow tightly. Whenever I had given him a responsibility, he had always taken it seriously. A very conscientious kid.

"Mom is still Mom, right?" he asked me.

"What do you mean?"

"Well, when people get married, they change what they are. Like, now Mom is your girlfriend, but after she is your wife. I didn't know if she turned into something else after, like a different Mom."

"No matter the words we use, the three of us are our family," I said. "She'll still be your mom no matter what."

"But not like my mother that died," he said. "She's different."

There was no drama in Juan's matter-of-fact statement. When a person grows up on a farm, their relationship to life and death is different than town kids'. Mortality is experienced young. Juan had already witnessed both birth and death in his eight short years.

"She was your biological mother," I said, "but a lot of people have more than one mom."

"They do?"

"Sure. It doesn't change what you meant to your other mom or what you feel about her. That will never change. Angie loves you and wants the job. She's marrying me to get to you."

"Is that how you tricked her into marrying you?"

I heard Bobby laugh behind me.

"Very funny," I said. "Keep a close eye on those rings. I've got some shady relatives."

"I will." Juan went back to talking up Kristi. She giggled at the first thing he said.

Bobby put an arm around me. "We could get some lessons from Juanito."

"Best thing that ever happened to me," I said. "Didn't know it at first, but now I can't imagine it any different."

"How you doing?" Bobby asked, a head tilt toward the flask in his hand.

"No fucking way," I said.

"The first marriage is always the hardest one," Bobby said. "It's okay to be scared."

"It's weird. I ain't nervous at all," I said. "Second to raising Juan, this is the smartest thing I've ever done. Ain't no one more important to me than Angie and Juan. I fucking love them."

Mrs. Davidson started up on the organ. Everyone found their places. It was like putting on an amateur production of a play. My mark was on the dais with Father Joe. He gave me a wink. I'm not sure what it was supposed to communicate, but I found it comforting.

It was really happening.

I was about to get fucking married.

The wedding played out how weddings do. It wasn't a night of improvisational comedy. It was predictably ritualistic. There were a few highlights. As Angie's parents had passed away a few years back, Mr. Morales gave her away. Bobby and Griselda—my best man and Angie's maid of honor—walked down the aisle, looking natural and beautiful together. At one point during the ceremony, Juan farted with insanely good timing. I would never be sure if it was on purpose or an accident. Either way, he got a big laugh and had done his old man proud.

In addition to the traditional vows, we had written our own. Ten drafts later and I still hadn't found a way to fully express how I felt about the woman I was about to marry.

Angie read her vows first. "Jimmy, we've known each other almost our entire lives. And through those ups and downs, we've ended up here. Crazy. A possibility when we were seventeen. Completely estranged by the time we were twenty-five. Fate, destiny, God, whatever. Here we are. That's the way life is. You can't plan it. It's unpredictable and wonderful and surprising. Life throws us curveballs. And you're the curveball that I want to spend the rest of my life with. You and our beautiful son, Juan. I love you, you big, dumb weirdo."

My throat was dry. I couldn't find any spit. Talk about setting the bar high. I was tempted to call bullshit on her consciously trying to make me cry.

Through a cracking voice that made me sound pubescent, I did my best. "Angie, first of all let me tell you how smoking hot you look right now. Father Joe knows what I'm talking about."

The crowd laughed. Father Joe gave me a disapproving look.

"Angie, you're an amazing woman, a wonderful mother, and an incredible friend. Being with you makes me feel like I won the lottery after getting struck by lightning. But not the kind of lightning that kills people. The kind that gives people superpowers.

"These are called vows, so I'm going to make some pledges to you, some for-real oaths of troth. I promise to be the man that I know I can be. The best version of myself. To be your husband and friend and co-conspirator. To protect you and let you protect me. To share love and adventure and laughter and everything in between. To always be there and to always have your back. I love you, Angie. Now, let's get hitched."

I may or may not have stuttered and cried throughout my vows. It's hard to remember. Lost to history. Snout cried enough for everyone. He had always been emotional. I allowed a brief pause so that Buck Buck could hand him a tissue. He blew his nose loudly. I love my moron friends.

The most important part of the whole wedding was that at the end of the ceremony, Angie and I were magically transformed into James and Angela Veeder. Husband and wife.

All that was left was the party.

It wouldn't have been an Imperial Valley wedding if someone hadn't ended up at the police station. We are a people that honor tradition. Conservative bookmakers would have put even money on Bobby. Three-to-one on Buck Buck or Snout. I proudly sat at five-to-one. Betting opened at a thousand-to-one on the arrestee being Angie.

But even a long shot comes in the money now and again.

It was strange to be the one reading back issues of *Guns & Ammo* in the police station waiting area with Angie cooling off in a jail cell. Married life suited me. Somehow, I had transformed into the responsible one.

I don't remember the last time I had been that happy. It wasn't alcohol-produced glee either, as my bachelor party hangover had limited me to only a couple glasses of wine. It could have been the questionable brownie that my teenage cousin made me eat, but I suspected it was something far deeper.

If it was me in the pokey on our wedding night, Angie would have motherfucked me the whole way home and for two weeks after. Considering the trouble I constantly found myself in, having this tomfoolery in my pocket for the rest of our married lives was the best wedding gift I could receive. Well, second best. It's hard to beat a George Foreman grill. It's so good, he put his name on it.

"How long you going to hold her?" I asked Ceja Carneros, the bigger half of the Holtville Police Department. Ceja was the Barney Fife to Bill Locher's Andy Griffith. Semiretired, Bill rarely set foot in the office. Still cutting himself a nice check, of course. HPD was a two-man operation in a town that needed one man or less.

"She kicked me, so I can't let her go right away. Or else everyone will start kicking police officers."

"I don't think that's going to happen," I said.

"It could start a trend," Ceja said. "I know it's your wedding night, but there's a principle here. She got mostly thigh. Missed my huevos by like an inch. Bigger balls and I'd be in trouble."

I used every ounce of restraint to not make the thirty jokes that jumped into my head.

"When do you got to be back?" Ceja asked. "You got a sitter for Juan?"

"Mr. Morales took him for the whole night. It's just me and Angie tonight."

"One more hour. No charges," Ceja said. "That'll be my wedding present. You can give me the salad spinner back. I need one."

"Sounds reasonable," I said. "You got any beer?"

"Six-pack on ice in the trunk of the cruiser. Tallboys. Maybe a bottle of something liquorer in the evidence closet," Ceja said. "If you're driving, I can't let you."

"I got the limo until morning," I said. "Driver's out front."

"I'll grab the beers," Ceja said, getting to his feet. "You want to shoot at bottles out back?"

"Of course. It's my wedding night."

I pieced together the events that landed Angie in the slammer. Not all the witnesses had been reliable by any standard. By the time shit went down, the die-hard wedding guests were all at least a bottle and a half of bulk wedding wine in. At eighty-nine cents a bottle out of the back of a panel van parked off the highway outside of Seeley, odds were that I had been responsible for poisoning my loved ones. The true grapes of wrath.

I hadn't been there for any of the action. Me, Bobby, and some of the boys were firing up some late-night knackwurst on the grill in back of the Swiss Club. Nothing like night meat to end an evening.

From all accounts, this was the gist of what went down: Someone, I'm guessing Jackie Apodaca—one of Angie's long-time frenemies—congratulated Angie, commenting that it was really good for her to finally take a risk and jump in the deep end, especially with a wild card like me. Angie took umbrage, asking what she meant by that, that she had taken plenty of risks in her life. Jackie replied saying that Angie was "you know, someone that never takes off her underwear."

Apparently, that phrase got under Angie's skin. "Never takes off her underwear."

That was the "Oh yeah!" moment. The bathtub wine vetoed any reasonable response. Angie looked around for her counterargument, saw a tractor in a nearby field, and got it in her mind that I wasn't the only crazy one in the family and that tractor was her ticket to demonstrating her spontaneity. The problem was that drunk Angie was more literal minded than sober Angie.

Angie took off her underwear.

She stripped down—dress, veil, gloves, even her fancy wedding chonies. Just proving Jackie wrong wasn't enough. No way. She hightailed it toward the tractor, trying to jump the canal between the road and the field. In place of a graceful leap, she face-planted in the knee-deep water. That didn't deter Angie. With her "friends" shouting encouragement and taking pictures—which were going to look awesome in the wedding album and on various social media accounts—Angie waded through calf-deep mud and made it to the tractor. She hotwired it—a skill I didn't know she possessed—and got halfway to town before she passed out by the side of the road.

Luckily for Angie, Griselda had to go back on duty and was the one that got the call. Responding to a complaint about a stolen tractor, she found my wife sound asleep, hugging the steering wheel and covered with so much mud that she didn't even know Angie was naked at first.

Griselda called me, but I had turned my ringer off for the wedding and never thought to turn it back on. She took Angie to the Holtville Police Department to sleep it off. The only clothes Ceja had in evidence were a fat man's jeans and a football jersey.

Griselda got the rubbery Angie into the ensemble. It wasn't a good look, but it covered her naughty bits.

The alleged kicking took place when Ceja woke up Angie to try to get some coffee in her. Angie has never been a morning person.

I didn't find any of this out until I finally checked my phone.

Ceja and I killed an hour by firing guns until a small pile of spent cartridges lay at our feet and a bunch of cans, bottles, light bulbs, and an old pumpkin were properly perforated and sploded. We must have woken up everyone within two miles of the station, but what were they going to do? Call the cops?

When we had tried every toy in the police arsenal and started eyeing the chicken hawks on the telephone line for lack of something better to destroy, Ceja decided that Angie had learned her lesson.

Angie slept the entire drive home, snoring and mumbling with me in the back of the limo. I stroked my wife's hair and watched her sleep with her head in my lap. Because the jeans Ceja had found kept falling off, she was forced to wear the filthy wedding dress that she had abandoned in the Swiss Club parking lot. It was going to take some serious bleaching to get it white again. I had planned on carrying her over the threshold, but now it was a necessity rather than a novelty.

The sun peeked over the Chocolate Mountains. It was tomorrow already.

"Your driveway is way too bumpy for this car," the driver said when we arrived at the house. "It damn near killed the suspension when I picked you up, and I'm pretty sure I fucked the muffler."

"You fucked the muffler?"

He gave me a look that told me he was too tired for my bullshit.

"You can let us off on the road," I said. "She's light."

I saw the black SUV in my driveway the moment I stepped out of the limo. Too clean for the desert, almost sparkling. It was either a really conscientious soccer mom or trouble. Not that a soccer mom couldn't be trouble, but that was more in a "Letters to *Penthouse*" kind of way.

I spotted a familiar ogre standing next to the car, cleaning his fingernails with a melon knife. Little Piwi, a driver and bodyguard for Tomás Morales. With the exception of his brother, Little Piwi was the largest human being I had ever been in the same room with. And I once had William "The Refrigerator" Perry sign my forty-five of "The Super Bowl Shuffle."

Tomás and I had been childhood friends decades before. Since that time, he had become one of the most dangerous men in Mexicali, if not Mexico. A criminal kingpin with his hand in a lot of illegal activities. Tomás and I had deep history. We had a falling out two years earlier over some trouble in Plaster City. I hadn't seen him since. Which is why his presence concerned me.

I leaned into the limo driver's window. "I need you to stay here with the engine running. I'm leaving Angie in the back. If things get weird, I want you to drive. Anywhere. In any direction. Away from here."

"What do you mean 'weird'?" He spotted Little Piwi. "Holy crap, that motherfucker looks like he ate a giant."

"It's probably nothing," I said. "An old friend."

"A friend that you're scared of?"

"I'm scared of most of my friends."

The ageless Tomás Morales got out of the back of the SUV as I approached. In a very sharp suit with coiffed hair, my childhood pal turned crime lord held a box wrapped in white paper with a red ribbon and bow.

"Hey, Tommy," I said, keeping my hands visible. "Been a while."

"I considered crashing your wedding but thought better of it," he said.

"I would have invited you—I considered it—but it didn't feel appropriate."

"Congratulations, by the way."

"Thanks," I said, pointing at the box in his hands. "Is that a wedding present?"

"In a way. I wouldn't have come here, bothered you, but some jobs you have to do yourself. This is about the past. Our past. Unfinished business that never sat well with me. I don't like questions. I've always been more of an answers guy."

"Well, that was cryptic."

"I thought it appropriate to wrap it for the occasion."

"You wrapped it yourself?"

Tomás laughed. "Of course not. It'd look like shit if I had done it. Little Piwi wrapped it."

I looked over at Little Piwi. He shrugged. A man of surprising talents.

"I give," I said. "What's in the box, Tommy?"

"You can unwrap it," Tomás said, "once we sort out the hombre with the shotgun pointed at my head."

THREE

The shotgun-wielding man who had rounded the side of the house had made no sound. Even Little Piwi—a henchman by trade—hadn't detected him. Little Piwi moved his hand two inches toward the inside of his jacket. The man with the shotgun shook his head and spit on the ground. Enough confidence for Little Piwi to think better of it.

The shotgun man smiled. Two bottom teeth accounted for his mouth's full inventory. A surprisingly friendly smile for mostly gums. Except for a small paunch, he stood skeleton thin. Shirtless in too-big jeans, it was hard to miss the three bullet scars that puckered his torso. He was forty-five going on seventy-five, leathered and cracked with skin the color of my Dewey Evans signature mitt. He looked like he had lived ten lives. All of them hard.

"It's okay, Joaquin. ¡Está bien!" I shouted, smiling and performing matching hand gestures. "Yo las conozco."

"Of course he's a friend of yours," Tomás said.

Joaquin spit again, gave Little Piwi a wink, and whistled sharply. A very large dog slowly emerged from behind the orange tree at the other end of the house.

"That is one big damn dog," Tomás said.

Joaquin's half-husky/half-wolf, Rufus, gave me and Tomás an icy stare. Tomás looked simultaneously impressed and concerned when Rufus nonchalantly sniffed his leg. I had never seen anyone intimidate Tomás, but apparently that didn't extend to animals. Rufus walked to Joaquin, and the two of them left toward the back of the house.

"You've added some interesting members to your crew," Tomás said. "An old Mexican ninja and a *Game of Thrones*–sized wolf-dog?"

"You watch *Game of Thrones*?"

"*Juego de Tronos*. Wouldn't miss it. You'd be surprised at the number of ways that it parallels my own business dealings. I've learned a lot from that show," Tomás said. "Where did you find those two?"

"They found me."

A year earlier, I stepped outside one morning and Joaquin was weeding the front yard. It's not that the yard didn't need it. Lord knows, it did. But I hadn't made any arrangements with him to do the work.

I waved and said, "Hola." He nodded and smiled, motioning with his hands to indicate that he had a lot of work to do and didn't have time to goof off talking to me. An hour later, I brought him a jug of water, a couple beers, and two carnitas burritos. At the end of the day, I paid him what I had on me. Probably less than minimum wage, but Angie and I were just getting by. I never actually hired him, but he was happy enough with the arrangement to show up the next day.

Joaquin had been with us ever since. He spoke no English, was stone deaf, and had the patience of Job's more patient brother. He always found work to do and never asked anything for it. He took what I gave him, accepting that it was what I could afford. I learned his name when he showed me his green card to communicate that it was his birthday. I was surprised at how young he was, and to be honest, that he was in the country legally. It was a pleasant surprise. After a couple months, I helped him fix up the abandoned Airstream on the side of the house. Rufus showed up soon after that. The dog didn't do any tricks, was damn near feral, but he loved Juan and Angie. He was indifferent to me. The first time I tried to pet him, he dragged me around the yard for fifteen minutes by my shoelaces. I took not killing me as a sign of affection. The best watchdog in the world. The meter reader and water guy found that out the hard way. Only Joaquin could control him. And he did it without speaking. If someone had told me they were psychically linked, I wouldn't have argued the point.

I had invited Joaquin to the wedding, offering him one of my suits, but he declined. I didn't press it. I would rather have had him there than half the people that I invited out of obligation. I saved a piece of cake for him. We'd have some beers later and laugh at jokes that were never spoken aloud.

Tomás handed me the wrapped gift. "Congratulations on your nuptials."

He and I sat on the low wall in front of the house to avoid all the chickens that had become curious by our presence. I wanted the deposit back on the tux, and Tomás's suit was pricier than my truck.

"I don't even know if you're still trying to track down your boy's family," Tomás said, "but I never stopped looking. My guy found a man he believes to be Yolanda Palomera's father. Juan's grandfather. In the box is all the information that he prepared for me. It's not much. A location, some news clippings. No phone number, but enough to go on."

I stared at Tomás and then at the box. "What?"

"I feel like that was concise. Should I repeat those same sentences?"

Allow me to clarify. Juan is my son, but my son is not my son. Okay, that sucked as clarification. Yolanda Palomera was my son's mother. My own father was my son's father. They had both died a few years back. On a family tree, Juan is my half brother, but I chose to raise him as my son.

I had never been able to learn Yolanda's whole story, find any relatives, or contact her family. After all the possible leads dried up, I had stopped looking. Mexico was too big a country, and the recordkeeping in the rural areas could be atrocious. Unless your name is Octavius Bartholomew Fuckwuckle, there are too many people with identical names. Over a thousand Palomeras lived in Guadalajara alone.

I wanted everything for Juan, and it bothered me that he would never know one side of his biological family and that his family would never know about Yolanda's death or the existence of her son.

"How?" I asked Tomás.

"Look who you're talking to. Being a criminal mastermind has its upside," Tomás said. "Mostly upside, really. With enough money, anything can be accomplished. Power manufactures results."

"I don't know what any of that means," I said. "And I don't want to know."

"Crime pays."

"Where is he?"

"Coatepec. It's a village in the mountains between Mazatlán and Durango."

"Mazatlán?" I said. "Isn't that a gringos-in-oversized-sombreros, drunk-frat-boys, fat-men-in-Hawaiian-shirts kind of place?"

"It's a Mexican city that Americans attempt to ruin, yes."

"Yeah, but one full of timeshare scam artists."

"I sell timeshares down there."

"Damn, you really are evil."

Tomás laughed.

"Why did you keep looking?" I asked.

"Because it was important to you."

I didn't know how to respond to that, so I said nothing.

Tomás hopped off the wall. The chickens scattered. He tap-danced around the chickenshit minefield as he walked slowly to his ride. I pushed myself off the wall and followed him.

"Before you give me a medal," Tomás said, "all I did was pay one guy to find another guy. We may have our differences, Jimmy. I can't afford your moral posturing and ethical delusions when it comes to my business. Maybe our choices don't allow us to associate. That doesn't mean we don't have history. I have plenty of friends that hate me. They're still friends."

"You're a fucked-up dude, Tommy."

"You're probably right." Tomás laughed. "You know, I've never met your bride."

"You've never met Angie? That's weird. I just picked her up from the police station. She's passed out in the back of the limo."

"Perfect for each other."

He nodded toward the end of the driveway. I turned to see Angie stumble-walking toward us. She held the hem of her filthy wedding dress in one hand, her shoes in the other. She looked like she'd been thrown out of a car.

"What in the hell did I drink?" Angie said as she approached. "Was that wine Uruguayan? I vaguely remember a tractor and a jail cell. Did fucking Griselda arrest me? That bitch. What happened? Forget it. I don't want to know."

"I'll show you the pictures later. The mugshot is pure gold. Your eyes are looking in two different directions. Like a cartoon pug or a beautiful Latina Marty Feldman."

"Don't get smart," she said. "You did just leave your fresh-from-the-factory bride in the back of a limousine. Who is this that he's more important than me?"

"Oh, Jimmy," Tomás said. "I like her."

"Say hello to Tomás Morales," I said. "He came by to drop off a wedding present."

She stopped in her tracks. "Tomás Morales? The one that . . ."

I nodded. "That's the one."

She looked Tomás up and down, looked back at me, and then gave Little Piwi a long stare. "You're a big one," she said to him. I could have sworn Little Piwi blushed a little. Angie turned back to Tomás. "I know a lot about you."

"Exaggeration, I'm sure. Jimmy has been known to goose his stories for effect. Either way, it's all hearsay." Tomás smiled. "None of it is admissible in court."

"You bringing trouble?" Angie asked, suddenly alert and sober.

Tomás turned to me. "She's good for you." He walked to the SUV. "Congratulations to the both of you. Have a great honeymoon."

"We haven't figured that out," I said. "Wedding was pricey. More of a staycation planned. One where we still work forty hours a week."

Tomás laughed and got in the back of the SUV. Little Piwi climbed in the driver's seat and drove away.

"What the shitting hell was that all about?" Angie asked.

I opened the box. A couple sheets of paper. Name, address, typewritten notes. Very sparse. Some newspaper clippings about a Mexican mayoral election. Also in the box were plane tickets, a hotel itinerary, and vouchers for parasailing and a brewery tour. At the very bottom was an envelope containing three thousand dollars in twenty-dollar bills.

"Beats the shit out of flatware," my wife said.

I was tired, but it was my wedding night/morning. I only planned on doing this the one time, so I was going to find the energy. How many women did I expect to fool into thinking that I was a responsible adult? I hadn't even convinced Angie yet, though she still went through with it.

Benefiting from the combined siesta in the jail cell and limo, Angie had hit that sweet spot between the worst of her drunk and the start of her hangover.

We kissed as I carried her over the threshold, only hitting her head slightly on the doorjamb. She acted like it hadn't happened, her first act of love in our newly minted marriage.

The living room wasn't how we had left it. I would have distinctly remembered having covered it in shaving cream, Silly String, balloons, an inordinate number of dildos, shitloads of glitter, scattered gummi bears, two interlocked, inflatable sex dolls (male and female, of course), a live chicken, and a sign that read "Just Marryed." My friends (and it had to be my friends, not Angie's) had outdone themselves. What really said congratulations like five hours of cleaning glittery chickenshit off hardwood and antique upholstery?

"I am going to kill Bobby," Angie said. "Kill him dead."

"You can kill him after I kill him."

"Get the chicken out of here. We'll deal with the rest later. After you wash your hands with soap and boiling water, meet me in the bedroom."

"You know how hot this farm boy gets when you demand I wrangle livestock."

"Seriously, that chicken is shitting like it's trying to win a bet. Your idiot friends probably tried to get it drunk."

"That sounds about right."

Naked, sweating, and slightly out of breath, Angie and I rolled to either side of the bed. I laughed a little, as I always did after really good sex. Angie turned and smiled. People that take sex seriously are doing it wrong. It is supposed to be fun.

"Wife sex is good," I said. "It's going to be a fluid adjustment. A fluid—"

"Yeah, I got it. Gross." Angie sat up in bed, crossing her arms over her bare chest. "I've been thinking."

"Oh yeah?" I said, getting sleepy.

"Taking that money, the plane tickets, or anything from that criminal is a mistake. The information is fine, but we'll find another way to meet Juan's grandfather."

"Can we talk about this tomorrow?" I said. "I'm basking in my sex glow. Kind of want to drift off and dream about more sexy sex."

"Okay, after you tell me that you aren't going to accept the money," Angie said.

"I haven't thought about it. I went from wrangling a diarrheic chicken to climbing your fine body. First to fifth gear, baby. My brain is a one-thing-at-a-time kind of machine."

"I don't believe you. You're working on a strategy, tactics." She shook her head. "You'll talk about how nice it would be to go on a honeymoon and the beach and the drinks and all that. And when will we ever be able to afford it."

"I haven't—that's not—"

Angie wasn't done. "You'll explain how important it is to find Juan's people. Which I agree with. You'll lay out all the pluses, fill that column. Ignoring the minuses, completely neglecting the fact that Tomás fucking Morales set this in motion. Which makes everything a minus. He exploits people. He kills people. For a living."

"I—"

"Quit arguing with me."

"That's literally the opposite of what I'm doing," I said. "You're arguing with yourself."

"It saves time."

"Let me think about it when I'm not out of it. Let's not forget that the reason we're up so late is because you Lady Godivaed on a tractor. Nothing wrong with thinking. We'll talk about it tomorrow. I mean today. Later today."

"When have you ever thought about anything before you did it?"

"That's a fair point," I said. "I'm maturing. It took us years to get married, didn't it? I didn't make a snap decision there. That whole time I was weighing the pros and cons of marrying you."

"There were cons?"

"Oh, baby. Tons of them," I said. "You don't rinse the dishes before you put them in the dishwasher. Which totally fucks up the filter. You've got that one gnarly corn nut toenail that plain freaks me out. I'm about two percent convinced that you pity-married me, if that's a thing. You like the Ernest P. Worrell movies. All of them. Which is fucking insane. But mostly, I didn't know if I could marry a woman that wouldn't accept a fat stack of cash and a free vacation. Which ended up being pretty relevant."

"First of all, *Slam Dunk Ernest* is a classic. That's a fact. Kareem Abdul-Jabbar plays an angel, an Oscar-worthy performance. And obviously I pity-married you. You're just so sad and pathetic and sad. Did I mention that you were sad? Like a puppy with wheels for back legs."

"We can keep talking about this, or fool around some more. I still got tons of energy."

"I don't know," Angie said. "I haven't decided. I have to think about it."

The next day, Angie and I had a civil discussion about the rightness and wrongness of taking a criminal's money to finance a trip to find our son's family.

No need to go into all the back and forth. Eventually Angie and I decided together that this was our best chance and if we missed this opportunity we would regret it. Angie made a point to announce to me that this was anything but playing it safe. Not something a person that didn't take off her underwear would do. Jackie had really gotten under her skin with that underwear business.

Because there was no way that I could jinx the trip, I found myself saying out loud, "What could possibly go wrong?" Even though my track record in Mexico in no way supported a level of confidence usually only associated with drunks and teenagers and drunk teenagers.

Two months later, Angie and I were wheels down in Mexico, and walking across the tarmac to the main terminal of General Rafael Buelna International Airport outside of Mazatlán.

She didn't do it for me. She did it for Juan. And maybe for Yolanda. She did it because it was the right thing to do for our family. Gangster money or not, there was a father out there that didn't know the fate of his daughter, or that he had an eight-year-old grandson.

FOUR

The first inhale off the plane felt like Mexico waterboarded me. Drowning in the thick humidity, I started having second thoughts. The heat was fine. Anything below ninety degrees was sweater weather in the Imperial Valley. It got muggy for a couple hellacious weeks in September, but mostly the desert was dry—which is what made it a desert. My shirt stuck to my back, and I broke out in hives. Maybe I was allergic to Mexico.

Angie had her misgivings about the trip, but she wasn't the kind of person that would insist on not enjoying herself to prove a point. Once she agreed, she was all in. Dare I say, underwear off. I deduced that from the assembly line of free margaritas she chain-drank on our short first-class flight out of San Diego.

We had considered bringing Juan with us but nixed it in favor of sticking our toes in the water first. We also selfishly wanted a honeymoon.

I called Mr. Morales on the walk through the airport to baggage claim.

"Bar," Angie said.

"Mr. Morales, it's Jimmy. We just landed. Checking in to see how it's going."

"I saw you this morning."

"Isn't this what a conscientious parent does?"

"Talk to your son."

The clunk of the receiver set down on the bar was soon followed by Juan's voice. "Pop?"

"Hey, Juano. You having fun with Mr. More-Or-Less?"

"We're watching *Santo Contra Las Lobas.* It's a good one."

"Movies with wrestlers and she-wolves usually are."

"And then we're going to go shooting."

Angie leaned in, whispering in my other ear. "How's it going?"

"Did you say Mr. Morales was going to take you shooting?" I asked Juan.

"Yeah, but only at targets. Not at like animals or nothing."

"Give me the phone," Angie said.

"Hey, Juano. Your mom wants to talk to Mr. More-Or-Less. I just wanted to tell you that I love you, I'm thinking about you, and I'll see you soon."

The shooting ended up being arrows, not guns. An archery lesson. Neither Angie nor I had a problem with a bow and arrow, but it was good to get clarification. Mr. Morales was on a haphazard mission to teach Juan the manly arts—Angie had still not forgotten the "Throwing Knife Incident" and the emergency room stitches that had followed—but I saw it as Mr. Morales's purview in his role as Juan's de facto grandfather.

If all went according to plan, Juan would soon have two old men spoiling him with presents and teaching him the swear words that fell in the gaps in my own vocabulary.

At the baggage carousel, a man stood with a sign that read "Beater." He was short and thick, but not fat. He had a three-inch-high flattop and wore a guayabera, loose pants, and huaraches.

"I think you may be here for me," I said. "¿Para que estás aqui?"

The man looked at a slip of paper in his hand. "Jaime and Angela Beater."

"I'm Jaime. Jimmy," I said. "That's us. Are you from the hotel?"

"No, señor. I am your driver. For the week. Para lo que necesite."

"Tomás hired you?"

The man shrugged and acted like the ceiling was interesting. He handed me a business card. "That is my number. For any time. Veinticuatro horas al día. Whatever you need. I know the city, the mountains, even the ocean, everything for a hundred miles."

I glanced at the business card. "Radical? Is that the name of your company?"

"No. My name. I am Radical."

I walked back to Angie, who was flipping through her phone as she waited for our bags. I pointed to Radical. "That's our driver. His name is Radical."

"Of course it is," she said. "I was concerned that it wouldn't be."

While Angie found a bathroom and Radical went to bring the car to the curb, I remained on luggage carousel duty. Bored in a minute, I scanned the old, white vacationing faces. None of the tourists looked excited to be on vacation. A couple of them looked downright pissed off. This crowd needed tacos and beer, stat.

That's when I spotted the dynamic duo. Through the crowd, I stared at the two men that I had seen in Mexicali on the day that Bobby had abducted me for my bachelor party. I had only got a glance at them outside the tux shop, but there was something memorable about their stares. Something more memorable about the big man's facial scar and the small man's ink.

Their presence could not be a good thing. Even worse, I had no idea who they were or why they were following me. I was being tailed by two shady fuckers, and they had been following me since before my wedding. All the way to Mazatlán.

"Fuck this fucking shit," I said, simultaneously showing off my patience and vocabulary.

A grandmotherly woman in neon pink shorts and a big hat gave me a nasty look.

"I didn't invent those words," I said. "I learned them from your generation."

Pushing through the crowd, I made a beeline toward the two men.

Teardrops caught sight of me and slapped Face Scar on the arm. They fast-walked in the opposite direction.

In my peripheral vision, I saw Angie walk out of the bathroom. My walk turned into a run. I gained ground, but the two men sped up their pace. Darting between octogenarians and roller bags, I chased them through the airport baggage claim area.

My eyes on the two men and not on my feet, I tripped on the edge of some kid's boogie board. It sent me sprawling and sliding across the floor on my stomach. I heard a few laughs, so it must have been a righteous face plant. My chin hurt, and my shirt had turned from white to beige. A human dust mop on the disgusting floor.

I rose and searched for the two men, catching sight of them heading out of the building. On the curbside, I ran into a thicker crowd. A half dozen tour buses loaded and unloaded Japanese and European travelers. I tried to use my height to see over the crowd, but there were too many Scandinavians in the bunch.

I lost them. They were gone.

I said "fuck" so loud that three people ducked.

I walked back to Angie, looking over my shoulder. She hauled one of our bags off the carousel. I quick-stepped and gave her a hand.

"Where'd you go?" she asked.

"I thought I saw Wilford Brimley."

She nodded like that was a completely normal explanation. The fact that she believed my shitty lie illustrated how many stupid things I was capable of uttering during the course of a day. If everyone thinks you're an idiot, you can get away with the dumbest excuses.

I'm not sure why I didn't tell Angie that two mysterious Mexican men had followed me from Mexicali to Mazatlán. It seems like one of those things that you should tell the person you're traveling with, especially the woman you love. In my caveman brain, I probably thought I was protecting her. As fucked up and stupid as that sounded, I thought it was better for her that she didn't know. I didn't want to ruin her good time.

Radical drove north into Mazatlán. With the ocean on our left, we passed a line graph of hotels along the ocean. Tall near the airport, lower at the edge of the city, and then rising again closest to the central area. As we neared the marina, the economic landscape shifted, the buildings pushed farther back from the road. Gated resorts and all-inclusives hidden by trees and walls. The swanky part of town, where the rich people only saw the minimum number of Mexicans. And those were the ones serving them drinks and handing them towels.

"Looks like Tomás did us right," I said.

Radical pulled up to a gated driveway and spoke briefly to the guard. A small brass sign on the wall simply read "La Playa Resort." The guard looked at a clipboard and nodded. The gate rolled inward, and Radical drove down the long driveway, past palms and manicured grass. A half dozen flamingos wandered in a small man-made lagoon.

If there was such a thing as a six-star resort, La Playa might have made the cut. The moment I hit the pool in my cutoff jorts, I expected to be quietly escorted off the premises by four burly men in dark suits hired to keep out the riffraff, which I most definitely was. I was the riffest raff there.

Radical's slightly beat-up Mercedes pulled up to the lobby entrance. Five employees circled, grabbing the luggage out of the trunk, opening doors, offering Angie a hand to help her out of the car. Before I said a word, someone handed me a margarita. I took a sip as much out of awe as thirst. Whisked away, that's what we were. Angie looked at me with wide eyes and a what-the-fuck-is-going-on-this-is-really-cool smile.

The resort minions parted and a statuesque Mexican woman walked toward us. "Welcome to La Playa Resorts. I am Verónica, your liaison. Right this way, Mr. and Mrs. Veeder."

"Mrs. Veeder. It's still weird," Angie said, and took my hand. We followed Verónica into the giant palapa that acted as the open-air lobby. I felt like Thurston Howell III. It only lasted a moment. I knew that I was Gilligan.

"How did they know who we were?" Angie whispered.

"I don't care," I said. "This is the best margarita I've ever had."

Angie took a sip. "Holy shit. Where's mine?"

No check-in necessary. Verónica assured us that everything had been taken care of. She walked us through one section of the grounds, which included another man-made lagoon, a hedge maze, several pools, and a private beach.

Our private cabaña did not disappoint. It was essentially a house with a huge veranda overlooking the Pacific Ocean, with stairs (or a fireman pole for the daring) that took us right to the white sand beach. This was going to be the nicest place that I had ever slept in my life. And I spent a night in Pauly Shore's guesthouse.

Verónica supervised the young man that had brought our bags. He put our clothes in drawers, opened curtains, and ran around making sure everything was just so. That was an expression rich people said, right? Just so. I wanted to make an effort to fit in. I considered affecting a British accent and holding my pinky out at random moments. I made a note to hit the monocle store later.

"Excuse me," I said to Verónica.

She turned with a smile that couldn't have been sincere but made me think she liked me. "How may I help you, Mr. Veeder?"

"How much does this room cost?"

"The room is prepaid, Mr. Veeder. As well as all the inclusive elements of the resort: food and drink, activities, golf, scuba, spa services. The folder on the dining room table has information on all the amenities of the resort."

"Did you say spa services?" Angie asked.

"This was a gift," I said. "I'd love to one day repay it. Can you give me a ballpark figure?"

"Of course," she said. "This luxury family cabaña costs fifty thousand pesos a night at this time of year. With a three-night minimum."

Angie turned to me. "That's around three thousand dollars. Three thousand dollars a night. Tomás paid twenty thousand dollars for the week."

Verónica laughed. "Mr. Morales did not pay anything."

"I don't understand," I said. "Why not?"

"Because Mr. Morales owns La Playa Resort, of course."

"Of course."

"Have you seen the bathroom? I could live in this bathroom," Angie yelled from—you guessed it—the bathroom.

As much as I loved a good bathroom, I could never match the enthusiasm that my bride had for an oversized tub, Jacuzzi jets, or any variety of steaming shower fixtures.

Immediately after Verónica left, Angie and I ran from room to room, marveling at the crazy decadence of the place. Picking things up and carefully putting them back down. Pointing at shit. There was quite a bit of shouting.

"There's a sauna, a whirlpool," Angie said. "One of those Frenchy ass-fountains."

"A bidet?"

"I tried it, which was interesting. I would definitely do it again, but not every day. Scary but refreshing. The soaps are all different shapes. Not like Travelodge rectangular, but beach themed. Mostly shells. But I saw a starfish and a seahorse, too. They smell like something called 'sea foam' or 'Pacific breeze.'"

"So taking the crime boss's money wasn't the worst idea in the world," I said.

“Don’t ‘I told you so’ me. I could ‘I told you so’ you just about every damn day of the year.”

“I was just saying that it turned out.”

“Okay. This place is crazy nice.”

“You may have to sit down for this, but I checked out the veranda, and there’s a whole ’nother hot tub out there. For naked outdoor action. And fluffy-ass bathrobes in the closet, which I’d go Axel Foley on if I wasn’t afraid of Tomás hunting me down to get them back.”

“We should leave the resort, go out, and do things,” Angie said, “but I don’t want to leave this room. I want to live and die in this cabaña.”

“Did you see the gift basket?” I asked. “No bullshit fruit and granola bars. There’s wine and cheese and chocolate and jalapeño jam and fancy crackers and a fucking Kindle. There’s an e-reader in the gift basket. Because why the fuck not.”

For the next hour, Angie switched back and forth between the outdoor hot tub and the indoor whirlpool bath.. It looked exhausting, but I enjoyed watching her prance around in the buff. I spread out on the enormous canopy bed and reread the papers that Tomás had given me.

According to the dossier—I’d always wanted to read a dossier—Tomás’s man had tracked down Yolanda’s father in a town called Coatepec, east of Mazatlán. A mountain village of a few thousand, it was well off the main highway and up a winding road into the Sierra Madre Occidental range. One of dozens of identical villages scattered all over this region. Isolated and only on detailed maps.

Fernando Palomera had grown up in the small town, moved away in his youth, and returned from Guadalajara. According to a brief mention in a Durango paper, he had recently been elected mayor of the town. There was an accompanying photo. The picture made him look like the Mexican Dennis Franz. Not exactly flattering.

Coatepec could mark the end of a long journey, a story that started five years earlier. One question hovered over everything: What had brought Yolanda to Mexicali in the first place? Why had she left? Had she fled from something? Okay, more than one question.

Yolanda hadn't carried herself like she came from a village. She had poise and a hint of upper class in her calm stride. However, when I had met her, she was living in a shantytown and working as a prostitute. To choose that life over whatever she left in Mexico was telling. I just didn't know what it told.

There was a chance that this would be a wash. That Tomás's man got his information wrong. Best-case scenario, I would meet the man, verify the relation, create a line of communication, and head back to Mazatlán and get drunk by the pool for the remainder of the week.

After an hour of enjoying all the possible variations of hot water, Angie crashed. She flumped onto the bed and within a few minutes was sound asleep. Her snoring sounded like a tiger purr. Mrs. Veeder vacationed hard.

I put on my swim trunks and a pair of the complimentary sandals (those, I was definitely going to steal) and sought out a swimming pool. There were four different pools in our wing of the facility, all enormous. The one I settled on was large enough to maintain three islands. Not some concrete brick bullshit, but real cartoon islands with one palm tree and a little beach. I swam to an unoccupied one and lounged on a lounge chair that was there for the purpose of lounging.

I closed my eyes and lost track of who I was. I pretended like I belonged at the resort. The divide between awesome and ridiculous had blurred. I went with it. I had never wanted to be rich more than I did then. The poor should never be able to experience that level of decadence. Revolution would follow. I wanted to live on my little island, the rest of the world be damned.

I concentrated on the red glow inside my eyelids, convinced that everything would work out. That this trip would be easier than a nymphomaniac recently released from prison. That it wasn't going to turn into a typical Jimmy Veeder shitshow.

As I drifted off, a shadow crossed my path, followed by an ice-cold sensation on my chest. I shrieked, snapped upright, and stared at Bobby Maves holding a glass of ice water and smiling like Dr. Teeth. His shirt and shorts were soaking wet.

"Are you kidding me?" I said. "You crashed my fucking honeymoon?"

Bobby laughed and made himself comfortable in the lounge chair next to me. "You knew I'd show up."

"No. I didn't."

"This place is fucking nice. Like Tim Cappello nice. Can't you imagine him lounging by the pool all oiled up? Playing his sax in the water?"

"How did you even get in here? They should have rich-people security here. Lasers and trapdoors and moats and shit."

"There ain't a prison that can keep me out. Wait, did I say that right?"

"Did you climb a wall, or tunnel in?"

"I devised an elaborate scheme that required two costume changes, a fake Peruvian accent, a series of wigs and mustaches, a hot air balloon, and thirteen ostriches as a distraction." Bobby laughed. "I told them I was a friend of yours. They called your room, and Angie vouched for me. She sounded really sleepy. I grabbed a cocktail at the bar, and here I am."

"I will be sure to make a note on the comment card that I was unsatisfied with their approach to privacy." I reached for his drink. "I'm surprised Angie wasn't mad."

"Oh, she was pissed. She called me a fuck-bucket." Bobby handed me the margarita. I took a huge swallow, regretting it immediately. The ice cream headache that followed felt like my brain had imploded.

"What the fuck are you doing here, Bobby? In Mexico?"

"Yolanda, man. I was there, too. If you're going to go find her old man, Juanito's grandpa, I want to be there. I'm a part of the story. I'm going to see this through, best friend." He shrugged. "Also, okay, I couldn't stand the idea of you getting to do funner stuff than me. I would've gone apeshit sitting in the fucking desert while you're Mexicoing it up down here."

"This is my fucking honeymoon. You couldn't let me and Angie go on our honeymoon without tagging along?"

"I'm the wildcard. I'm unpredictable." Bobby shot me a fake grin. "You just got wildcarded, bro."

"You can't crash in our cabaña, if that's what you're thinking. We're planning on doing sex things."

"Relax. Me and Gris are staying at a shitbox down the road. I got a deal. We have to listen to some slimeball try to sell us a timeshare or some shit for a couple hours Saturday morning, but the price was right. I can daydream through the fuck's spiel using the power of my imagination. Reminisce in my brain about my favorite pornographies while I eat free huevos. Boom. Who wins? This guy."

"Griselda is here, too? Where'd you get the money?"

"Unlike you, bro," Bobby said, "I'm a successful farmer. I had some hay money in my safe. Couldn't figure out what else to do with it."

"Hay money?"

"What the gubment don't know keeps me out of jail." Bobby winked. "Cheating on your taxes is as American as steroids in baseball. I still pay too damn much for shit I don't want. Politicians can go fuck themselves."

"That sounds about right."

I took a slower pull from the margarita and handed it back to Bobby. "I'm glad you're here."

"Of course you are. You don't know how to have fun without me."

"I'm being followed."

Bobby gave me a dubious look. "Is it because of the secret files, or the stolen diamonds? Who the fuck would follow you? You're boring. I've never been followed, and I'm exciting as fuck. People would pay for the privilege to ride shotgun on a Mavescapade."

"That day you grabbed me in Mexicali, my bachelor party—fuck you very much for that, by the way—I saw two guys across from the tux place. I saw those same guys at the airport a few hours ago."

"Us Mexicans, we can look alike to you gringos. Were they wearing ponchos and sombreros? Did they have leaf blowers on their backs?"

"It was the same guys. First in Mexicali, now here."

"What do they want?"

"No idea."

"Let's find out." Bobby cracked his knuckles.

"What does that mean? I don't know what that means. I hate the sound of it."

Before Bobby could answer, we were distracted by a woman in a bikini swimming to our island and stepping onto its small beach. Bobby and I stared, trying and failing to not come off as creepy. Sad men looking at something they could never have.

"Mr. Veeder," the woman said. "Can I get you or your friend anything from the bar or kitchen?"

"Island service," Bobby said. "This place is uptown."

"I would love a beer," I said, trying to focus my eyes on her face, despite the fact she was leaning over. "A Pacifico."

"This place is all-inclusive, right?" Bobby asked.

"For guests," she said.

"Do you have lobster?"

"We do. Maine lobster flown in fresh daily."

"Mr. Veeder would like a half dozen lobster tacos, the hottest hot sauce you got, and ten beers." He gave her a wink. She smiled.

"Bobby," I said, embarrassed. "I don't—"

"I'll be back with your order." The woman returned to the water and swam away. It was a sight to behold.

"I'll eat the tacos that you don't. So they don't go to waste." Bobby smiled. "When you get a guest pass to heaven, you sure as shit got to steal a halo and a harp for the drive back to hell."

"I knew when I married you, I married that maniac, too," Angie said when I returned to the room full of tacos and beer. I would classify her anger level at peeved, not as mad as I had expected. A four, tops. Usually devoted to the times when I farted in bed and tried to convince her that she did it.

"I didn't ask him to come down here," I said. "I want you to know that."

"Uh-hunh."

"You won't even notice they're here. We go to dinner with Bobby and Gris tonight. He comes with us to Coatepec tomorrow. The rest of the trip is you and me and drinks and sex and parasailing and complimentary Bikram yoga and donkey rides on the beach or whatever the hell people do down Mexico way."

"You're going to do yoga?"

"If it makes you happy."

"Can I take video? That would definitely make me happy."

FIVE

Radical pulled the car to the front of the Bahía Del Sol Kwality Resort, a concrete bunker with two fake palm trees on either side of the front entrance. The plastic foliage looked like it was dying. The faded, hand-painted sign had taken a beating from the wind and sea. A shirtless man with his pants hanging off his ass hosed down two garbage pails, greenish-brown sludge running through the mortar of the driveway bricks.

"I would poke fun," I said, "but this is where we would be staying if I didn't have an in with the human incarnation of the devil."

"It pays to know evil people," Angie said.

Bobby and Griselda walked out from the lobby, all smiles and waves. Bobby hopped in the front seat. Griselda joined us in back.

"It's not as fancy as your digs, but there are perks," Bobby said. "A quality selection of condom flavors in each bathroom vending machine. The papaya is bracingly tangy."

Griselda gave Bobby a light smack on the back of the head. We all agreed.

"I want you both to know that I was against coming down here. And against not telling you," Griselda said. "But you know how he gets."

"Some children need to scream in the aisle until you buy them Oreos," Angie said.

"That was the one time. And they were Double Stufs," I said. "This is Radical. He's our driver."

"How did you get the name Radical?" Bobby asked. "Is it because you're radical?"

Radical pulled out of the driveway. "When I was younger, I was—¿cómo se dice?—un alborotador."

"A troublemaker," Bobby said.

"Sí, I made trouble. Fighting and drinking. And the women. All the things that young men do."

"And some older men who should know better," Griselda said.

"One night, some güeros—surfos—they want to fight me. Three of them, only me. But they fight for fun. They don't fight because they need to. After it's over, I'm standing with one of their shirts in my hand. All their blood is on it. The shirt said Radical on the front. I wore that shirt all the time. Like a prize."

"That's a fucked-up story, Radical," Bobby said. "You're going to fit right in."

"Who we are as boys is not who we are as men," Radical said. "That is the lie we tell ourselves."

During the drive on the Malecon from Zona Dorada into Centro Histórico, Bobby kept an eye on the side mirror. I wanted to turn around and look for my Mexican shadows, but I resisted. I didn't want to raise any alarms in the car or outside it.

Griselda and Angie were deep in a conversation about how awesome the bathroom in our cabaña was. I was getting jealous. If it came down to me or that bathroom, Angie's choice was clear. I had better step up my game. I made a mental note to buy Angie a churro later.

Bobby gave me a glance and a nod. I took it to mean that we were being followed, but we really hadn't worked out a functioning system of signals and gestures. He could have been indicating that he felt thirsty or dyspeptic.

I made it clear to Radical that we wanted a restaurant with real Mexican food in a real Mexican neighborhood. We might hit the tourist area at some point to do our ceramic frog and cheap serape shopping, but when it came to Mexican food the salsa had to be spicy and the flavors correct. The gringo tourist traps salted up and blanded down the food to match the El Torito mentality. If I wanted to go to a Hooters or Hard Rock, I would have stayed in the United States and shot myself in the face.

Radical pulled up in front of a restaurant. A simple sign read "Beto's." Stucco walls and a terra cotta roof. Cerveza signs for Pacifico and Victoria beer on the walls. The sound of live tambora music from inside. It sounded like a mariachi/polka band made up of circus musicians.

"You will like Beto's," Radical said. "Best seafood in Mexico."

I asked Radical to join us, but he shook his head. "Gracias, no. There is a chica that I want to see. Take your time at dinner." He gave me a completely unnecessary wink.

"Radical is about to get radical," Bobby said.

Getting out of the car, I gave my best nonchalant look over my shoulder, catching sight of a black SUV parked at the end of the block with two people inside. I couldn't make out their faces, but who just sits in their car?

The four of us dined on the second-story patio overlooking the modest shopping district. Radical hooked us up. The dorado, wahoo, and shark were fresh and cooked perfectly. The Pacifico was cold and had alcohol in it. The old lady that made tortillas in the corner was exactly the right shape. So were the tortillas. I don't care how that sounds. Thin women made inferior tortillas.

We talked and laughed and settled into the trip. It stopped being a big deal that Bobby and Griselda were there. It felt good to share the moment with family. I no longer felt like I was on a mission. The whole trip had become about fun and family, and those are the two words that I thought of when I thought of Bobby and Gris.

After dinner, Angie and Griselda decided to check out some of the shops. That gave me and Bobby the perfect opportunity to deal with our Mexican shadows and see if they would take the bait.

We walked through the narrow streets, getting farther and farther from the well-lit commercial district.

"They still behind us?" I asked without turning around.

"A block back. Caught sight of them when we turned that corner," Bobby said. "Don't worry. I got a plan."

"If you described the plan to me, would it be something along the lines of 'When they get close, we fuck them up'? Or just a series of sound effects and karate chops?"

"Shut your taco hole. You're in my wing of the mansion now."

"Is that a phrase?"

"It is now. Trust the plan. We're going to have a nice constitutional. Find a dark alley. Wait for them, and then bing, bang, boom, they tell us why they're following you."

"You literally combined the two things I said. 'When they get close, we fuck them up' with some sound effects. Nice to see you go uptown with the word 'constitutional,' though."

"Word-a-day calendar. I'm growing as a word talker."

"In your wing of the mansion."

"Where the awesome people hang out."

"What is my role in this elaborate plan?" I asked.

"I'll take the two on the left."

"There's only two of them."

"Exactly," Bobby said.

We made our way into a neighborhood with flickering streetlights. A few pedestrians roamed the streets. People sat on tables outside cantinas. We kept walking until we found an industrial area. Fewer people around. Bobby gave me a nod. We ducked into the next alley, disappearing in its shadows. It reeked of standing water and garbage.

With my back against the damp wall, I readied myself. My heart beat loudly in my ears. My mouth got dry. My hands shook. The moment before any confrontation, my brain and heart react with all the subtlety of a coked-up Jerry Lewis.

Bobby on the other hand appeared as calm as a really calm thing. Seriously, that calm. His breathing stayed slow and steady. He smiled. The man loved fighting. I was tempted to look down to see if he had a pup tent. He pulled a bottle of beer from the wide pocket of his carpenter jeans, popped the top, and took a deep swig.

"Are you kidding me?" I said.

"You didn't grab some fight beers before we left?"

Before I could refute the concept of "fight beers," the two men from the airport turned the corner. Three feet away, they froze, surprised to see us. The big man with the scar appeared incapable of closing his mouth, panting heavily from the walk. The smaller man started to say something but stopped short.

Bobby took one last pull from his beer and then broke the bottle against the ear of the bigger man. The giant stumbled backward, holding his bleeding melon. He tripped on the uneven sidewalk and fell on his ass.

The smaller man took a few steps back and pulled a gun. Bobby stopped. The gunman didn't bother to check on his friend. He motioned for us to move back deeper into the alley.

"I don't want to nitpick," I said to Bobby, "but your plan had flaws."

"Kind of a dick move to 'I told you so' me now," Bobby said.

The bigger man rose, slowly moving to the gunman's side. He held his hand to his ear, blood oozing through his fingers.

"What do you want?" I asked. "Why are you following me? ¿Por qué me está siguiendo?"

"We speak English, ese," the small man said with an East LA accent. "Don't with the white-bread Spanglish bullshit."

"I know, right?" Bobby said. "It's embarrassing."

What happened next. As the kids say, I can't even.

Griselda appeared from the mouth of the alley and tackled the guy with the gun, hitting him in the back of the knees. Fifteen-yard penalty for clipping. The gun fired into the air, a loud crack echoing down the alley. The small man landed on his knees and fell forward with Griselda on his back.

The big man took a step toward them but turned at a sound. Angie hit the big palooka in the face with a rock or a brick, something that made a squishy thud where the man's nose had once been. He fell like the bones had vanished from his body.

Sitting on the back of the small man's legs, Griselda kidney-punched the shit out of the little fella. He gasped and grunted, arms flailing. He attempted to lift the gun, but Bobby put a foot on his wrist and pried it from his hand.

Bobby laughed. "You seeing this shit, Jimmy? Our women are badass."

"I think he's had enough, Gris," I said. "Bobby's got the gun."

Griselda gave him one more for good measure, pushed his face into the sewagey ground, and stood. She brushed off her jeans and turned to Angie. They high-fived in a moment that should have been freeze-framed.

"Where did you two come from?" I asked. "That was nuts."

"We knew you two idiots were in some kind of trouble," Angie said. "You're that predictable."

"No, we're not," I said, but that was the extent of my argument.

Angie laughed. "We saw these two jokers following you, so we tagged along. That's when we saved your sorry asses."

"Hey, Michelle Yeoh. I had everything under control," Bobby said, walking to the bloody and barely conscious big man. The man tried to stand but fell back down. Bobby grabbed his foot and dragged him next to the littler guy.

I checked the men's pockets for more weapons but only found a Swiss Army knife, the thirty-two-tool version with the magnifying glass and toothpick. I had the same one when I was eight.

"Bummed I didn't get to scrap," Bobby said. "Guess it's ladies' night."

"You hit a guy with a bottle."

"That was just to get their attention," Bobby said. "I told you my plan would work."

"Your 'plan'?" I made quotes with my fingers.

"Only assholes use air quotes."

"Yeah, okay. My bad."

"Only assholes say, 'My bad.'"

"Who made you the asshole police?"

"Shut up, shut up, shut up," Angie said. "Do you two ever stop?"

"Have you ever done anything without that annoying eighties action movie banter?" Griselda asked.

"Of course not," Bobby said, looking at me like she was crazy.

"Just because you couldn't think of a good catchphrase," I said, "doesn't mean you need to be mad at us."

"We should go," Griselda said. "That gunshot will draw attention. Although I doubt police response in Sinaloa is speedy."

"Who are these guys?" Angie asked. "What's going on?"

"Dunno." I shrugged, leaning down and helping the smaller man into a sitting position. "You going to tell us what this is all about?"

"This is bullshit," the small man said. "That's what it is. We're like protecting you and shit."

"Protecting us?" I said. "You pulled a fucking gun."

"Because the guy with the fucked-up hair hit Jorge with a bottle, pendejo. I wasn't going to let that shit happen to me."

"Instead, you got your ass kicked by my lady," Bobby said. He turned to Griselda. "Seriously awesome, by the way. Sexy as shit. We might have to role-play that later."

"You motherfuckers are all violent motherfuckers," the man said.

"You were following me in Mexicali," I said. "What's going on?"

"Wait a minute," Angie said. "What now? These dumbasses have been following you for how long? And I'm hearing about it now?"

"You stepped in that one, bro," Bobby said. "It's going to take some scouring to get that shit off your shoe."

Angie gave the small man a soft kick. "You said you're protecting Jimmy. Who from?"

"No one. Mexico, I guess. This is a fucked-up country. Mexico is way dangerous and shit."

"Tomás hired you," I said, not a question. Who else?

The guy didn't say a word, just stared.

"I can call him and ask," I said, reaching for my phone. "It's no problem."

"Shit, man," he said. "Don't do that. We fucked up the last thing. This would be our second fuckup. We got jacked up by your ladies. Ain't that enough?"

"It must be a really important assignment if Tomás sent the best of the best," Bobby said.

"Normal people don't hit other people with beer bottles."

"You obviously haven't been to one of my family reunions," Bobby said. "And my family is totally normal."

"Let's take this indoors," Gris said. "That gunshot might draw attention. You two going to give us any trouble?"

They both shook their heads, looking like scolded children.

The upside of a great dive bar—apart from the obvious wonderfulness of a place devoted to drinking—is that no one gives a shit about who you are or what you're doing. As long as you aren't a dick or a loudmouth, a dive bar is a place you can sit and be left alone.

Not to be confused with one of those faux dives that hipsters flock to. A place that used to be slightly shady, but now serves wine in mason jars and infuses things. Where the bathrooms are clean and the graffiti is clever. There's nothing wrong with that kind of place, other than everything. It's a vacation spent in clean dirt. Class tourism, slumming in the shadows.

A real dive is effortless. Working class, a few barflies, a jukebox that hasn't changed in decades, and a take-no-shit bartender. A place with fewer than three choices of beer and where the wine just comes in two colors. A cracked-leather, outlaw shithole where anonymity is the only ID. While you aren't exactly welcome, you know whether or not you belong.

Mexico knows how to do dive bars. When your party of six included two bleeding hostages at gunpoint, that was important.

Cerveza probably wasn't the name of the place, but the handwritten sign was the only clue we had to go on. No need to brag about a name with something as bourgeois as a sign. Dark and smelling of body odor and grease, Cerveza only had a few customers. Nobody—including the bartender—gave a shit about our presence. The six of us crowded around one of the two small tables in the back.

"Six cervezas?" Bobby asked us, moving toward the bar.

"A Coke," the small man said. "I don't drink."

"I knew I didn't like you," Bobby said.

When Bobby returned with the drinks, we all stared at each other.

"We kind of lost our momentum, didn't we?" I said.

Bobby glanced at the bar, then pulled the pistol halfway out of his pocket. "My old man used to own a Trejo. The first handgun I ever fired."

"Like Danny Trejo?" I asked.

"Yes, Jimmy," Bobby said, dismissing me. "Like Danny Trejo. These little babies are nasty. Las fabrican en Mexico. Used to see them all the time. I don't think they make them anymore."

"Couldn't bring anything in," the small man said. "It's what we could get."

For all the gun violence in Mexico, guns aren't always easy to come by. The cartels don't have a problem, obviously, but for most, it's a matter of knowing the right person—or wrong person, depending on your point of view. Drugs move north. Guns and money move south.

"Let me take a look at your nose," Angie said to Jorge, the big man.

He shook his head. "You crazy? You're the one that did this shit."

"She's a nurse," I said.

The big man gave her a suspicious look but nodded. As she inspected what I could tell from across the table was a very broken nose, I turned to the smaller man.

"What's your name?" I asked.

"Luis."

"Okay, Luis. Tell me what's going on."

Luis sighed, glanced over at Jorge, and shrugged. "Fuck it. Me and Jorge, we got in some shit in LA. Had to get out of there. Heard there was work in Chicali. Been doing small jobs for Morales. Paying our dues. Mostly errands. When you saw us in Mexicali, we were supposed to give you a fucking present. Like a wrapped box with a bow. The easiest fucking job. You disappeared. Went in that tux place and poof. Like Where's fucking Waldo and shit."

"Now I understand." Bobby laughed. "You guys are fucking idiots."

"Real fucking funny, Mexican Elvis," Luis said. "Morales gave us a cakewalk job, and we fucked it up. We looked like assholes. He sent us down here to do a few other things. He didn't say for sure to like guard you, but I got this feeling if anything happened to you, we were fucked."

"I don't want you following me no more," I said. "I don't need protection."

"You ain't been listening, ese. I work for Tomás Morales. Not you. We fucked up in Mexicali. We fucked up tonight. If something happens to you, we're like triple-fucked."

"Jimmy ain't asking," Bobby said, still holding the gun.

"I ain't worried about you two backward-ass country fucks. I'm fucking scared of Tomás Morales. I've heard stories. Like horror movie stories."

"Nothing is going to happen to us," I said. "We're here for a family reunion thing."

"It's still Mexico." He turned to Bobby. "You going to give me my gun back?"

"The fuck I will," Bobby said.

Griselda held out her hand to Bobby. "Yeah," she said. "I better hold on to that."

"Come on, baby," Bobby said. "Not in front of the guys."

Griselda gave Bobby her cop stare. Bobby put the small automatic in her hand.

Luis closed his eyes and squeezed the bridge of his nose. "Who the fuck are you people?"

Radical showed up a half hour later. I had called him to pick us up, but he ended up having a few beers with us. He knew Jorge and Luis but wouldn't let on the exact nature of their relationship. It was all mysterious and shady, but they worked for Tomás. What else could I expect? Whatever side business they were involved with had nothing to do with us. We were there to see my son's grandfather.

Bobby wanted to let Luis and Jorge go fuck themselves, but I had empathy for their position. A shitload of beers and a few Cokes later, we worked out a compromise. I'd been on Tomás's bad side, and it wasn't a place I ever wanted to be again. They might be thugs, but who was I to fuck up their lives?

The Numbnut Twins agreed to stop tailing us within the city of Mazatlán. It might have been in Sinaloa, but Mazatlán was one of the safest cities in Mexico. Old people retired there. However, they insisted on joining us on the trip to Coatepec. In their mind, the country was where bad shit could go down, and they wanted to be there if it did. Who knew what kind of nonsense went on out in the rural Sierra Madre?

I figured no harm having an extra couple people. Whether Mexico or the US, small towns held their own secrets. And their own screwy form of danger. Cue the banjo music.

"I don't like you, but we can't let nothing happen to you," Luis said. "If Tomás Morales wasn't our boss, I'd mess up your buddy for that bottle shit."

Bobby laughed. "Why is it guys that think they're tough always start sentences with 'I'd fight you, but . . . '?"

"When this is over, homes," Luis said, "and your women aren't around to protect you, we'll go."

"That's going to be fun," Bobby said.

Angie looked at Griselda. "Men are fucking morons."

"Stupid fucking morons," Griselda said.

SIX

I don't like to get up early when I'm on vacation. And by early I mean before noon. I compromised, and we set out at eleven. My hangover was manageable, nothing that two aspirin and sunglasses couldn't handle. The simple trip that I had planned had somehow become a clusterfuck of organizational bullshit.

Griselda was the only person not complicating things. She chose to bail on the trek and lounge by the pool—to, quote, keep away from you morons and stay out of Mexican jail, unquote.

Bobby wanted to stop for some road beers. We weren't driving, so I thought it was a good idea. Angie did not. She was already throwing off our rhythm. Bobby and I had a way of doing things, and that almost always required beer.

When two people go to Disneyland together, there are no arguments over what rides to go on. Three people, and there's always that person who wants to ride the Teacups first thing in the morning. Because apparently they enjoy the taste of puking up scrambled eggs and Jimmy Deans.

I reminded myself that this trip wasn't one of Bobby's Mavescapades but was supposed to be me and Angie. Bobby was the third wheel. Angie and I were married now, and this trip was for our son. I wanted her to be there, and I wanted her input. That said, I bitched and moaned until we stopped for beer, but just a sixer.

Radical was the only one in the car that had his shit together. He was quiet and professional, but I could tell by his stoicism that he would have preferred a hot-sauce-covered finger in the eye to our bickering.

To avoid any headaches, I called Luis and Jorge. Traditionally, one didn't call the shady people following them, but those morons were mostly harmless. They waited on the street when we pulled out of La Playa. Once on the highway, they passed us and took the lead. Our caravan of two cars and six people finally left Mazatlán on a field trip into the Mexican countryside.

The neighborhoods of the east side of Mazatlán were a strong reminder of the economic imbalance within Mexico. The farther we got from the ocean, the more run-down the buildings, the shittier the streets, the sketchier the neighborhoods. Not much different than most US cities, only more pronounced. The people that worked for cheap wages in those fancy resorts and hotels had to live somewhere.

"That's Lomas del Ébano," Radical said, as if reading my mind. "Where I live. If you are from there or Ricardo Flores Magón or Valle de Urías or any of the barrios, you were born with your hands already in fists."

"I don't doubt it," I said.

"Most turistos, they don't come this way. Why would they? Nobody to take care of them. You liked Beto's, yeah? Good food. If you want, when we come back, we stop and get tortas and queso fundido. The best in Mexico. Or maybe you don't."

"That sounds radical, Radical," Bobby said. "I can't stand that Señor Frog's horseshit. Mexicans being the Mexicans that white folks want them to be. Might as well be sleeping on the street with their knees up wearing a big ol' sombrero, all Speedy Gonzales."

"Actually," I said, "that better describes his cousin, Slowpoke Rodriguez."

Bobby turned, looked at me, and gave me an eye-roll that would have impressed a teenage girl.

"Ándale, ándale. Arriba, arriba. Epa, epa. Yee-haw," Radical said, doing a spot-on Mel Blanc.

"Do you know a place we can get chapulines?" Bobby asked.

"Sí. There's a Oaxacan. He makes them."

"You got to try them," Bobby said to me and Angie. "Grasshoppers."

Angie made a face. "Do they come with a side of ants?"

"Not ants, no," Radical said, "but you could get escamoles."

"Those are ant eggs," I said.

"Stop talking," Angie said, grimacing. "I'm losing my appetite."

The city vanished, transforming into hills and scrub. The foothills of the Sierra Madre range turned more mountainous at every bend. My ears plugged as we climbed. The four-lane road appeared new, well-maintained, and smooth. The tires purred. Every mile or so we traveled over a bridge or through a tunnel. If something got in the way, the Mexicans who built this road went through it or over it. Never around. It's the same strategy I employ. I'm a straight-ahead guy, regardless if that's the easiest or smartest path. Forward is the direction that makes the most sense to me.

I leaned forward between the seats to talk to Radical. "Last night you never told us how you knew Luis and Jorge. Same employer. Did you know they were following us?"

"I saw them once, but I did not know," he said. "I had other business with them. Some introductions. A favor. Business not related to your business."

"Business for Tomás Morales?"

"This is all new," Radical said, pointing up ahead. "New road. New bridge up ahead. Very high. Very long. Now you can drive from Mazatlán to Durango. Much easier than before. It's good. Progress. Mexico continues to grow."

Radical was not a subtle man when it came to avoiding a question. I was about to press him about Tomás, but as he spoke, a new but muddy Jeep Wrangler attempted to pass us on the left. As there was an open lane to our right, it didn't make sense to get in the oncoming lane. Once alongside Radical's car, the Jeep slowed and maintained the same speed. The four men inside wore cowboy hats and sunglasses. They all had mustaches and semiautomatic rifles—AR-15s and AK-47s, according to my action movie acumen. The men stared directly at us. Even the driver, his eyes off the road.

"What the fuck is this?" Bobby said, not moving his head and barely moving his lips.

"Do not move your hands," Radical said, staring straight ahead. "Be calm."

"What's going on?" Angie said. "Who are those men?"

"It's going to be fine," I said, hoping I wasn't lying.

"The car is too nice for bandits," Radical said. "Narcos. Maybe borrachos playing games."

I glanced over without moving my head. The four men remained motionless, still staring. Cars rushed past in the far oncoming lane, horns blaring.

"If something is going to happen, it will happen on the bridge," Radical said.

Radical took his foot off the accelerator. I felt the car slow down, falling behind the Jeep. The Jeep slowed as well, readjusting to remain beside us.

"Well, something's going to happen," Bobby said, nodding forward.

Through the windshield, I saw two cars coming into view in the oncoming lanes less than a quarter mile ahead. The man in the passenger seat of the Jeep lifted his sunglasses and smiled. He waved the driver forward. The Jeep sped up and passed us just before the other cars zoomed past. Radical let the car slow more, in no hurry to catch up.

"That was really scary," Angie said.

"Do you want to forget this?" I said. "Head back to Mazatlán?"

"No," she said. "They had their fun."

We turned a corner, and the view changed drastically. The mountains opened up to reveal an enormous ravine. The giant bridge that Radical had mentioned spanned its length ahead of us.

"Baluarte Bridge," Radical said. "Sinaloa on one side, Durango on the other. Four hundred meters to the bottom."

"How much is that in American?" Bobby said.

"About thirteen hundred feet," I said.

Bobby whistled.

The chasm below the bridge might as well have been bottomless. It was impossible to see the whole drop from our vantage point. Definitely one of the highest bridges I had ever seen, and it looked about a half mile long. One of those wonders-of-the-world kind of bridges.

"You said if something was going to happen, this is where it would happen," Angie said, pointing ahead. "It's fucking happening."

"Fuck me," I said.

Before the bridge, the Jeep pulled a similar maneuver alongside Luis and Jorge's SUV, moving to pass but keeping pace instead. At least this time, it wasn't in the oncoming lane. I couldn't tell what was going on, but it appeared that the men in the two cars were shouting at each other, having a conversation. Dramatic arm gestures were involved. The vehicles swerved a couple times, almost hitting each other.

"We should bail," Bobby said. "Two cars full of tough dimwits. There's only one possible outcome."

"I agree," Angie said.

"Me, too," I said.

Radical looked in the rearview mirror and grimaced. "Ya valió madre."

We drove onto the bridge. Four lanes with a thick metal railing separating the oncoming traffic. Thirteen hundred feet above the ravine. Nowhere to go.

Then the shooting started. And all holy hell broke fucking loose.

I only caught a glimpse of the beginning of the action before Radical slammed on the brakes, sending the car spinning. There was a barrage of gunfire from the Jeep's window. Jorge and Luis's SUV swerved to the right, then to the left, slamming into the Jeep. A gun flashed from the driver's side of the SUV. One shot. A man fell from the Jeep onto the road in front of us, his limbs already loose at his side. The man's body bounced off the shoulder and folded in a way that would give me nightmares for a long time.

That action took two, maybe three seconds. But I swear it happened in slow motion. Then all I saw was spinning, the world streaking by from left to right. Radical's car bumper tapped the bridge rail enough to remind me how high up we were. I peed a little. We came to a stop facing the wrong direction, the sound of the gun battle behind us. Another Jeep Wrangler appeared on the road in front of us. It stopped at the edge of the bridge.

Our car became a cacophony of swears and yelling in at least two languages. Angie, Bobby, and I upped our creative profanity game, overlapping into a solid piece of slam poetry.

"Is everyone okay?" I yelled, although it had already gotten quiet. My hands shook uncontrollably.

Angie looked confused, but she nodded.

"What in the fucking fuck, man?" Bobby said.

We all turned to look out the back window to assess the aftermath of the fight. Jorge and Luis's SUV had crashed into the railing and come to a stop. The Jeep drove ahead to the opposite end of the bridge and stopped. The man's body remained in the middle of the road. His neck was bent at an angle that necks didn't bend.

"I wish we weren't on a fucking bridge right now," Bobby said. "A very high-up fucking bridge."

"Coño, coño, coño," Radical said, showing emotion for the first time.

We all turned back to the front windshield, facing the direction that we had come from. The newly arrived Jeep crept forward toward us.

"We should check on Luis and Jorge," Angie said.

"Yeah, no," I said. "We're not doing that."

"No offense, Angie, but the fuck we should," Bobby said. "The only thing we should do is get the fuck out of here. Like now."

I started to say something, but Radical didn't want to debate our options. Apparently his car was a dictatorship, not a democracy. He performed a quick two-point turn, and then floored it in the direction that we had been heading. He drove straight toward the first Jeep Wrangler. He did his best to swerve around the man on the road but failed, catching part of the dead man's arm. I barely felt the small bump, but it still made me queasy.

As we passed, I glanced at Jorge and Luis's crashed SUV. A glance was all it took to see that both of them were dead, a bloody mess. At least a dozen bullet holes perforated the driver's side door and front fender. Luis's arm dangled out the driver's side window, still holding a pistol. They hadn't stood a chance.

"Uh, Radical," I said. The "uh" meant to explain that I had some trepidations about our quickening approach to the ready gunmen standing behind their Jeep at the far end of the bridge.

"They won't shoot," Radical said.

"Uh," I said again. This "uh" inquired about how he could possibly know with enough certainty that his course of action was the correct of the infinite choices that he had to choose from. My "uhs" carried a lot of subtext.

"They would have shot us before," Radical answered. "They didn't. They want to kidnap you."

"Kidnap?" Angie said. It hurt me to hear her afraid.

"They'll kidnap the three Americans," Radical said. "They'll kill this stupid Mexican. Hold on."

The most unnecessary "hold on" in the history of reckless driving. He yanked on the parking brake, forcing us into another spin. It was so abrupt, the car tilted for a second on two wheels, threatening to roll. The car leveled out and traveled backward toward the Jeep for twenty yards. The back bumper of Radical's car slammed into the Jeep's front end. Steam immediately rose from its radiator. The seat belt dug deep into my shoulder. My neck whiplashed forward.

The Jeep on the other end raced toward us, swerving slightly to avoid the dead man in the middle of the road.

A man appeared at the window beside me. I jumped in my seat—and may or may not have shrieked. He held a rifle but looked glassy eyed and not at all sure of where or even who he was. Blood ran down his forehead.

Radical didn't wait to trade insurance information. He punched the gas. The car went into reverse and pushed the Jeep to the side. Once clear, Radical spun the car around and headed quickly down the road in the direction of Durango, only a ten- or fifteen-second head start on the other Jeep. The metal of the trunk had folded forward, but it didn't look like the damage affected the car's performance.

"Missed a great opportunity," Bobby said. "You should have said 'It's time to get Radical!' before you crashed into them."

Past the gorge, the road twisted farther up into the mountains. Forty-five-kilometers-an-hour warnings sat posted at most turns. The views would have been amazing, but they were lost on me in my panicked state. While Radical drove, we all kept our eyes out the back window.

Off-road, a Jeep would be the better vehicle. But on a mountain highway, Radical's Mercedes had the advantage. Jeeps aren't known for their acceleration, and they handle for shit on turns. The one war in which the Germans beat the Americans. If we were lucky, our pursuers would accidentally drive off a cliff. One could dream. Radical put some distance between us and them.

All the action on the bridge had taken less than thirty seconds. As all of us tried to absorb our current situation, talk seemed stupid. Of course, that didn't stop me from talking. Or being stupid.

"What the fuck do we do?" I asked no one in particular. "What happens now?"

"We head to Durango," Bobby said. "Get to the city."

"Radical?" Angie said. "You know the area. Do we go to Durango?"

Radical thought for a moment, concentrating on each turn. "Too far. Maybe men up ahead. I know a road. There's a silver mine. A town not very far from it. From there somehow we find our way back to Mazatlán."

"Whatever you think," I said.

"What's going on, Jimmy?" Angie said. "Who are those men?"

"I have no idea."

A mile and a half later, Radical turned the car off the main highway onto a one-lane mountain road that wound through the scrub and trees. Paved once and then forgotten, it was a minefield of chuckholes and depressions. Since it was the width of a single truck, if traffic came from the opposite direction, we would have to pull into the brush to allow the other vehicle to pass.

Radical slowed down to navigate the rustic path, swerving as best he could to make the ride smooth. Every thirty seconds, the car bottomed out with a loud bang and Radical swore. I hit my head on the roof every time.

"You think they'll follow?" I asked, glancing over my shoulder.

"Not at first," Radical said. "They will watch the highway. Or they will give up. If they are determined, then they will search the mountain roads. There are many of them. An easy place to get lost."

"Has anyone tried their cell for a signal?" Angie asked.

I looked at Bobby. He looked at me. We both checked our phones. Nothing.

"What's the plan?" Angie asked. "Get to some village, find a phone, call the Mexican army, report the shooting, request an escort back to Mazatlán, and then take the first flight home?"

"You sure you haven't done this before?" I said. "I had the 'Get to some village' part and 'Find a phone' percolating, but after that, it was all circus music. I say we go with what Angie said."

"Be careful who you contact," Radical said. "If the man wears a uniform, he can be bought. Durango is not Sinaloa. Not one cartel in charge. There is a war here. Both have eyes and ears in la policía estatal, los federales, and los militares. You cannot trust anyone."

"Who do we call?" I said. "How do we get out of this?"

"Tomás Morales," Radical said. "I also have a cousin that can help."

"Great," Angie said, unconvinced.

"Don't look at me," Bobby said. "I hate running. Putting off the fight for later is all you're doing. Procrastinating the violence. I say mix it up now. Stop the car and fight."

Radical pumped the accelerator, but the car slowed down on the uphill road.

"I don't know about fighting," Radical said, "but we are stopping."

It wasn't immediately apparent whether the crash at the bridge or the rough road was the cause of our automotive issues. It didn't matter. We weren't moving. Which made fleeing considerably more difficult.

The four of us stood around the open hood with our hands on our hips like we knew what the fuck we were looking for. We stared at the hunk of metal that had once been a car.

"Do you smell gas?" I asked.

"Sorry," Bobby said. "I had chorizo and eggs for breakfast."

I hunched down and inspected the underside of the car. "It's a drip now, but from the pooling I'd say it was a big leak. Either the gas tank or the fuel line. Either way you're empty. And even if you had a gas can, it'd be like pouring water in a colander."

"I don't know what a colander is," Radical said, "but I guess it is something with holes."

I stood up and glanced back down the road, waiting for the Jeep to turn the corner. Standing in the middle of a secluded road in rural Mexico felt like the pinnacle of vulnerability.

Angie held her cell phone over her head, checking for a signal. She turned in a full pirouette. With an audible harrumph, she jammed the phone back in her pocket. "How far is the next town?"

"Thirty-five, forty kilometers," Radical said. "It is far. Not to do in one day."

Bobby looked at me.

"Twenty, twenty-five miles, give or take," I said.

"We better get walking," Angie said.

"We can't leave the car here," Bobby said. "If those narcos head this way, they'll know we went in this direction. Better to keep them guessing. It ain't a chase no more. Now we're playing hide-and-seek."

"This car is my work," Radical said. "It is my car."

"Sorry," I said. "It could mean our lives."

"A la verga." Radical nodded, kissed his palm, and touched the hood of the car. He reached inside, threw it in neutral, walked to the back bumper, and pushed.

Bobby and I joined him. Angie moved to the driver's side and cranked the steering wheel toward the side of the road. We put our backs into it and pushed the car until we were as deep into the brush as we could go.

"We have to hide those tracks," Angie said as she pulled at branches to cover the car.

"She's adjusting well to the situation," Bobby said. "I knew Angie was Mavescapade-ready."

"It ain't funny to me at all," I said. "I hate that she's here, in any kind of danger."

"I wouldn't mess with her," Bobby said. "And she's smarter than us."

Using a thick branch as a lever, Radical and I wedged open the smashed trunk. We pulled whatever supplies he had. Bobby and Angie gathered branches and brush to camouflage the car. As we walked back to the road, we kicked at the tire tracks and dirt. When we were done, the car was invisible from the road. Even when I stared right at its location, I couldn't see it.

"How many hours do you think?" Bobby asked. "Twenty miles."

"Uphill, most of it," Radical said.

"Eight. Ten hours if it's more than twenty miles," Angie said. "That's without breaks."

"Bobby Maves doesn't need breaks," Bobby said. "What time is it?"

"A little after two. I doubt we can beat the sun," I said. "Traveling in the dark will be dangerous."

"Won't be the first time I slept outside," Bobby said.

"The first time sober, I bet," Angie said.

Radical loaded us down with the supplies. It was a good thing he kept his trunk stocked. I carried a couple gallon bottles of water. He had also dug out a map of the area, a flashlight, an electric lantern, two rolls of toilet paper, a bag of oranges, and a bag of Sabritones (the single worst snack product on the planet—and I had once tried Tuna Mayonnaise Doritos in Japan). I was going to have to be starving to eat those. They tasted like a hippie with a yeast infection smells, but with a hint of lime.

"In twenty kilometers, you will reach a silver mine," Radical said. "I will draw it on the map. "There is freshwater near there. Listen for it. Before dark you can sleep in the mine."

"Wait," I said. "You're not coming with us?"

"The men, they do not care about me," he said. "They want you. It is not safe for me to be near you."

"What are you going to do?" Angie said.

"I will walk to the highway. Someone will drive me back to Mazatlán. Another Mexican on the road. Nobody cares about me."

"Makes sense," Bobby said.

"What happened on the bridge, those men planned it. You were their plan. I will tell Tomás Morales. If anyone can help, he can."

"When you get to Mazatlán, find Griselda, my girlfriend from last night," Bobby said. "You remember her?"

"Sí," Radical said.

"Tell her what happened and where we are, but make sure to tell her not to come after us," Bobby said. "Tell her to stay in Mazatlán. To stay in her hotel room and not answer the door for anyone. She could be in danger."

"Sí," Radical said. "I will tell her. And I will call my cousin."

"Is your cousin Batman?" I said. "If not, leave him out of it. We've already put you in danger. Might as well keep the rest of your family out of harm's way."

"Pepe is not concerned with danger."

"Thanks for your help," I said.

"Buena suerte," he said, and walked back down the hill.

SEVEN

For the first hour of our hike, we trekked in silence. I had no idea what was going through everyone else's head. I couldn't help reliving that half minute of violence on the bridge. The shock of witnessing a shootout and the dead bodies that followed. I didn't know Jorge and Luis. I met them the night before. We weren't anything close to friends. But they were real people. Two dumb guys doing a stupid, shitty job for a person they were afraid of.

I whistled the tune from *Bridge on the River Kwai*, but I got a quick, in unison "Shut the fuck up" from Bobby and Angie. So much for levity. When things get scary, I make jokes. I was tempted to switch to "Whistle While You Work," but there are limits to my assholery.

"It's got to be Tomás," Angie said, answering a question that hadn't been asked. "This is all his fault. Has something to do with him. Why else would we be in the middle of this shit? I'm a nurse, and we're fucking farmers."

"I'm just glad we decided to leave Juan back home," I said. "I can't even imagine this happening with him here."

"Of course it's Tomás's fault," Bobby said. "The dead guys were his guys. That shit on the bridge was fast, furious, and fucked up. Cartel or government or CIA. Something big and scary and organized."

"He's the worst person you know, Jimmy," Angie said. "He's probably got enemies all over the world. Most of them in Mexico."

"I'm not disagreeing," I said, "but this is sounding a lot like an 'I told you so,' which both of you gave me shit for doing. What do we do with that knowledge? How does knowing it's Tomás help us?"

"I don't fucking know," Bobby said. "I'm just agreeing with your wife."

"I'm not blaming you, Jimmy," Angie said. "I want you to know that."

"Even if it is my fault," I said.

"Let's just get home," she said.

We heard the Jeep before we saw it. The silence of the remote road saved our asses. We had been walking for hours. My knees and back ached. The car's engine was quiet, but the crunch of its tires announced the oncoming vehicle long before it came into view.

It could have been any car, for all we knew, but I wasn't willing to wait around and find out. I grabbed Angie's hand. The two of us darted for the edge of the road, rushing deep into the sparse scrub. Mostly oaks and chaparral. The dry branches scraped my exposed skin. I searched for the densest area. Twenty yards off the road, I hit the deck and pulled Angie down into the dirt with me. We lay partially hidden by a tree, but still too exposed. Bobby had fled to the opposite side of the road.

"It's going to be okay," I said, turning to Angie. "Fuck. Crap."

"What?" she asked. "What is it?"

Angie's white shirt might as well have been a thousand-kilowatt beacon, bright against the browns and greens that surrounded us. I shoveled leaves and dirt on top of her with both hands.

"Hey," Angie said. "New shirt."

"It's too white," I said. "Too unnatural. Too easy to see."

She looked down, and then without hesitation she took off her shirt and shoved it underneath her body. "Brown enough now?"

I nodded. She had always been smarter than me.

We stayed low, waiting. Through the branches and leaves, I could just make out the road. It felt like ten minutes but was probably ten seconds. Eventually a Jeep Wrangler rolled past. No way to tell if it was one of the Jeeps from the bridge, but I didn't believe in coincidences. It traveled slowly, bouncing up the road. Angie and I remained completely motionless.

It never stopped. Just crept past. And then it was gone. Up the hill and around a corner. Out of view, but somewhere in front of us, in the direction we were headed.

Angie and I remained on the ground for another minute. After a look and nod, we sat up and brushed the dirt and dead leaves off our bodies. Angie shook her shirt and put it back on. Pulling it away from her stomach, she thumbed at the dirt smeared all over it.

"Sorry," I said. "I'll buy you a three-pack when we get home."

We made our way to the road, one eye in the direction of the Jeep. Bobby emerged from the brush on the other side. Leaves in his hair and grass stains on his clothes.

"Was that them?" Bobby said. "I couldn't tell. If it was, they're going to be more trouble. Makes them on a damn mission. A mission to fuck with us."

"It was a Wrangler for sure," I said, "but I couldn't see much more. They went up the hill. Means they could come back down. Maybe next time we don't hear them quick enough. We can't stay on the road."

"Not how shit works, bro," Bobby said. "We have to stay on the road. It's the road. The only fucking road."

"They could be waiting for us up ahead," Angie said.

"How long have we been walking?" I asked. "It's going to be dark soon. Are we getting close to that silver mine?"

"No idea. My guess, about two hours away," Angie said. "We bust ass, we can make it there before sundown."

"Then let's bust ass," Bobby said.

We started walking again, picking up our pace to late-for-work strides.

"I can't believe we're going to sleep in an abandoned mine in the middle of the Mexican jungle," Angie said. "If we're lucky."

"It's not really a jungle," I said. "Mostly oak trees."

"You know what I mean," Angie said.

"It's not how I pictured our honeymoon either, but what are our options? Those bastards are looking for us, and we won't be able to see jackshit once the sun goes down."

"How does trouble find you two so easily?" Angie shook her head and fast-walked away from us up the rocky road.

Bobby looked at me. "At least this time we weren't looking for trouble. That's something, isn't it?"

Only one other vehicle passed on our walk up the road. Six hours' total walking time and only two vehicles, including the Jeep. Not exactly a main thoroughfare.

We jumped into the scrub for cover like before, but it ended up being an old pickup truck headed down the mountain with a ten-year-old kid at the wheel. I yelled after him, but the kid was long gone by the time I scampered out of the brush. Bobby had the same idea. And the same luck.

"Damn," Bobby said. "That could've been our ride."

"Nothing we can do about it now," Angie said. "We need to keep moving. The sun is almost down, and we still got about a mile."

A half hour later, Angie stopped and pointed to the side of the road. "This has to be it. That's a trail, right?"

In the dim twilight, I could just make out the almost-imperceptible trailhead. There was a wooden sign, but whatever words had once been written on it had long faded. The trail was easy to miss, but once I caught sight of it, I could see the path that wound up the mountain away from the road.

"It's getting dark fast," I said, turning on the flashlight.

"We're really going to do this?" Angie said. "We're going to spend the night in an abandoned silver mine?"

"Too Scooby-Doo for you?" Bobby asked.

"Only if it's haunted," she said.

"Duh. All abandoned mines are haunted. That's like Ghost 101," Bobby said. I'm pretty sure he was being serious.

"We'll get through this, Angie," I said. "We always do."

"Pardon me if I don't share your confidence," Angie said. "This is my first Veeder and Maves train wreck of a shitshow."

"A Mavescapade," Bobby said. "We're on a Mavescapade—*R* with a circle around it."

Angie stared at Bobby for a moment and then turned on the lantern and headed up the trail.

Bobby shrugged at me. "What? What did I say?"

"Anything," I said. "You said anything."

A short, uneventful hike later we were finally there. I had nothing left, dog tired and glad the day was finally going to end. It was amazing how much suck could fit in one day.

I didn't have a lot of experience with abandoned mines—although I'd heard some stories about some morons searching for gold back home in the Chocolate Mountains. My mental image of a mine had probably come from cartoons and old movies. The reality—like so often in life—was a letdown. It was a glorified cave. No real indication of a mining operation aside from some abandoned lumber near its mouth. Time had made its appearance more natural than man-made. I wouldn't even be able to stand completely upright inside, which all but assured more bumps on my noggin.

"That's it?" Angie said, sharing my disenchantment. "Our hotel for the evening?"

"Give me the lantern," Bobby said. "I'll get some wood for a fire while there's still a little light. We're in the mountains. It's going to get cold tonight."

"I'll get the s'mores fixins together," I said, which made me hungry. Which made me realize I was going to have to eat some of those Sabritones. Which made me not hungry anymore. The circle of life.

An hour later, we had a fire going at the mouth of the cave. The three of us stared into the flames. I held Angie close, my arm around her. I tried to act like I was keeping us warm and comforting her, when I knew full well that her presence made me feel safer.

"What's the plan?" Angie asked.

"You've asked that before," Bobby said. "You're giving us too much credit. Once the fire got built, all my plans for the future had reached fruition."

"Ignore him," I said. "Tomorrow bright and early, we walk to the next village—cautiously, safely. We find a phone or a ride or a car or something. We get back to Mazatlán. Then get the fuck out of Mexico."

"They could be waiting for us," Angie said. "We don't know what they want. They killed two people."

"They don't know for sure we headed this way. We hid the car. There are dozens of little villages in these mountains. They can't wait in all of them. Mexico is a big country."

"What about that Jeep that headed up the road?" she asked.

"Like Bobby said, it's one of the only roads."

"It didn't drive back down."

"They'll eventually stop looking when they don't find us," I said.

"Or head back to Mazatlán." Bobby stood up quickly. He glanced around in a bit of a panic. "Griselda is a sitting fucking duck. They went after us, they could go after her. We have to get back. We have to warn her."

Bobby practically ran in place. He pushed against the cave wall, went outside, and then came back inside. Wanting to go, but nowhere to go. Ready for action, but only darkness in front of him.

"Calm down, Bobby," I said. "Of all of us, Gris can take care of herself the best. They didn't try anything in Mazatlán. Gives us reason to believe she's safe."

"What do you think she'll do when we don't show back up or call?" Angie asked.

"She'll assume we're the fuckups that we are," I said. "She'll assume we screwed things up."

"But what'll she do, Bobby?" Angie said.

"It wouldn't be the first time I didn't come home at night and didn't call," Bobby said. "She'll assume we got drunk or something equally stupid. Stayed the night in town, but got no phone signal. She'll be pissed but won't start worrying until tomorrow. Then she'll come looking for us."

"Unless Radical made it back to Mazatlán and found her," I said.

"That's a big if. The bad guys could get to her first," Bobby said. He sat down and picked up a rock, then hit it against the ground. "This is why running is always bullshit. You never know where you stand. We should've grabbed their fucking guns on the bridge and finished it. When you fight something head-on, you know who is winning. I fucking hate this shit." He threw the rock out of the mine and into the darkness.

"Did you hear that?" Angie said.

I heard it, too. A unique sound rose from deep within the mine. It started as an odd buzz but gained a car-alarm quality as it neared. Nails on a chalkboard combined with scissors cutting a roll of tinfoil, shrill and slightly metallic.

"I told you all mines were haunted, Velma," Bobby said.

"Velma?" Angie said. "I'm Mexican Daphne, for sure."

"Get low," I said. "As low as you can. We got bats."

I had traveled enough in Mexico, Belize, and Guatemala to have experienced the world of bats. As creepy as they can be, they're small and mostly harmless. Cute even, when there are only a couple of them. But there are never only a couple of them. Thousands of anything flying in your direction is mostly going to be terrifying. A swarm of ten thousand butterflies advancing with intent would be threatening. Even more frightening when the creatures are screeching like the schizophrenic wing of the Home for Criminally Insane Castrati.

The blackness of the mine grew blacker, but with flickers of movement. Out of that darkness, the top three-quarters of the cave filled with bats.

Angie screamed as I pulled her low next to me.

Bobby put his hands over his ears, but I could see he was smiling. He said something that I couldn't hear over the clamor.

It lasted for less than a minute, and then they were gone. A few stragglers flitted here and there. I imagined their screeches meaning, "Hey, guys. Wait up."

"That was a lot of bats," Bobby said. "That might have been all the bats."

"You both okay?" I asked.

"Are they coming back?" Angie asked, shaken.

"They live here, so yeah," I said, "but probably not until morning."

"Then we're up and out of here before then," Angie said. "That was crazy."

"Batshit crazy, to be specific," Bobby said.

"Shut up," Angie said.

"What did you say?" I asked Bobby. "You said something, but I couldn't make it out."

"I said, 'And that's the day I devoted my life to fighting crime.'"

Bobby and I both laughed harder than we should have. Angie stared at us.

"Come on, baby," I said. "Look at the bright side. It's a part of Mexico that most tourists don't get to see."

"You need to shut up, too," Angie said. If I listened close, I could hear the love in her voice. It was there. I had to listen really, really close, though.

I woke up at first light when the bats returned to the cave. Angie and Bobby slept right through their return. Nothing like a twelve-mile hike for a good night's sleep. Letting them sleep some more, I grabbed a roll of toilet paper and went into the scrub on my morning vision quest. The mountain air was brisk but refreshing, warmer than in the cave.

Like a dog sniffing at every bush, I wandered aimlessly through the brush looking for the right spot. With my luck, I would get lost. The vegetation opened up to a pond with a brook emptying into what I would describe as a "right nice swimmin' hole." The mini-waterfall on the end kept the flow of water moving. It was an idyllic location. Private, pristine, beautiful. Even though I knew other people had been there, it felt like I had discovered it. I dug a small hole to take a shit in.

Hunkered down, I daydreamed like usual. It relaxed my body. I thought about crafting a Segway or helicopter from fronds and bat guano. But this wasn't *Gilligan's Island,* and I didn't have the know-how. I already knew I wasn't Mr. Howell. I most certainly wasn't the Professor either.

On the other side of the pond, a bobcat appeared out of the bushes. It stopped when it spotted me. At a safe distance, with the water between us, I still chose to remain motionless in my vulnerable position. My usual reaction when I was in the presence of something that could kill me. Especially when I was in the middle of growing a tail.

The bobcat took slow, tentative steps along the shore, pacing back and forth. Its eyes never left me. Beautiful and piercing. I waited for lasers to fire from those eyes. The bobcat stopped, lapped at the water, and continued pacing.

When I inadvertently let out a loud fart, the bobcat growled and snarled enough to make my heart race and sweat form on the top of my head.

"I'm almost done," I said.

The bobcat jumped in the water and swam toward me.

"I'm done," I said.

I gave myself a superficial wipe, pulled up my pants, and got the fuck out of there. I tore through the brush, not looking behind me. I tripped on a root and scrambled to my feet, fighting through the stubby trees and bushes.

When I finally stepped into the open area in front of the cave, I felt relief. At least I knew where I was. The relief lasted less than a second. I was immediately reminded that bobcats weren't the only predators in the Sierra Madre Occidental.

Four men stood at the mouth of the silver mine. They held rifles on Bobby and Angie. One of the men spoke in Spanish. I couldn't make it out from the distance. Angie and Bobby shook their heads.

With the bobcat somewhere behind me and these men in front of me, I froze from indecision.

"Mira," one of the men said, turning his rifle in my direction.

"Fucking fuck," I said.

"Run!" Angie yelled.

I'd rather take my chances with the bobcat than these assholes. I took two steps back toward the brush. A gun fired. Dust kicked up inches from my feet. I stopped and raised my hands. My escape attempt had gotten me one stinking yard.

EIGHT

The two-hour truck ride was even bumpier than in Radical's car. Uphill, downhill, the back of the stake truck felt like we were inside a clothes dryer. The two armed men back there with us didn't seem to notice. Probably their usual commute. One of them fell asleep for a stretch, his head bobbing around loosely. Bobby, Angie, and I sat on the floor sliding around into each other. With my hands tied behind my back, it was difficult to stay in one place.

Mexican abduction number two wasn't going any better than the first one.

"Where do you think they are taking us?" Angie asked.

"Probably not Disneyland," Bobby said. "Maybe SeaWorld."

"Or Parque EcoAlberto," I said. "That's the place I was telling you about, where you can pay to simulate an illegal border crossing."

"The jokes aren't helping," Angie said.

"Cállate," the not-sleeping man said, his voice more tired than authoritarian. Like he'd had a long day at work and the last thing he needed was grousing kidnap victims.

I was tempted to tell the guy that if he didn't want us to talk, he should have gagged us. But it was rude to tell someone how to do their job. He was the professional, after all. Also, I didn't want to be gagged.

When the truck came to a stop, my body felt like I had gotten off a roller coaster. Shaky and weird and unbalanced. The two men hopped out of the back and waved for us to do the same. Pushing my shoulder against the side of the truck, I wrestled my way to my feet. Water pooled in the truck ruts of the muddy road. I jumped down, slid in the mud, and landed on my ass.

"Help her," I said, seeing Angie trying to figure out how to get down. "Ayúdala."

One of the men reached out a hand, taking Angie's elbow. She jumped out of the truck. The man stabilized her landing so she didn't fall.

Bobby waited for the same help but didn't get it. He jumped and managed to keep his footing, although he slid a good two feet.

"Sígueme," one of the men said, pointing to a large shed made of scrap wood and corrugated tin. It looked like a shipwreck, old and weathered and rotted. Either a hundred years old or built from hundred-year-old trash. The primary building materials appeared to be rust and decay. It stood out of place in the beauty of the small valley.

"It's gorgeous here," Angie said.

"You know what those are, right?" I said.

"Oh," she replied.

The poppies in the fields that surrounded us were indeed gorgeous. Big, red flowers filling the landscape. I took in a deep breath. Nothing. It felt like it should smell wonderful and fragrant, but apparently poppies have no smell. All I got was dirt with a mild afternote of manure.

Hoping that we had somehow driven to Amsterdam by a miraculous shortcut via wormhole, I knew the reality of our situation. If there had been any question that these men were with a drug cartel, it had been answered by the field of opium poppies.

Men worked in the fields. Farmers like me, but nothing like me. Not a single one of them looked in our direction. They did their job and hoped to survive the day, the week, the year. I envied the hard work but wouldn't want their lives. Not that things were going so great for me at the moment.

"Ándale," the man said.

We did our best to pick up the pace, but the mud gripped our feet. The sucking noise threatened to steal a shoe with each step.

The inside of the shed was nicer than the outside would have suggested, but not by much. A half dozen cots, a woodstove, a table, and some chairs. A crash pad for the farmers. Well used, but also well maintained. The men who temporarily lived here did the best with what they had.

Once inside, the man untied our hands and left. He gave us no orders or directions. He didn't have to tell us to stay put. It was implied by the fact that we were in a shack in the middle of a cartel-run opium poppy field.

I wanted to tell Angie that everything was going to be okay. That this misunderstanding would soon be sorted out and we would be able to get back to our vacation. But that would have been a lie. The moment Jorge and Luis were killed on the bridge, our honeymoon was literally over. I had no idea what was going to happen next. I had no reason to believe that we would live through the day. And I was scared shitless.

"This is all a big mistake," Angie said. "It has to be."

I put an arm around her and gave her a squeeze. She put her hand on mine. It all felt like not enough. I wished I had superpowers. One power that was enough to keep my friends and family safe.

"Any ideas?" Bobby said, rummaging through kitchen stuff on a shelf. He held a wooden spoon for a moment, testing its weight, but chucked it back.

"Do we got any choice but to wait?" I asked. "See what they want, what this is about. There's a conversation going to happen. That's why they grabbed us."

"We could just be hostages," Bobby said. "Trying to get money for our safe return."

"Who from?" I asked.

"Who do you think?"

Two of the men entered the shack. They held Radical by the elbows and pushed him forward. He landed on the ground in front of us. Radical looked like he had gotten tuned up pretty good. He had a black eye, and the cheek below was red and swollen. Dried blood caked his nostrils and upper lip. I helped him stand and sat him down on one of the cots. His head hung low. His hands shook.

"Lo siento," Radical said. "It was survival."

Angie sat on the cot next to him. She delicately put her hand under his chin and lifted his face. She turned to the men in the doorway. "I need a towel and some fresh water."

The men walked out. I didn't think they were going to bring either.

"I tried," Radical said. "I fought. It is harder to fight when you are not a young man. I sent them to the mine."

"What else could you do?" I said.

"I work for many people in Mazatlán. Not just Tomás Morales. These men know me. I have a family."

"Shit, man," Bobby said. "You didn't owe us nothing. I ain't mad. Glad you're okay. Or alive, I guess. That beating is on us."

"What do you know about these men?" I asked.

"We are in Durango, but these men are from Sinaloa. In this area, it is not one cartel that controls it. A war. They fight for control. One town, one valley, one road at a time. That's all I know."

"Do you know where we fit into all this?" Angie asked.

"No sé," Radical said. "Only that they wanted to find you."

"Rest," Angie said. She helped to lower him onto his back. He closed his eyes.

The short man that walked into the shed an hour later wasn't the same rank as the others. If they were pawns, he was at least a bishop, maybe a rook. He looked like every personal trainer I had ever seen. Three-hours-a-day-at-the-gym muscles bulged from a polo shirt. He was in his mid-twenties, wore an expensive watch, and looked like he had gotten a haircut an hour earlier. The kind of guy that liked to work out and fuck in front of a mirror. He brushed away a fly and took in the scene.

The two men that had brought us to the shed walked in behind him. Nothing good was going to happen next.

"El güero," he said, pointing at me.

"Jimmy?" Angie said.

The two men walked to me, each grabbing an elbow. They roughly pulled me from my chair, not letting me get my balance.

"Hey, hey, hey," I said, because that was totally going to make them stop.

"Let go of him!" Angie screamed.

Two other men ran into the shed. When Bobby took a step forward, fists up, one of the men raised his rifle, the butt ready to drop on Bobby's head.

"Do it, motherfucker," Bobby said.

I found my footing and moved with the men toward the door. "I'll go. Take it easy."

"If you hurt him," Angie said to Polo Shirt.

The man stared down Angie. He spoke without an accent. "Be careful who you threaten. Mexico is a dangerous place. Especially for women. The stories you've heard. They're all true. Worse. Terrible violence. There aren't any laws or rules."

"I'll be okay, Angie," I said.

"I love you," she said, which made me sadder than I'd ever been.

I left the shed with the men, taking one last look at my wife and best friend. They pushed me down the muddy road away from the shack. Polo Shirt followed, cursing at the mud that had engulfed his shoes.

I wanted to beat the living shit out of the son of a bitch for threatening my wife, but I held my rage in check. I needed to be smart. I would wait. I needed this guy to tell me what the hell was going on before I shoved his Rolex down his fucking throat.

Of course, that was all contingent on me not getting killed in the next five minutes.

Polo Shirt and his toadies walked me to a clearing in the center of the poppy field where four roads intersected. What I had to assume was Polo Shirt's ride—of course it was a black

Hummer—was parked in the center. The car looked like it had just gotten mud on it for the first time. Shiny on top, filthy on the bottom, the vehicular equivalent of a mullet.

Polo Shirt didn't bother with any small talk. He immediately hit me in the stomach with a hard right. It doubled me over, but I kept my feet. I put a hand on the hood for balance. Gulping in air, I looked up at Polo Shirt through watery eyes.

"Tell me about Tomás Morales," he said. "Tell me everything."

"I know him," I said, gulping breaths, "but I don't know jack-shit about him."

Polo Shirt grabbed me by the collar. He pushed me against the Hummer, my feet sliding in the mud underneath me. He was a foot shorter than me, but stronger. "Why did Tomás Morales send you to Sinaloa? What is his interest here? What are his plans in Mazatlán? Is he making a play into Durango? What is his next move?"

"Easy, easy," I said. "You got it wrong. I don't work for Tomás. Me and Tomás know each other. We're friends, I guess. That's it."

"You're lying," he said, his face close to mine. His breath was minty. "Tomás Morales does not have friends. He's not capable of friendship."

"Yeah, okay, I can see how you would think that," I said. "I knew him when we were kids. We grew up together. Even guys like Tomás were kids once."

Polo Shirt let go of me, stepped back, and pulled a pistol from the back of his pants. He held it to his side, but the threat was loud and clear. "He sent you here. To Sinaloa. He paid your way. That is more than friendship. He sent you up into the mountains. Why?"

"I know how bananas this is going to sound," I said, "but it was a wedding present."

The man stared at me like I had just farted. I might have. I have been known to fart when I get scared.

"I'm telling the truth," I said. "Even if the truth sounds ridiculous."

"You traveled with two men that work for him and another man that works for everyone." He pointed the gun in the vicinity of my knee. "How does that fit into your lie?"

"I didn't know any of that until the other night. Until I was in Mexico. Tomás sent them. That's true. But for our protection. Without my knowledge."

"Is that woman your wife?" He nodded in the direction of the shed.

I kept my mouth shut. Everything I wanted to say would definitely get me shot.

"She is a beautiful woman," he said. A threat. I felt like throwing up.

I kept my voice metered. "I came to Mexico to tell a man that his daughter had died. Five years ago, a woman I barely knew died. Her family never found out. That is all. Tomás found that man for me. He lives in a town called Coatepec somewhere in these goddamn mountains. Or some other mountains, because I don't know where the fuck I am right now. That's where we were headed when all hell broke loose on that bridge. I came to Mexico to give an old man bad news."

The term "pistol-whip" doesn't do justice to the act. "Whip" suggests that it is a slashing blow. It most certainly is not. It felt more like someone had hit my cheek with a brick. Which is what a gun is, a brick that shoots bullets. "Pistol-bludgeon" was more accurate, but too unpoetic a mouthful.

I tasted a mouthful of blood as I took a knee. My face hurt like a motherfucker, and it was difficult to see out of my left eye. It was a small miracle that my eyeball was still in its socket.

"Get up," Polo Shirt said.

I rose slowly, a little rocky. With one hand clutching at the side of the Hummer, I made it to my feet.

Polo Shirt grabbed my chin, tilted my head, and looked at my eye. "This is not torture. I'm not torturing you. You'd know if I was torturing you. That was a sampling. I wanted you to know what it felt like, how much it hurt. So that when I do the same to your wife, you'll know how much pain she is in."

That was it. I couldn't listen to any more of this asshole's bullshit.

"Fuck you, you yoked-up midget," I said. "I've told you everything I fucking know, and you threaten my wife? You're nothing but a weak-ass motherfucker. Steroid muscles with a two-inch dick. Without that gun and your boys, you're nothing but a scared bitch."

"Tráeme a la mujer," Polo Shirt said to his soldiers. They turned toward the shed.

"Leave her alone. Damn it. I don't know what to tell you. I don't know anything. I hadn't talked to Tomás in years. He came to me. He sent me down here. He gave me Fernando Palomera's name."

On hearing the name, Polo Shirt turned to his men and said, "Espera."

They stopped and waited.

Polo Shirt turned back to me, slightly confused. "Fernando Palomera? In Coatepec?"

"Yes. I came to Mexico to see him. He's the mayor there."

"Yes, I know." The well-dressed man laughed. He couldn't stop laughing. It wasn't the kind of laughter that was contagious. It was the kind of laughter that you'd hear coming from a dark cellar in a nightmare.

The men took me back to the shed. Angie got up from the cot, ran to me, and grabbed me in a hug. My middle was wonky from the gut punch I took, but I wasn't about to let go. Holding her was the only thing that mattered at that moment, pain or no.

Releasing me from her grasp, she took a look at my face. It must have been bad, because she winced at the sight of it. It takes a real mess to make a nurse wince.

"Those sons of bitches," she said.

"It hurts, but not as bad as you'd think," I lied.

"What happened?" Bobby said.

"They think we're working for Tomás," I said.

"I knew it," Angie said, dabbing at my face with the edge of her shirtsleeve.

"They thought beating the shit out of me would make me talk."

"Idiots," Bobby said. "They don't know that getting the shit beaten out of you is the one thing that you're good at. It's kind of your thing."

Angie gave Bobby a look, but I appreciated the humor in an otherwise humorless situation. I had never been in a situation where humor didn't help.

"I talked," I said. "I just didn't have anything to tell them. Told them we came to see Fernando Palomera in Coatepec. All the fucker did was laugh."

"He knows him?" Angie asked.

Bobby walked to the door of the shed and glanced outside. He turned back to us.

"I don't want to sound like a pessimist," Bobby said, "but we need like fuck to escape. This shit is real. I don't want to end up in a ditch with my severed dick in my mouth."

"Come on, man," I said, looking at Angie. "Take it easy with the horror movie imagery."

"It don't do no good to protect her from reality," Bobby said. "Mexican motherfuckers are creative when it comes to violence. Angie needs to know that there's a good chance these fuckers are going to kill us. Or worse."

"I'm right here, Bobby," Angie said. "And I understand the gravity. I'm scared, but I'm not a damsel in distress. You don't got to protect me any more than Jimmy does."

I took her hand.

Six men rushed into the room.

"Here it fucking comes," Bobby said, grabbing a pan from the stove and throwing it at one of the men. It bounced off the guy's chest, knocking him down. Bobby squared up to fight, but the other men had a step on him and were able to grab him before he threw a punch.

Angie and I didn't fare any better. They roughly grabbed us and threw sacks over our heads. We shouted and struggled but eventually gave in to the momentum and moved wherever they moved us. We walked out of the shed. I slipped in the mud but got pulled up quickly.

Someone wrapped tape over the top of the sack, over my eyes and mouth. The second time in the last few months. I was going to have to compliment Bobby on his technique. This guy was a brute. I could barely breathe. We climbed in the back of a truck. I couldn't see or talk. Hearing was tough. I tried to control my breathing, every lungful a challenge.

What had I gotten Angie into? If anything happened to her, I wouldn't be able to forgive myself.

NINE

I held on to the idea that if Polo Shirt had wanted to kill us, he would have already done it. We had been in the perfect spot: a remote, illegal drug field. Three birds with one stone and some free fertilizer in the process. Something else was happening, and it had everything to do with Polo Shirt's reaction to Fernando Palomera's name.

We drove for hours. I was starving, thirsty, and generally cranky from the experience. Bumping around with a sack over my head gave me time to think, to regret, and to worry. No matter what happened, I had to find a way to get Angie out of this. I would die to keep her free from harm. At least Juan was safe back in the Imperial Valley. The only good decision I had made recently was leaving him at home.

When the truck finally stopped, the first thing I heard was the laughter of children. Faint shrieking giddiness. A playground maybe. Everything else was muffled, but the high-pitched laughter pierced the burlap. I had no idea what to do with that sound.

With more gentle hands than those that had loaded me into the truck, I was helped out of the back and leaned against its side. A hand took my elbow and guided me. We walked, transitioning from outside to inside, turning a few corners, and descending a flight of stairs.

When the tape and sack were removed from my head, I stood in a basement. My hands remained tied behind my back. My handler, a guy I hadn't seen before, sat me down on a bench. I watched as two other men did the same for Angie and Bobby.

My left eye was completely closed from the pistol bludgeoning. I had to turn my head to get the full view of our surroundings. The room was filled with shelves of canned food and dry goods, enough to supply a restaurant or a survivalist's end-of-the-world sanctum. Barrels and bags of rice and beans sat stacked on pallets against one wall. No dust, like it had all been delivered recently. No windows, only brick walls. We were definitely underground. Bare bulbs lit the room in distinct pools of light, the corners bleeding into darkness.

My handler took three water bottles off a shelf, handing one to each of the other men. They screwed off the caps and tilted the water into our mouths. I drank slowly, water dripping down my chin.

"Where are we?" Angie asked the man standing over her when she had finished drinking.

The three men walked out of the room without answering. The heavy door locked behind them.

In comparison to the rough treatment that we had received at the poppy field, these men had done their level best to be courteous. If I was asked to fill out a comment card after this kidnapping, I would commend them on handling themselves in a professional manner.

Once the men were gone, Bobby awkwardly rose to his feet and walked to the first row of shelves. "My hands are tied with rope, not zip-ties," he said. "I think I can get loose if I keep working them."

"Maybe there's something sharp in here," I said, standing on my second try. I looked at the items on the shelves.

"The edge of a can would be sharp," Angie said.

"We'd need a can opener," Bobby said.

"What happens if you get the ropes off?" Angie asked.

"What do you mean?" Bobby said.

"First we get them off," I said.

"But then what happens?" Angie asked. "We don't know where we are. There are men with guns outside. What good does not being tied up do? Do you plan to fight your way out with your fists?"

"If you watched Korean action movies," Bobby said, "you'd know that everything is a weapon. We'll have the element of surprise."

"Being untied is better than being tied," I said. "One victory at a time. That's how this kind of thing works."

"'This kind of thing'? What kind of thing is this kind of thing?" she said.

"We don't know what's going on," I said, "but can we afford to wait around and find out? Plans are great, but we don't got one. We have to focus on what we can change. Anything. A small thing. Right now these ropes are the battle. Maybe we can change that, check that off the list, then see what's next."

"I don't like any of this," Angie said.

"Neither do I."

Bobby stopped what he was doing. "Shit changed when you said Fernando Palomera's name to Muscles McMexican, right? No more questions."

"Yeah," I said. "I told him we were in Mexico to tell Palomera about Yolanda. That she had died."

"So we know where we are," Bobby said. "In Fernando Palomera's basement."

"You didn't mention Juan, did you?" Angie said. "Tell me you didn't mention his name."

"No, I don't think so," I said.

"Keep his name out of this," she said. "Nobody here needs to know anything about him. We don't know who this Fernando Palomera is, what he's like."

I nodded. I didn't really care if the man was his grandfather anymore. If Fernando Palomera was involved with the cartels, he wasn't going to have anything to do with Juan. There had to have been a good reason Yolanda, Juan's mother, had decided to live in Mexicali as a prostitute rather than be in his life. A warning that I chose to ignore.

"It would make sense that we're in Coatepec," I said. "As much as any of this makes sense."

I went back to fumbling with some cans, immediately dropping a whole stack onto my foot. It was that kind of day.

"Are any of the cans self-opening?" Angie said. "You know, like soup with pull tabs or sardines. You won't need an opener, and the edge will be sharp."

"There's our female MexGuyver," Bobby said.

"Doing my best to get into the spirit of the thing," Angie said with no enthusiasm.

"Holy shit," Bobby said, one shelf over from where I was.

"What?" I asked, walking to him. "What is it? What did you find?"

He pointed at the shelf. "There're three different kinds of apple soda in front of me. Amazing."

"You're a fucking idiot," I said.

"Hold your judgment, bro," he said. "Maybe it's a clue. Usually people have a favorite brand when it comes to soda. They're a Coke or Pepsi person. Or a freethinking RC maniac. Three apple sodas tells us we're dealing with someone that appreciates nuance. There's Sidral Mundet, of course. A classic. But Manzana Lift and Manzanita Sol, too. Whoever's place this is, he really likes the taste of green Jolly Ranchers. Someone that's trying to get diabetes the easy way. A complicated man."

"Or an insane one. You're like Sherlock Holmes, but with a cerebral hemorrhage." I had walked away during Bobby's first sentence. Not that it stopped him from talking. Then I saw it. "I got one. A can with a pull tab. Pickled jalapeños."

"Who cares what's in the can?" Angie said.

"I thought it was interesting. Fucking Bobby got to ramble on about apple soda."

"It's an underappreciated flavor," Bobby said.

The shelf was too high for me to grab it with my bound hands. I moved the can of jalapeños to the edge of the shelf with my nose, and then, using my chin, I knocked it onto the ground. I awkwardly bent down onto my knees, leaned to the side, and picked up the can. Maneuvering the can into my tied hands was like a puzzle. I had to do everything by feel. Once I got it in one position, I couldn't quite reach the pull tab. I could solve a Rubik's Cube faster than get that fucking can open.

The locks turned, and the door opened. A fat man in a windbreaker entered the basement. He wasn't visibly armed and didn't look particularly dangerous. For a moment I thought it might be Fernando Palomera, but this man was closer to his mid-forties. He had a bushy mustache and a big stomach. One of those guys that had to decide if the beltline went over or under. He chose under.

He shook his head at the sight of me. Not my best moment, on my knees with a half-opened can leaking jalapeño juice onto my back. Bobby was in the process of trying to open a bottle of apple soda with his teeth, which I thought was more embarrassing. It wasn't a competition, but if it had been, he would have lost. Angie was the only one who came out of the situation looking poised.

"A sus pies," he said. "Debo hacer que usted coma."

I did what he said, not particularly interested in eating a whole can of jalapeños on an empty stomach. Pickled ones, at that.

The man untied our hands and walked us up some stairs and down a long hallway. The house was big and nicely furnished. Boxes lined some walls, like the occupant was still in the process of moving in. A few cracks in the plaster, but considering the rest of the decor, they may have been intentional. None of the art on the wall had any sense of modernity, all Old Mexico art and artifacts. Yet at the same time, I saw a huge TV in one room and a high-end exercise treadmill in another.

We were brought into a large dining room with a heavy wooden table and solid chairs. Whoever built them had made them to last. This furniture would be here a thousand years from now. The fat man pulled out the chair for Angie. A touch of class. That's quality henching.

Food covered the table. A basket of bolillos. A variety of cheeses with some sliced-up longaniza. A stack of steaming tamales. Chicken in dark mole. A molcajete filled with guacamole. Tomato and tomatillo salsa. Tortillas. And a stew that smelled incredible.

"Coma," the fat man said.

He didn't have to tell us twice. We hadn't had a proper meal in a day. I stuffed my face, wrapping my arms around my plate like a prisoner. It hurt to chew, but I didn't care. Eating too quickly, I almost choked twice and bit my lip once.

When I was on my thirds, a man in his early sixties entered the room. Bald and wearing glasses, he looked like the guy who did my taxes. One of his eyes might have been glass. Wonky, at the least. He held a bottle of wine in one hand and a bouquet of wineglasses in the other. He set them down gently.

We stopped eating. I wiped my grease-covered chin with the cloth napkin in front of me.

"Thank you for the food," I said. "Gracias."

He smiled at me and then turned to Angie. "El vino?" His voice was gentle, nonthreatening.

She shrugged and nodded. I could tell that she didn't want to give him any kind of deference and had even given me a look when I thanked him. But I had also never seen Angie turn down wine.

"Hacer un doble mina," Bobby said.

The old man smiled, poured four glasses of wine, and handed each of us a glass. He sat at the end of the table.

"Don't drink until he does," Bobby said to Angie.

"We already ate all the food, dumbass," Angie said.

The man took a drink and nodded. Satisfied with the vintage, he took another look over the top of his glasses at the label on the bottle.

We all took big gulps from our wine. I'm sure that Bobby had started to become concerned that this whole ordeal wouldn't involve any alcohol.

"My compliments on your apple soda collection," Bobby said. "El refresco de manzana."

The man looked at Bobby for a second, and then said, "Ah. Sí. Me gusta el sabor a manzana. Soy como un niño."

While I would have preferred English, it wasn't my place to ask everyone to change for my benefit. That would have been the gringoest thing I could have done. Besides, I got no indication that Palomera understood English. So, except when speaking to each other, Bobby, Angie, and I spoke Spanish. I had improved my skills lately, learning with Juan. I got the gist of what was said.

"Apple is a flavor that hasn't caught on in the US," Bobby said. "It is only served as a nonalcoholic alternative for champagne. And that's real apple juice, not the artificial sweet stuff that you got."

"Yes," the man said. "Martinelli's."

After that, we sat silently and drank our wine. I needed to piss, but the timing was weird. Although pissing my pants wasn't going to break the ice any better.

"I can't do this," Angie said in English, and then spoke to the old man in Spanish. "We were abducted. My husband was beaten. Men were killed. I demand we be brought back to Mazatlán."

"So much for small talk," Bobby said in English.

"Have you all had enough to eat?" the old man asked.

"We deserve to know what is going on," Angie said.

"Tavio," the old man said over his shoulder.

The fat man left his post at the doorway and came to the old man's side.

"Women should speak less than they do," the old man said, nodding toward Angie.

"That's not going to go over well," I said.

"What the fuck did you say?" Angie said.

"Señora?" Tavio put one hand gently on Angie's elbow. She shrugged it away.

"I wish to speak to the men at the table," the old man said.

"Fucking macho sexist bullshit is what that is," Angie said.

The man looked taken aback. "Out!"

Tavio took her elbow a little more forcefully. Both Bobby and I stood from our seats. Four other men came in the room from who knows where. Bobby held the small cheese knife ready to cheese-knife someone. Everything froze for a moment.

"I'll go," Angie said. "I hate it, but I'll do it."

Angie gave the old man her best death stare, knocked the chair down when she stood, and walked back in the direction we had come, not even bothering to let Tavio catch up. The fat man fast-walked after her.

"She will not be harmed," the old man said.

"That's going to cost me," I said. "She's going to take that out on me."

"She has garras," the old man said.

I didn't know that word. I looked at Bobby.

"Claws," he said.

"Like a fucking tiger," I said.

The man took a drink of wine and said, "I was told that you came to Mexico to give me a message."

"You are Fernando Palomera?" I said.

"Sí," he said.

"The man that brought us didn't give you any message?"

"Porfirio? No."

"It is about your daughter," I said, "Yolanda. You have a daughter named Yolanda, yes?"

"Yolanda," he repeated. For a moment, his facial expression grew softer, sadder. He nodded. "You know where she is?"

I nodded. "I'm sorry. She died. Five years ago. She was living in Mexicali, on the border. I live on the other side, near Calexico. We met not long before she died."

He took a big gulp of wine and then stood up, his eyes staying on the line where the wall met the ceiling. He set his empty wineglass down. "How did she die?"

I took a second. There was no good way to tell it. "She was murdered."

He winced and then spoke through gritted teeth. "And the person who did it? The person that killed my daughter?"

"He paid for the crime."

"His name, what is it?" he asked. "What prison is he in?"

"Alejandro. I never knew his last name. He's dead, too."

The man looked down from the ceiling and stared directly in my eyes.

"The police?"

"No." I shook my head. "They did not care about what happened."

"You?"

I held his eyes but didn't react. No reason to confess to murder, even in this circumstance.

Bobby said, "The only way he's leaving the desert is in the belly of a vulture."

For the record, "in the belly of a vulture" sounds a lot better in Spanish. En el vientre de un buitre.

"You came to Mexico to tell me this?" Palomera said. "Five years you waited?"

"You were difficult to find."

"There is more," Palomera said. "Tomás Morales paid for your trip. What is the real reason you are here? People I know have concerns."

"That is all," I said. "Your daughter died on my land. I cared. Tomás Morales helped me five years ago. He helped me with Alejandro. I thought her family should know what happened. It took me this long to find you. Tomás was the one that tracked you down. That is why I'm here."

"I have not been hiding," the man said. "I am not hard to find."

"I thought she was from Guadalajara," I said. "I was looking for relatives there."

"Where her mother was from," he said, almost to himself.

"Yolanda had said that her father was dead," Bobby said, some venom in his voice.

"We've been through a lot," I said. "Look at my face. Whatever you think we're here for is wrong. If I was involved in some criminal shit, would I bring my new bride? I'm stupid, not crazy."

"You brought another man on your romantic trip?" Palomera asked.

"I came on my own," Bobby said. "I was there five years ago, too. For everything with Yolanda and after. My reasons ain't always got to make sense, but I know when I got to do a thing."

"People don't go through this much trouble for other people," Palomera said. "That's not how people are."

"Maybe not the people you know," Bobby said, "but that's how we do things where we're from. Why did Yolanda leave in the first place?"

Palomera stared at him but didn't answer.

"What are you doing, Bobby?" I asked in English. But I knew what he was doing. Bobby was a scrapper. If he couldn't fight with his fists, he was still going to get in some shots.

"You haven't asked about her life at all," Bobby said. "Seems like some bad shit must have happened for her to end up living in Ciudad Perdida in a hovel working as a fucking hooker."

"¡Cállate!" Palomera shouted, walking across the room. He reached to the wall and tried to pull a decorative sword out of its display.

"Bobby," I said. "Knock it the fuck off."

"I've had it with this motherfucker playing Pablo Escobar," Bobby said to me in English, and to Palomera in Spanish, he said, "I don't like having guns pointed at me. I don't like bags over my head. Being tied up. I don't like being held against my will. I don't like being threatened. And I don't like people fucking with my friends."

Palomera gave up on the sword, swore, and walked toward the back door.

"All we want is to go home," I said to him. "That's it."

Palomera gave both of us a stare and left the room. Bobby and I looked at each other.

"Why did you have to antagonize him?" I asked.

"Because he's a fucking asshole," he said.

Tavio walked me and Bobby back down into the cellar. If Palomera was going to get in the habit of holding people against their will, he should seriously consider investing in a proper dungeon. It didn't seem hygienic to store people and food in the same location. The door closed and locked behind us. Angie rose from the bench, still fuming.

"Are you okay?" I asked. "They didn't hurt you or anything, did they?"

"No," she said. "What happened?"

"I tried to explain, and then Bobby got snotty."

"He's a dick," Bobby said. "Fuck that guy."

"You didn't tell him about Juan, did you?" Angie said. "You kept Juan out of it."

"The last thing I want is for that guy to know about Juan," I said.

"What's going to happen?" she asked. "How does this end?"

"I honestly don't know," I said.

"One of two things is going to happen," Bobby said. "He's either going to let us go or—" He stopped short of finishing the sentence.

"Or we're fucked," Angie said.

"Time to fight," Bobby said.

"We make it out of here," I said, "our next trip is to Europe. Or Asia. Or fucking Phoenix. And I hate Phoenix. Anywhere but Mexico."

"We need weapons," Bobby said. "Look around. See what you can find. Next person that walks in the door, we bum-rush them."

"For once I agree with Bobby," Angie said. "If we wait too long, it might be too late. It's time to get aggressive. Try to escape."

"We're in Coatepec," I said, combing the shelves for anything that could be used as a weapon. "At least we know where we are."

"We know where we are, all right," Bobby said. "We're on this guy's plate, and we're the filling in a shit sandwich."

"That makes us the shit," I said. "Shouldn't we be the bread?"

The cellar door opened, and Tavio entered while we were still in the process of discussing our next move. The thing about bum-rushing was that it required planning. He rushed our bum-rush.

Palomera only wanted to talk to me. Bobby and Angie stayed in the basement, most likely forging primitive spears from mop handles.

Tavio took me to an open courtyard that had a fountain in the center and a small flower garden. An eight-foot wall that probably led to the street stood in front of us. An armed man stood by the only door. He might as well have been twenty men. The outside was that far away.

The sky overhead was dotted with clouds. Birds flew in the air. It was peaceful. The sound of children laughing came from the other side of the wall.

Fernando Palomera sat on a concrete bench next to the fountain. Polo Shirt stood a little behind him, taking frequent pulls from a vape pen. I hated that guy's fashion sense, but I hated him more.

"I didn't know you stuck around," I said to Polo Shirt.

"You don't know anything," he responded.

Palomera motioned for me to sit next to him.

"Tell me about Juan," Palomera said.

"Fuck," I said in English, because I needed that "K" sound.

The mention of Juan's name had taken me by surprise. I was sure it showed on my face. I mumbled some incoherent sounds as I tried to construct a lie, but for whatever reason no lie came. I lied all the time. I couldn't understand why nothing was coalescing. It was a hell of a time for my lie generator to go on the fritz.

I knew that Mexican people had air-conditioning and indoor plumbing and computers and cell phones and Wi-Fi and every convenience. Not the whole country, but definitely those with some money. And the cartels were not lacking money. Still, my ethnocentric mind expected a pickup with a bed full of farm workers instead of—well, microphones in storage cellars, as an example.

"Your woman said that she did not want me to know about Juan," Palomera said. "Which means that I very much want to know about Juan. Who is Juan?"

Nothing. Still no solid lie. And I was taking too long. They would have to know that whatever I said next was a lie if I didn't get my shit together.

Polo Shirt stepped forward. "What is Juan's last name? Is he your contact in Mazatlán? One of Tomás Morales's soldiers?"

"Nobody," I said. "Juan is nobody."

"Nobody is nobody," Palomera said.

"I can't," I said.

"I will hurt you," Polo Shirt said. "I will hurt your woman." No emotion, matter of fact. The threat of hurting Angie seemed to be his go-to tactic. Admittedly, it was effective.

I stood and faced him. In English, I said, "You touch her and I will kill you. I will fucking kill you."

"No, you won't," he said. "I will do what I want, and you can't stop me. Or punish me. I hurt who I choose to hurt."

"I'm not saying a fucking thing about Juan or anything," I said.

Polo Shirt turned to the fat man. "Tavio, tráeme la mujer."

"The fuck he will," I said, pulling the sharp lid of the jalapeño can out of my pocket and putting it to Palomera's throat. Tavio drew a pistol gunslinger-fast. I got Palomera's body between me and him, pressing the sharp edge deep enough to draw a little blood. Palomera's glasses slipped off his face. Polo Shirt smiled but remained still.

The old man struggled, managing an elbow into my midsection, but when I pushed even deeper with the sharp edge, he stopped resisting.

"Okay," Palomera said, not scared but accepting. "Calma, Tavio. Calma."

"Bring my wife and my friend," I said to Tavio. "Bring them here. We are leaving."

Tavio looked to Polo Shirt and then to Palomera.

"Don't look at them," I said. "Go get them."

"I am curious how this plays out," Polo Shirt said. "Should be interesting."

He nodded. Tavio left the room. I got a better grip around Palomera's neck, moving the two of us together so that my back was against the wall. Patting him down for a better weapon, I found nothing. Powerful men never carried weapons themselves.

"This will not end how you want it to," Palomera said.

Polo Shirt laughed. "Come on, Fernando. You have to admire the gabacho's huevos. Neither of us anticipated a fighter. Something you would have done."

"You threatened my wife, motherfucker," I said. "Nobody gets to do that."

Tavio returned with Angie and Bobby. The problem was that he also returned with six armed men. Because my plan was stupid. Worse than that, it wasn't a plan. It was a reaction. I never had a fucking plan.

Angie and Bobby had guns to their heads. I was reminded why improvisation was rarely a good idea, in comedy or in life.

TEN

As the only gringo invited to the Mexican standoff, I felt self-conscious about whether or not I was doing it right. I was more accustomed to being the aggressee rather than the aggressor. I put on my best sneer and pushed the jagged edge harder to Palomera's throat.

"On three, kill the Mexican," Palomera said. His voice was calm, what you'd expect from a villain commanding his men to shoot your best friend on the count of three.

"Bro," Bobby said. "That's me. I'm the Mexican."

The man holding the gun to Bobby's head cocked the hammer of his pistol. Bobby struggled, but the other two men had a good grip.

"Your man shoots Bobby, you die," I said to Palomera, and then turned to Polo Shirt. "I got nothing to lose. I'll kill him."

"This is not how I die," Palomera said. "One."

It was going to come down to who blinked first. I slid the blade across Palomera's neck, hoping I didn't cut one of the important arteries or veins. I needed to send a message. Blood ran down onto his white guayabera in a thin line.

"Two," Palomera said, unperturbed.

It finally hit me. Palomera was crazy. You can't play chicken with crazy. Crazy doesn't swerve. My leverage held no weight against Palomera. There was no way to win. The game was rigged.

"Fuck," I said, dropping the can lid onto the ground and letting go of Palomera. "Fuck," I repeated, because it warranted two fucks. Maybe three, but I would save the third one for later.

Palomera lifted a hand to his neck and looked at the blood. "I should shoot your friend for this."

"Let's not do that, Fernando," Polo Shirt said. "He did what you would have done. You gave him no choice. It was a desperate but understandable reaction."

Polo Shirt waved for the men to lower their guns. They did, but nobody looked relaxed.

Palomera picked up his glasses, cleaned them on his shirt, and hit me across the face with the back of his hand. Hard enough to force me to take two steps to the side. At least it was on the right side of my face. Maybe it would balance out my coloring, make my whole face purple. I stayed on my feet, but barely.

"Don't hurt him," Angie said. "Don't."

"It's okay," I said.

Bobby had been right. Getting my ass kicked sat squarely in my comfort zone. I had few skills, but taking a beating was one of my distinct talents.

The next time Palomera hit me it was with a closed fist, and I fell. More cheek than chin, it still turned my head enough for me to see small bursts. The next one was going to fuck me up. My face was on its way to looking like a smashed grape.

"Weak pussy bitch," Bobby mumbled, struggling against the two men that held him.

"Goddammit," Angie said. "Stop." She cried openly, which didn't happen often. Not sadness, but frustration. There was no worse feeling than watching a loved one get hurt and not being able to do anything about it.

Palomera raised his fist to hit me again. I let my face go slack and prepared to move with the blow. This one might do permanent damage.

"Fernando, stop," Polo Shirt said. "This is taking too long. I have other work."

Palomera put his fist down. He glared at me, breathing heavily through his nose.

"I have more important shit to do today," Polo Shirt said to me. "I thought this would be interesting. Tell us who Juan is."

I shook my head.

"Don't make me get violent," Palomera said.

I laughed a little. "I came here to tell you about Yolanda."

"How can I believe anything when you keep this secret? I will find out who he is, even if we have to start all over."

"I can't."

Palomera pulled out a small pocketknife. He cleaned some dirt out from under his thumbnail. Then without a word he stuck it in my leg about an inch deep.

It hurt, but not as bad as you would think. More than acupuncture, but less than getting stabbed with a larger knife. I grunted but kept it under control. Tears filled the one eye that worked.

Palomera left the knife in my leg. "I don't think that you and your friends are dangerous to me, but I am a man of principle. You are tourists. I can see that. But you have a secret that might affect my friends. You don't get to have that. I get what I want. I once sent ten men to Michoacán to get a goat that had been stolen from my neighbor. I didn't like the man, but I decided that he should have his goat back."

It had hurt when he stabbed me with the knife. When he twisted it, I screamed.

"Who is Juan?" he asked again.

"He's your grandson!" Angie yelled to Palomera. "Juan is your fucking grandson, you evil fuck."

"Not what I expected," Polo Shirt said, "but still not interested by all this."

"Angie, don't," I said.

Palomera looked dazed. "What did you say?"

"Your daughter, Yolanda, had a son before she died," Angie said. "He would be about eight years old now."

Palomera removed the knife from my leg. He distractedly took out a handkerchief and placed it on the bleeding wound. I pressed down on it with both hands.

"Mi nieto," Palomera said, his voice quiet. He nodded his head, staring at his feet. "I have a grandson. An heir. A legacy."

"Waste of my time," Polo Shirt said. "Family bullshit." He walked into the house.

Palomera turned to the remaining men. He waved both hands in the air. "Go. All of you. Go."

The men slowly disappeared through one door or another. Only the guard at the gate and Tavio remained in the courtyard. Palomera walked to him and reached out his hand. Tavio put a pistol in it and walked inside. Palomera kept it loose at his side.

I stood with an eye on Palomera. He didn't object. I took a seat on the concrete bench. If I tried to stand for too long, I was sure I would fall. The bleeding in my leg was down to a trickle, but it still hurt like hell. The only upside was that I wasn't thinking about the pain in my face.

"I have a grandson," he said. "Where is he?"

"He was adopted by an American family," Angie said.

I let Angie do the talking. Not only was I one head rush away from passing out, but she was going somewhere with all this. My personal lying skills had failed me, but I knew the start of a good lie when I heard one.

"Who?" Palomera said. "What are their names? How do I find him?"

"I don't remember," Angie said. "I don't know. It was five years ago. There was a lot of chaos after Yolanda died. I didn't know her—we didn't know her—very well. Our lives mostly crossed after she died, after Jimmy found her body. I heard about the adoption from a friend of a friend. I might have the parents' names written down on a piece of paper in a drawer somewhere back home."

Well played, Angie. Well played.

"Why did you fight so hard to not tell me about him? Take so much punishment? Why did you tell me about Yolanda and not my grandson? Why the secret if you have nothing to do with him?"

"Are you joking?" Bobby cut in. "Maybe it was the guns and the murdering and the kidnapping and the hitting and the stabbing? You're a bad guy. You can't hurt a dead woman. But a kid? That boy is better off with you not in his life."

"I love children," Palomera said, offended. "I would never harm a child. Especially my own blood."

"Before we even got here," Angie said, "we witnessed two people murdered. Ran for our lives. Grandson or not, why would we help you find a child? I wouldn't be able to sleep at night knowing that I put any kid in your sights."

"I am family. Family is all that matters. Family is blood. I have no grandchildren. Now I have Juan."

Polo Shirt walked back outside. He looked annoyed and impatient. "Fernando."

Palomera walked to Polo Shirt. The two of them talked in whispers. Palomera walked back to me.

"Our original plan was to come here and tell you," I said. "About Yolanda. About Juan, but shithead here's mistaken assumption that we were involved with Tomás Morales fucked all that up."

"You can locate the boy?" Palomera asked.

"Maybe," I said. "When we get home, back to the US. We might have the information in the house. The name of the family that took Juan in."

"I have a phone," Palomera said. "Call someone, tell them where to look. Where to find the information."

"Obviously, you've never been to our house," I said. "That would be like looking for a specific grain of rice in a very large pile of rice."

"We're slobs," Angie said. "It means that slip of paper is where we left it. Because we don't clean. But it also means it's covered with a hundred other slips of paper. Because we don't clean."

Palomera walked back to Polo Shirt. They talked again in whispers. It was fucking excruciating. There were machinations happening so far above my head, it made me feel like an ant waiting for a boot to crush me.

That's the way the world works. Most people are nobodies, ordinary schmoes like me. We're never made privy to what's really happening, what powerful people talk about behind closed doors. Or in whispers. Big decisions that affect every aspect of our lives. Governments, criminals, corporations. We never even know half the decisions, only their impact.

The only part of the conversation I made out was the last thing Polo Shirt said: "I don't care."

"Okay," Palomera said, turning back to us. "Tavio will drive you to Mazatlán. You will return to your pigsty house. You will contact me with information about my grandson, Juan."

"Are you kidding?" I said. "Just like that?"

Palomera nodded.

"Absolutely," I said. "Deal. Give us a number where we can reach you."

"Thank you," Angie said. "I can't believe this nightmare is over."

Bobby wasn't a thanker in these kinds of situations. Not after having a gun to his head and ostensibly being one second away from oblivion. He was correct in not thanking anyone, because Palomera wasn't even close to finished fucking with us.

"When you contact me, I will return your wife," Palomera said. "Until then she will be my guest here in Coatepec."

"The fuck she will," I said.

"You talk like you have a choice," Palomera said.

"I have plenty of choices. I can pick that can lid up off the ground. Cut your fucking throat."

Palomera looked at the pistol in his hand.

"I don't give two shits about your fucking gun," I said. "There's no way I'm leaving without my wife. No fucking way."

Palomera started to raise the gun.

"There's no need to fight," Angie said. "It's a bad plan, Mr. Palomera. If you want to find your grandson, you'll need both of us looking. We're going to have to tear the house apart. Jimmy can never find anything. He's borderline worthless when it comes to these kinds of things."

"I am," I said.

Palomera nodded. "I have been married. I understand that well."

"You have our word," Angie said. "We promise to call you when we get back and find the information."

Polo Shirt laughed out loud at that statement. I had almost forgotten that he was there.

"Carajo," Polo Shirt said. "It's obvious. Let the woman go. Keep the idiot."

Bobby and I looked at him and then each other.

"Which one of us is the idiot?" I asked, feeling like an idiot.

"That's what you get for crashing my honeymoon," I said to Bobby.

Bobby, Angie, and I waited in the big room with the TV. We had been moved there while arrangements were being made. A soccer game played on the television. Two armed men stood by the door. I considered attempting an escape on the next goal, but it ended up being a scoreless tie. Ninety-plus minutes ending in zero to zero. No wonder soccer is so popular all over the world.

"At least the food here is good," Bobby said.

"We got some time," I said. "We'll figure something out. We'll get you home safe."

"If you can't, I'm okay with that. I understand." After our last conversation was heard, we had to talk around everything. "I'm not going to get defeatist, but no matter what happens, make sure Gris is okay. And let Lety and Stacy know that I love them."

"We'll get you out of here," I said. I wished I knew how.

"I know you," Bobby said. "You're that cop that goes by the book, while I'm the ruggedly handsome wildcard. You're going to want to go to the cops or feds or whatever. Resist that urge.

That ain't the right move. Up in these hills, they can disappear me long before anyone knocks on the door."

"I'm not going to leave you here," I said.

"Let's not pretend I'm not fucked," Bobby said.

"I'll come up with something."

"Sure, Jimmy," Bobby said. "I'm sure you will."

It took them hours to figure out what the hell they were doing. When they finally got their shit together, Angie and I were ushered into a Jeep. Angie sat in the backseat. I reluctantly got in the passenger seat next to Tavio.

I turned back to the house. Bobby stood next to Fernando Palomera. No gun to his head. Not physically restrained. They were underestimating an uncertified maniac, but he wouldn't try anything until he knew that we were safe. Bobby would absolutely try something, though.

Bobby's sacrifice was admirable, but I also knew how Bobby's brain worked. He had probably already devised an elaborate plan that involved romancing a Mexican señorita, tunneling one hundred yards, karate-chopping a guard, and every other cliché that he'd ever seen in a movie. Bobby hadn't watched the movie *The Rock* one hundred times to not be prepared for this exact kind of situation. Every time he sat me down and made me watch *The Raid: Redemption* or *Crank: High Voltage* or some other action flick with a colon in the title, he would turn to me and say, "Research. Enjoy, but learn." Most people lie to themselves about who they are. Bobby was not most people. His life was a cartoon, and he knew it.

I just hoped that the stupid that he attempted—and there was no doubt that it would be stupid—wasn't stupid enough to get him killed.

That made the race against time not just about Juan, but about Bobby. I had to do something slightly less stupid before his inevitable escape attempt. I needed a proper plan. Not exactly my forte.

Angie and I had three days—seventy-two hours—to get the information about Juan to Palomera. That was the deal. It was all bullshit, of course. The information didn't exist. We knew where Juan was, and there wasn't a chance in hell that we'd reveal the truth. Lies stacked on lies.

The best plan I had was straight out of Bobby's playbook: to get to Mazatlán, put Angie on a plane back home, coordinate with Tomás and whoever he knew in Sinaloa, organize a crack commando team, and bust Bobby out of this Escobar-lite's compound. Go full Chuck Norris on his ass. Somehow do all that under the watchful eye of Tavio, Henchman Extraordinaire.

I knew how outrageous it sounded—the word "outrageous" being generous. Once Angie was safe, I could release the hounds. Or free the doves. Or whatever fucking animal that would get Bobby out of Palomera's clutches.

Tavio started the Jeep. I flashed Bobby a pair of heavy metal devil horns. Mostly because a wave didn't seem appropriate and finger guns would have been offensive. Bobby grinned, stuck out his tongue, and went full Lemmy, returning the gesture with both hands.

"See you soon, buddy," I said.

"Fuck yeah, you will," Bobby said. "If not sooner." He winked. God help us all. He already had a harebrained scheme mapped out.

ELEVEN

Life is unpredictable. That isn't news, but at those monumental shifts, we are often reminded in the worst way. We go about our days, worried that we're down to the last roll of toilet paper or that rent won't get paid on time, and then something huge happens. Something big, life-changing, catastrophic. A death in the family, a medical diagnosis, a car accident. From that moment on, everything shifts. Priorities are immediately altered. All the bullshit on the top of the to-do list becomes the bullshit that we unconsciously knew it was all along.

As the rest of the world goes about their mundane lives of worrying about getting enough fiber in their diet or spending too much money on car insurance, it's like living on a different planet. Inside catastrophe, normal lives feel quaint, distant, and foreign. It's hard to understand how anyone could care about those miniscule concerns when life-and-death shit is happening.

Survival is resilience. The tragedy passes, and we eventually get back to the world and take everything for granted again, not even realizing how much of a luxury it is, stressing about bullshit that we won't remember six months later.

That's a bit what it feels like when your best friend is being held for ransom for information that doesn't exist and you have three days to figure out how to get him out of the hands of a Mexican cartel or else he will be killed. You know, that kind of day.

Coatepec was larger than I thought it would be, maybe a half-mile square, probably housing a few thousand people. There was a density to it that you usually find only in cities. Like it had once been a fortress of some kind. A few two-story buildings poked up among the mostly squat structures. Narrow streets with no sidewalks. It was hard to guess the age of the Mexican town, but it was definitely built in a time before the electric and telephone lines that ran overhead—the only sign of modernity other than the few pickups parked here and there.

Palomera's compound was on the top of a hill, an eight-foot wall surrounding the entire property. Children played on the street outside, getting out of the way of the Jeep as we passed.

There was nothing extraordinary about the town, which made it all the more haunting. Women, children, old men. Shops and taverns. A fountain in the central plaza. A big, old church. I wanted it to be something else. A ghost town. An occupied territory. When I was frightened by something, I wanted it to look frightening.

The town was just a town. Its mayor and the people that he worked with were the monsters. The story of modern Mexico. Those who have power never deserve it and rarely know what to do with it. It's not that power corrupts. It's that power is corruption.

"Tavio?" I asked, speaking in Spanish. "Is Fernando Palomera a fair man? Can we trust him to keep his word?"

Tavio said nothing.

"If we help him, will he keep his word?" I asked again. "Will he hurt our friend?"

"Fernando Palomera is fair to me," Tavio said. "To everyone. He will do as he said. He is an honest man."

"An honest criminal?" Angie said.

"Yes." Tavio saw no irony in that phrase. In a place where criminality is de rigueur, morality is relative.

The town receded behind us. The dirt road cut straight through the cemetery at the edge of town. Simple crosses and ancient headstones jutted from the ground at skewed angles on either side of us. A few markers were adorned with fresh flowers, the only sign of life.

A mountain road approached, a tunnel in the overarching trees and brush. Goodbye, Coatepec. For now.

"We'll be back home soon," I said to Angie. I knew it sounded dumb, but I wanted to say something—anything. I wanted to be the good husband, comforting and helpful. All that came to mind were platitudes. Positive thinking was worth about one centavo.

"Yeah," she said, appropriately unenthusiastic.

"If anyone gets through this, it's Bobby."

"Cállate," Tavio said.

"Fuck you, Tavio," Angie said, and then in Spanish, "We aren't driving two fucking hours to fucking Mazatlán in fucking silence. We aren't sitting in this Jeep and watching the scenery. If we want to talk, we'll talk. Try to do something about it. I'm serious. Fucking try."

Tavio looked like a five-year-old whose mother just caught him stealing money from her purse. I felt a little bad for him, but then I remembered the situation we were in. So yeah, fuck you, Tavio.

"What were you saying?" Angie said calmly, turning back to me.

Tavio did not object. He concentrated on the road.

"Bobby has been in a billion dangerouser situations in his life. This kind of thing is nothing new to him. It's his comfort zone and his danger zone combined. He always comes out of it with some scratches and an embellished story."

"Until he doesn't."

"Way to jam a pessimism pin in my optimism balloon," I said. "Dream shatterer."

It wasn't the same road that Radical had driven up when we had hightailed it off the highway, but it could have been its twin brother. A rough, one-lane slab of asphalt that descended steeply down the mountain. Scrub and oak trees on either side, sandwiched between large rocks. Not picturesque, but not ugly either.

We turned a sharp corner. Tavio slammed on the brakes. The Jeep slid to a stop in front of a large extended cab pickup stopped in the middle of the road. The stalled truck filled the narrow stretch, no way around it. Its hood was raised, and we got a really good view of a woman's backside. In short shorts, no less. Ba-boom.

Tavio and I took a moment to admire the view. The woman didn't turn around.

"You both are pigs," Angie said.

"Do not move," Tavio said. "Stay in the car." He pulled the pistol from the holster on his belt and got out of the Jeep. He kept the gun against his leg, out of view.

Out the front windshield, Tavio walked cautiously around the Jeep. He said something to the woman. I didn't make it out. She waved him over to help.

"What's going on?" Angie said, leaning between the seats to get a better view.

"Get the fuck out of here," I said. Not to Angie, but to the situation.

The woman had turned enough for me to see her face. It was Griselda. For some reason she was dressed in a full-on Daisy Duke costume, the shorts and the shirt tied in a knot at the bottom, showing off ample cleavage.

"¡Suelta el arma!" Griselda shouted. "Drop the gun."

Tavio looked at the pistol in his hand. He laughed, not able to figure out why he would listen to an unarmed woman.

That was, until two men in balaclavas and full camouflage walked out from the trees. They carried assault rifles. One of the men was gigantic. Tavio dropped his gun and put his hands in the air.

"She totally Daisy Duked him," I said. I held up my hand to give Angie a high five, but she was transfixed on the action outside.

"El teléfono también," Griselda said to Tavio.

Tavio dropped his phone next to the pistol. She made a gesture with her hand, brushing him back. Tavio backed up a few steps. Griselda picked up the phone and pistol. She kept the pistol and chucked the phone in the bed of the pickup.

I got out of the Jeep. Angie right behind me.

"Hey, guys," Griselda said.

The bigger of the two masked men set his rifle down and walked to Tavio. Griselda handed him a pair of handcuffs. The big man twisted Tavio against the hood and handcuffed his wrists behind his back.

"Where did you come from?" I asked. "How did you know we were here?"

Griselda put a finger to her lips, yanked Tavio off the hood, and guided him through the brush. They disappeared into the woods.

I turned to the two silent masked men. "Hey. What's up?"

The smaller man lifted up his balaclava. Radical smiled through his busted-up face.

"Radical?" I said. "How are you not dead?"

"I have value." He shrugged. "I work for no one and for everyone. For the cartel and the enemies of the cartel. A competitor on Monday can become a business partner on Tuesday. They had two choices. Kill me, or let me go. They decided that they can kill me whenever they want, so they let me go."

"But Griselda? How did you guys meet up?" I asked.

"I had told your friend that I would find her. I do what I say. She was in Mazatlán, about to come here."

"Why would you come back?" I asked. "It's a dangerous move."

"They gave me a beating," Radical said. "Nobody gets to win a fight against me. I always get back up. This is my cousin Pepe I told you about. He owns the guns, but he wanted to help."

Pepe kept his balaclava on but nodded and grunted in response. He was bodybuilder big, forearms thick with ropy scars.

"I had heard 'Fernando Palomera' and 'Coatepec,'" Radical said, "so that's where we came. We arrived in the town, saw them put you in the Jeep. We drove here five minutes before you. This was not a planned plan."

"Had you ever heard of Fernando Palomera?"

"Not until I made a call."

"Tomás Morales?"

"He didn't know the name as anyone to know," Radical said. "Except that he had given it to you. Five minutes later, he had talked to some people, wired me money, and sent me here to get you."

"So it wasn't just the goodness of your heart," Angie said.

"Nothing ever is."

Tavio had better have a chiropractor or acupuncturist on speed dial. The way Griselda had his arms handcuffed around the trunk of the big oak tree looked like it was torquing his back in ways that hurt. To make it even more uncomfortable, Griselda stuffed a sock in his mouth. The cherry on the bondage sundae.

"So I got to ask," I said. "The outfit? Kind of elaborate."

"This is what I was wearing when Radical found me. I'm on vacation."

"Sorry," I said. "And the handcuffs? Do you always travel with handcuffs?"

"Bobby and I like to—" She stopped. "Where's Bobby? Why isn't he with you?"

I shook my head. "He's still up there. At Palomera's."

During the whole procedure, she talked to me with the nonchalance of doing the dishes. "You left Bobby?"

"We didn't have a choice," I said. "I swear we didn't."

"Let's not talk around this guy," she said.

Griselda double-checked her work and gave Tavio a pat on the head. We walked back through the bushes to Radical and

Pepe, who watched the road for cars. As I explained the arrangement that we had made with Palomera, Angie searched the Jeep.

"The only plan I had was to get Angie on a plane," I said to Griselda. "Selfish as that sounds, Bobby was priority two. Or maybe three. Angie and Juan first. Those were Bobby's priorities, too. Or else he wouldn't be where he's at. Once Angie was in the air, I was going to see if Tomás had any boys down here. Go full *Dogs of War* on Palomera's ass."

"I don't know that one," Griselda said. "Is that a movie?"

"Con Christopher Walken y Tom Berenger," Pepe said.

"There is no time," Radical said. "Me and Pepe. That is your army."

"Palomera's going to be expecting a call from that guy in the next hour," Griselda said. "When he doesn't get it, what happens?"

"Maybe this rescue wasn't a great idea," I said. "I had three days to figure something out. Now we only got an hour."

"I didn't know he was taking you to the airport, dumbass," Griselda said. "I assumed he was taking you out to the woods. That you were in danger. You're welcome, by the way."

"Sorry. Thanks."

Angie joined us, carrying a rucksack full of supplies that she had found in the Jeep. The bag held another gun, some road flares, and a bottle of tequila. She set down the rucksack, pulled out the tequila bottle, and took a swig. She handed it to Griselda, who took a pull herself.

"If we're going to get Bobby out of there," Griselda said, "we've got to do it now." She handed me the bottle.

"The house is walled on the outside," I said. "There were at least six guards—maybe more—polo shirt guy, and Palomera himself. I'm not sure how we get in."

"It's Bobby," Griselda said. "We have to try."

"My whole plan was to keep Angie safe," I said. "She's not going back there."

"Fuck you, husband," Angie said. "You don't get to decide if girls are invited or not. I've shot a gun before. I can fight, too."

"Who the fuck are you? Where's my wife? I ain't going to apologize for wanting to keep you out of danger. You have a fucking kid now."

"That's a bullshit argument," she said. "So do you."

Radical and Pepe took a step back, staying out of it. Smart men.

I stared at my wife. I didn't care if she was right. I didn't want to get Bobby out of danger by putting Angie in danger. The math didn't add up to me.

"I'm not a fragile thing that's going to break," Angie said. "I make my own grown-up decisions."

"Okay, fine. Fuck. I'm not used to this. It's usually me and Bobby doing this shit."

"Kiss, hug, fuck, whatever you need to do," Griselda said, "but do it now. We're running out of time."

I nodded. "We aren't going to shoot him out of there. We have to be more clever than that. Palomera's got too many men, and the place has got that wall around it. We're going to have to do this stealthy. Somehow sneak him out of there."

"They still think you're on the road to Mazatlán," Griselda said. "This is our only shot. Let's do it."

"Do what?" Radical asked. Which kind of took the wind out of our sails.

With Radical and Pepe piled in the backseat, we drove back into Coatepec. The desolate cemetery had extra meaning, reminding us of the real possibility that we would end up in that very dirt.

Who was I kidding? It was far more likely that we'd end up in an unmarked hole in the middle of the surrounding scrubland. No reason to sugarcoat the stupid we were about to do.

We were still shy one plan to get Bobby out of his predicament. Which was going to become a big problem very soon. We had the nerve, but no direction. What we really needed was Bobby. He was our resident shit-stirrer. Preposterous or not, he'd have a plan.

"Tell me you got something brewing, Gris," I said. "'Cause I got nothing. Even if we get Bobby out of there, we got to somehow make it out of this town and to the highway."

"One road in and out," she said. "It's about ten, fifteen miles but takes at least a half hour. Means we have to either sneak him out and get all the way back to Mazatlán before they know he's gone, or somehow incapacitate everyone."

"When we were there," I said, "there were a load of guys standing around, at least a half dozen. I can't figure how to do either of those options."

"It's what we got, not what we want," she said. "And we're running out of time."

Angie looked out the windshield, the furrows in her brow deep enough to hold a playing card. For Angie this must have been as foreign as agreeing to capture a unicorn. She was a nurse, for fuck's sake. This was outside of Griselda's normal weekend, but she was a cop. While she never dealt with this situation, she knew mayhem. I had always been around chaos. Expecting normalcy would have been insanity for me.

"Maybe there's a secret way into Palomera's compound," I said.

"The courtyard was walled off," Angie said. "I doubt it."

"Bribe one of the men?"

"Pick the wrong guy and we're screwed," Griselda said. "That's the kind of thing that requires time that we don't have."

"Then it's a bust and run," I said. "And we're going to have to do it in broad daylight. Can't ninja our way in."

Griselda nodded. "I agree. But just so you know. 'Bust and run' isn't an expression."

"If we pull this off, it will be," I said. "Wait a minute. It's almost dinnertime."

"We don't got time to eat," Angie said.

"No," I said. "Palomera served us a nice spread. He sure as shit didn't prepare it himself. He's got a bunch of men up there, too. They got to eat. That means there's people inside that compound that cook the food. They're our way inside."

Angie, Radical, and I stayed out by the cemetery. If the wrong person recognized us, everything would go to hell. Pepe and Griselda went into town to get the supplies we needed. Pepe seemed hesitant to take the balaclava off, but even he knew that it would be suspicious looking.

We had a plan. It was a train wreck plan, but it's what we had.

"Pepe seems like a nice guy," I said to Radical.

"He's not. He's the most violent man I've ever met. Why would you even think that?"

"I don't know," I said. "Making small talk."

"He is here because he enjoys hurting people, and this sounded like a good opportunity."

"Is Tomás paying him, too?"

"Just me," Radical said. "Pepe was bored."

The sound of trucks approached from town. The three of us ducked behind a low stone wall. I peeked through the gaps in the mortar. Two Jeeps headed out of Coatepec. Polo Shirt sat in the passenger seat of the lead car. I hated that fucking guy. Both Jeeps were full of the men at Palomera's home. The cartel soldiers were leaving.

With me and Angie gone, and the drama pretty much over, Polo Shirt must have figured that all that personnel was no longer required to keep an eye on Bobby. After all, there was a drug empire to run. Messing up our lives was extracurricular.

When the Jeeps had passed, the three of us stood, staring at the cloud of dust.

"Fucking A," Angie said.

"You said it," I said. "Like a fucking Christmas present."

"We may not die now," Radical said.

"Loving the optimism," I said. "Let's go get Bobby."

Griselda and Pepe came back fifteen minutes later. They had bought some dresses at a local store but failed to find out who did the cooking at Palomera's place. The elaborate plan we had concocted had involved costumes and foreign accents. Griselda and Angie would pretend to be cooks and sneak into the compound via the kitchen. The dresses looked more appropriate for portraying Mexican peasants in a middle-school play about Pancho Villa. Costumes for tourists. Which was strange in a town that looked like it got a dozen tourists a year. And half of them because they got lost. The other half were like us. They had gotten abducted.

"Fuck the old plan," I said to Griselda the moment she was in shouting range. "The narcos are gone. Most of them, at least. Just drove out of town."

Griselda looked at Angie, as if she was more likely to not talk out of her ass.

"We watched them drive out of town," Angie said. "The handsome guy and at least six of his men."

"You thought he was handsome?" I asked, hating him even more. I didn't think that was possible.

"Not as handsome as you," Angie said in the most insincere, demeaning way possible. She might as well have pinched my cheek as she said it.

"We don't know how many men are still up there," Griselda said.

"Less," I said. "We know that. There's five of us. It's as even as it's going to get."

Griselda nodded, then turned to Pepe and Radical. "You two good with this?"

"The old bust and run," Radical said, giving me a punch on the shoulder.

"See. I told you it was a thing."

"You shouldn't encourage him," Griselda said to Radical.

"Ahora es el momento," Pepe said. "Yo quiero ir. Yo quiero luchar."

Nobody argued with Pepe. Now was the time. The time to go and fight. We all climbed in the truck and headed up the hill to Palomera's compound to free our friend.

TWELVE

“I swear this is the last time,” I said, “but I have to express my reservations about the two of you doing this—putting yourself in danger. I don’t care if it sounds sexist or it is sexist. Radical, Pepe, and me. We got this.”

“Do not involve me and Pepe,” Radical said. “This is between you and your wife and this lady and not me.”

“You’re sure that’s the last time?” Angie said. “Because that bullshit is getting old. Your concern is touching, but I told you, I’m a grown-ass woman. It’s shut-the-fuck-up o’clock, and we’re going with the plan we have.”

“It’s fucking dangerous,” I said. “I’m not being unreasonable.”

“But you’re still talking,” Griselda said. “Your wife was pretty articulate. What part of ‘shut-the-fuck-up o’clock’ didn’t you understand?”

“Apparently the ‘shut’ part. And the ‘up’ part,” I said. “I got the ‘fuck’ part loud and clear, though. The ‘o’clock’ part doesn’t really make sense.”

Pepe and Radical looked at each other. A look that communicated concern about tying their wagon to the idiots in front of them.

I don't know why I didn't shut the fuck up. The arguing about it had been long over on the short drive up the hill. I lost every tack I took. I knew that Angie was an adult who made her own decisions.

We stood around the truck parked in an alley two short blocks from Palomera's walled compound. There was nothing imposing about the eight-foot-high adobe wall. It looked like all the other courtyard walls around the town. Knowing what was behind it was what made it feel like a glance into 1970s East Berlin. The Stasi waited on the other side for us to make our move. No Checkpoint Charlie, but a whole lot of no-man's-land.

A dozen children played in the street outside the house. The rocky dirt street seemed like a strange place to play, but it wasn't a town that got a lot of traffic. The single door leading into Palomera's courtyard opened, and Fernando Palomera himself stepped out.

I ducked back deeper into the alley and watched.

Palomera held a basket under his arm. All the children ran to him. He handed each of them a tamale wrapped in a paper napkin. He gave some of them coins. As soon as they got their food, they ran off, found a curb, and ate. When Palomera's basket was empty and all the children were fed, he went back inside.

"The people of Medellín loved Pablo Escobar, too," Griselda said. "It doesn't take much to sway people who have nothing. It's hard not to like someone who feeds children. This town was probably starving. He brought money, found the men work, sold some hope. The cartels use the people, but they get more than a labor force. They get loyalty. It's why it's so hard to get rid of the cartels. They give. The government is hated more, because they only take."

"Los dos lo pueden jugar," Radical said, and ran down the road into town.

With a freshly purchased bag of Mexican candy, Radical got the children to follow him a few blocks away. If there were going to be any shenanigans, we didn't want kids to be anywhere near Palomera's place. Apparently these children's parents never told them not to take candy from a stranger. Maybe they assumed he was one of Palomera's men. Either way, Radical—a.k.a. el Flautista de Hamelín—cleared the street of children.

Griselda and Angie, in their new Mexican peasant dress costumes, walked in front of the door to Palomera's. They both took their places, inhaled deeply, and screamed at each other in Spanish.

"¡Puta fea!" Angie yelled.

"¡Perra gorda!" Griselda yelled back.

"No me jodas. Peleare contigo."

"Chíngate, chocha."

And it went back and forth like that, breaching the limits of my Spanish expletive vocabulary, which was extensive. I wanted to write some words down for future reference. They kept at it until the door opened. A man poked his head out. Angie slapped Griselda. Not lightly. The sound echoed down the street. I flinched and softly said, "Oh, shit."

The man watching smiled, threw the door wide, and leaned against the frame. Who didn't like a catfight? He nodded, silently willing more violence. Maybe a blouse would get torn off. The ultimate fantasy of all girl-fight enthusiasts.

Griselda grabbed Angie's hair, and the two of them hit the ground, punching and pulling at each other. If I didn't know this was all part of the plan, I would have thought they were playing out some deeply repressed emotions over some long-forgotten grudge. I wondered if Angie was still pissed about Griselda tossing her in a jail cell on our wedding night.

The man at the door leaned his rifle against the wall and whipped out his phone. The modern reaction to practically everything. He stepped closer and filmed the fight, already imagining his future YouTube fame. I probably would have been one of the viewers, but I would have been ashamed the whole time I watched it.

Pepe—back in his balaclava—appeared from around the corner three steps away from the amateur cinematographer. He easily got behind the distracted man. The butt of Pepe's rifle came down hard on the guy's head. Harder than I would've hit him, but Pepe looked like he only had one setting. I kept my gun trained on the door. The man was out before his body hit the bricks. Radical grabbed him quickly and dragged him into the closest alleyway.

Another man ran out the door. He saw me and Pepe and immediately dropped his rifle and put his hands in the air. No hero, this one. Pepe picked up his rifle, took his phone, and pointed to where Radical stood in the mouth of the alley. The man nodded and walked toward him with resignation in his stride.

Griselda and Angie had stopped fighting, breathing heavily with their hands on their knees. They had put everything into the show. Their faces were scratched up and knees bleeding from rolling around in the street. Blood dripped from Angie's lip. They looked at each other like they weren't done.

"You two okay?" I asked.

They both nodded.

"Who won?" Angie asked.

"I'm not stupid enough to answer that," I said.

Angie looked at Pepe. "Who won?"

Pepe aimed his gun ahead of him and rushed through the door into the courtyard. He would rather throw himself at danger than answer her question. Smart man.

I held my breath, shoved my fear as low as it would go, and followed him.

The courtyard was empty. The only sound came from the water splashing in the fountain. We hadn't raised any alarms. Nobody shot at us. Not even harsh language. So far, so good.

Pepe stepped quickly through the courtyard and into the house, his rifle moving as he scoped out the area.

It occurred to me that we hadn't discussed shooting people. I wanted to avoid shooting people, because I considered it to be bad. I especially didn't want to kill anyone. Which I also considered to be bad. Very bad. All I wanted was to get Bobby out of there and get back to my boring life as a dirt farmer. I swore to never complain about digging up gopher holes or baling hay at three in the morning again.

Griselda and Angie were right behind me. Griselda had a thousand-yard stare, pistol in front of her in two hands. Angie looked completely out of place, trying to imitate Griselda's stance with a pistol of her own. They entered slowly.

"Watch the door," I said to Angie. "And our backs. Radical has the street."

Angie nodded, eyes darting around. Griselda pointed toward the door Pepe had entered. I nodded, and we cautiously stepped into Palomera's house.

I was painfully aware I didn't know what I was doing, what I was going to do, or whether or not I was going to be able to do it when the time came. I was accustomed to being under-prepared, but the stakes were higher than the disastrous time I tried to make flan without a recipe. Luckily, Pepe had the bulk of the badassery covered. The unconscious guy on the floor of the dining room was a good sign. Another guard taken out silently. I checked his pulse. He was alive.

Griselda tied the man's hands and stuffed a cloth napkin in his mouth while I kept watch.

"The cellar is this way," I said quietly. "Probably where Bobby's at."

I led Griselda through the house and down the stairs. I had expected a guard in front of the heavy door, but they weren't anticipating any trouble. I unbolted the big, medieval metal bar that ran across the door, threw it open, and walked into the food pantry.

Bobby stood up from the bench, ready to fight. He held a half-empty bottle of Manzanita Sol in one hand, wielded like a knife. He relaxed when he saw me.

"Traffic was a bitch," I said.

"Not funny, bro," Bobby said seriously. "I thought I was going to die here."

"Sorry. I thought—"

Bobby broke out laughing. "I'm fucking with you. I really did think I was going to die, but that doesn't mean I lost my sense of humor."

Griselda entered the room behind me. Bobby's eyes watered up when he saw her.

"Come here," he said.

They held each other more tenderly than I thought Bobby capable of. He kissed her forehead. I looked back to the staircase to give them the moment.

"The worst thought I had," Bobby said, "was that I might not see you again."

"Not a chance, stupid. I love your dumb ass too much."

"What happened to your face?" Bobby said, examining her black eye. "Who did that to you?"

"Angie," Griselda said.

Bobby smiled and nodded. "Catfight for a diversion. Classic."

I turned back. "Time to get the fuck out of here."

Bobby wiped his wet eyes. "Let's show these assholes what it means to fuck with someone from the Imperial Valley. You bring a gun for me?"

Walking back up the stairs, I was greeted by a gunshot and plaster chipping inches from my head.

I screamed "Fuck" and slipped down two steps. Bobby casually walked past me, put his back against the wall, turned quickly, fired a round, and put his back against the wall again.

"Good form, honey," Griselda said, "but if you get shot, I'm going to kill you."

Two more shots fired in our direction. Bobby pointed to the door across the hall. I nodded, stuck my gun at the very bottom of the doorframe, and fired two shots in the direction of the gunfire.

Bobby shouted "Catchphrase" and jumped across the hall into the other room. He smiled and gave me a thumbs up.

"Did you just say 'Catchphrase'?" Gris asked.

"I couldn't think of anything, but when I tell this as a story later I'll fill in a good one. Like a placeholder. It counts."

"Find a way to flank whoever's shooting," I said.

"Yeah, about that," Bobby said. "This is a closet."

"Flawed plan," I said. "You went from being trapped here to being trapped in a different place. Five feet away."

"Something like that."

"Will this be a part of the story when you tell it later?" I asked.

Bobby didn't answer. Two more shots fired from the hall. One splintered the doorframe near Bobby's head.

"Oh, fuck this," Bobby said. Then for emphasis he repeated it: "Fuck. This."

"Don't," Griselda said. "Shit."

Too late. Bobby stood up, took three quick breaths, and ran down the hall in the direction of the gunfire. His screaming voice Dopplered away from me and then abruptly stopped.

I rolled into the hall, gun ready to give him some backup.

"Well, that's disappointing," Bobby said, his voice around the corner. "I didn't get to do nothing but get shot at."

"What's going on?" I shouted.

"Come on out," Bobby said. "It's all over."

Griselda and I walked down the hall.

"I didn't get to shoot anyone!" Bobby yelled. "I didn't even get to hit anyone." His voice carried through the house. "Didn't get to stomp a guy's foot really hard. No, I got to sit on a stool, wait for a few hours, and then run around with a gun. I can do that shit at home. What the hell?"

We found Bobby. He was with Pepe and the man that had been shooting at us. Pepe held the man at gunpoint. The man was Fernando Palomera.

Palomera's body shook in anger. It looked like he was going to explode. Spit flew from his mouth as he spoke. "Mi nieto es su deuda para mí."

Pepe grabbed a cloth napkin and shoved it in Palomera's mouth. When Palomera reached to pull it out, Pepe pulled both his arms behind his back and tied him up.

"I assumed that Mexican Rambo was with us," Bobby said.

I nodded.

"La casa está claro," Pepe said.

"He made it look easy, bro," Bobby said to me.

"Actually," Griselda said, "you guys make it look difficult."

Mi nieto es su deuda para mí. That's what Fernando Palomera had said. My grandson is your debt to me. That did not bode well.

We should have immediately hightailed it. Every second that we stayed, there was the off chance that Polo Shirt and his narco army would return. For all we knew they ran out to buy smokes. However, there were some disagreements on how to close out our little mission.

The biggest question that arose was what to do with Fernando Palomera. Radical and Pepe insisted that the best plan of action was to leave his men tied up and to kill Fernando Palomera. Their argument was that Palomera would continue to be a direct threat to us and them, but the men were just soldiers. They were doing their job and knew it wasn't personal.

With Palomera and his men tied up inside, we tried to hash things out in the courtyard. I couldn't get behind killing Palomera. It wasn't just that he was my son's grandfather—though that was a factor. It was that it was murder. He had threatened and kidnapped Bobby, but at that moment, he wasn't a threat anymore. It might turn out to be a mistake, but I couldn't kill a man for vengeance. And I couldn't kill a man because of a hypothetical.

I had killed two men in my life, and I knew the weight those decisions carried.

"Killing is often necessary," Radical said. "He isn't a threat now, but he will be a threat to you. And maybe me."

"This isn't only my non-murder policy," I said. "If we kill him, someone will want retribution. Polo Shirt knows who we are.

There's no way the cartel would let it go. Breaking our friend out, that's what anyone would do. Killing him will bring the wrath of God on all of us. I can't murder a guy just because he might do something."

"Not might," Radical said. "He will."

"What would I tell my son? I would have to lie to him. And the only lies I'm comfortable with are the tooth fairy and Santa Claus. Even those he knows I'm bullshitting. He just doesn't want to call me on it and risk not getting the money and presents."

"Just because you're the gringo, that doesn't make you the leader," Radical said. "You don't get to make the decision."

"I'm with Jimmy," Griselda said. "I can't allow it either."

In a symbolic gesture, Griselda and Bobby stepped behind me. Pepe stood behind Radical. The tension rose a notch, which was bound to happen during a civil discussion about murder.

"To be honest, I'm on your side, Radical," Bobby said. "This guy is high on my extensive shit list. I'd off the bastard, but I love this lady. And this dude's my best friend. So whatever they say is the right play, that's what's happening."

Radical stared us down. He nodded and took Pepe aside. They talked for a minute, or rather Radical talked and Pepe mostly shrugged.

"Before I forget," I said to Griselda, "remind me to tell one of the guards where Tavio is tied up."

"Good call," she said. "That would've been messed up to leave him out there."

When they were done with their huddle, Radical returned and said, "It is a mistake, but Pepe and I wore masks. Nobody saw our faces. We are safe. You are the ones in danger, so it's your decision."

"Thanks for all your help."

"I got paid," Radical said.

"Still. Thanks."

"Do not be fooled," he said. "Fernando Palomera will come after you. And he will come after your boy."

With that statement on full repeat in my brain, the four of us borrowed one of Palomera's vehicles and drove straight to the Mazatlán airport. No stops along the way. We wanted to get out of the country as quickly as possible. The drive back over the Baluarte Bridge reminded me of every frightening moment of the last couple days.

Radical had contacted Tomás Morales to make travel arrangements for us to return to the US. Verónica met us at the airport. She had our passports and luggage and walked us to the Aeroméxico ticket counter. Everything was ready for us. Four tickets to San Diego. Verónica apologized that the tickets were coach class. I laughed at that.

We checked our bags and headed straight for the gate. Three hours early for our flight, but I would take sitting in an airport over being held captive any day. It wasn't until I walked through security that I relaxed. For the first time, airport security and their metal detectors made me feel safe rather than annoyed.

The four of us strolled through the terminal in the general direction of our gate.

"The bar?" Bobby said. "I need drinks. Fully alcoholized drinks."

We all nodded. That was easily the best idea anyone had ever had ever. We looked for an airport bar, but the best we could do was a Mexican restaurant named Flap's in the food court. The phrase "full bar" had never been more welcome. Bobby ordered for the table, tequila shots and beer chasers all around. And for the fuck of it, some nachos, taquitos, and ceviche.

When the drinks came, we belted the shots and drank half our beers, no toast or ceremony. The alcohol burn in the back of my throat was the same kind of good pain as when I cracked my neck. If I may quote Mr. Cougar Mellencamp, it hurt so good.

"Fucking Mexico, right?" Bobby said.

Even if I knew it wouldn't last, it always felt good to laugh.

"What the hell happened?" Those were the first words out of my mouth when I finally got Tomás on the phone.

After a quick call to Mr. Morales to tell him we were coming home early, I called Tomás. I tried to keep my anger in check over what we had endured, but it boiled over.

"Jimmy," he responded evenly.

"You sent me down to Mexico to meet a guy mixed up with a drug cartel. No fucking warning. My wife was with me. How did that fucking happen?"

"An oversight," Tomás said, his voice even. "I didn't know anything about the man besides his name."

"The mighty Tomás Morales didn't know something? I thought your whole shtick was that information was power or some shit. Where was that precious information?"

"What do you think? That there's some kind of IMDb for Mexican gangsters? None of that shit is written down. My guy finds his name, because he's looking for a woman's father. He finds his address. That he's some politician. You know how many people in Mexico are named Fernando Palomera?"

"I don't know," I said. "Six?"

"Now that I've had some time to investigate, I've pieced together some background on Mr. Palomera. If I would have known, of course I would have told you. The man has been retired for years but was a big deal when the Guadalajara Cartel fell apart. His glory years were before the Internet, so I would've had to hit the microfiche."

"A lot of good that information does me now," I said. "You put Angie and Bobby and Griselda in a lot of danger."

"From what I can tell, the cartel set him up as mayor for his past service to the organization. There's a lot of loyalty there. People owe him. The mayorship isn't just a retirement plan either. Coatepec has strategic importance between Sinaloa and Durango."

"I don't care anymore."

"Once I started talking to people from Guadalajara back in the day, I learned a lot," Tomás said. "The guy is a narco legend."

"Great. Still don't care."

"Back then, they called him 'El Loco.'"

"That's something that would have been good to know," I said. "Fuck me."

"You should have killed him," Tomás said. "His death was your best—maybe only—option."

I lowered my voice and cupped my hand over my mouth. "If murdering my son's grandfather and killing a member of a drug cartel was my best option, I'm fucked from the get-go. I've seen movies. You don't kill a cartel guy and walk away. Wouldn't his friends want revenge? Come after us?"

"Better the cartel than Palomera," Tomás said.

"That can't be true."

"For the cartel, it's business. Something I could throw money at and make go away. But I'm not going to have any pull over Palomera. If he gets it in his head that he wants his grandkid at his side, what lengths will he go to? People do stupid things when they think they're fighting for principle." Tomás laughed. "Such a dumb reason to fight. He went through the trouble to hold Maves to get Juan. He's definitely going to come after him again. They didn't call him El Loco because he wasn't crazy. Mexicans don't do irony."

"I can protect my son. Back in the US, on my turf, I can protect him," I said. "There are cops and feds and people that exist to make sure bad shit doesn't happen to kids."

"Let's hope so," Tomás said, and hung up.

The first—and really only—thing that both Angie and I needed was to see our son. See Juan and give him a big hug and know that he was okay. After a silent and contemplative flight from Mazatlán and drive from San Diego, we returned to the Imperial Valley.

When Angie and I walked into Morales Bar, Juan and Mr. Morales looked up from what appeared to be a heated poker game. A pile of pennies and a few nickels filled the pot. Juan wore a green visor that I didn't know he owned.

"Don't peek at my cards," Juan said sternly, giving Mr. Morales an untrusting eye. He set the cards down but then decided to bring them with him when he ran to me and Angie. The three of us hugged and held each other for a while until Juan squiggled out of it. I would have held him for another hour if he would have let me. His hug felt like home.

"Did you miss us?" I asked Juan.

"Sure, I guess," he said. "You weren't gone that long. Was that a whole week?"

"You're playing for money?" Angie asked, walking Juan back to the table. "Didn't we talk about this?"

"Mr. More-Or-Less said it was okay." Juan smiled. "He owes me eight dollars and twenty-six cents."

"If you're winning," Angie said, "I guess it's okay."

"Eight dollars?" I said. "It looks like you're playing for pennies."

"We are," Mr. Morales said. "The kid is a damn shark."

While Angie helped Juan put his pennies into paper rolls, I gave Mr. Morales a full account of our trip and the various shenanigans that had occurred down Mexico way. Mr. Morales made a face every time Tomás's name came up. His grandson's career path had soured their relationship. They weren't about to patch up their differences anytime soon, so long as Tomás Morales was still the kingpin of all things criminal in Mexicali and its environs.

"Not one to agree with my nieto," Mr. Morales said, "but he was right. You should have killed the man."

"Is everyone a Monday morning murderer?" I said. "It's easy to say that, but you—like most people—have gotten this far in life without killing someone."

Mr. Morales stared at me but didn't say anything.

"Or. Okay. But just the same."

"The situation called for it. The rules in Mexico are different."

"That's what everyone keeps telling me," I said. "My Spanish is crappy, but I'm a hundred percent sure that murder is still illegal there."

"Self-defense."

"The man was tied up."

"Wait and see," Mr. Morales said.

I wasn't enough of an optimistic idiot to believe the nightmare was over. To believe that me or my family were completely safe. Palomera had kidnapped and held Bobby in hopes of being united with Juan, and he hadn't even known of his existence an hour prior to that. Now that he had time to let it stew, he would do something. Add in the embarrassment of us storming his castle and holding a gun to his head. The likelihood that a man nicknamed El Loco would let that go sat right at zero.

Fernando Palomera remained a danger to me and my family, but at least for that moment, we were together and safe. The snake would eventually come out from under his rock. It was in a snake's nature. I only hoped that when that day came, I was ready.

I had worked and fought for my family and what little else I had, and I wasn't about to let anyone take it. Juan was my son, and I would fight to my last breath to protect him. My plan was simple: keep my family close, my eyes wide open, and my firearms fully loaded.

PART TWO

THIRTEEN

We did our best to get back to our boring lives. Boring felt good. Nothing like a series of near-death experiences to slow a person down. Work, school, farming. Simple and satisfying. Family was everything. The only thing that mattered. The maybe of our future floated in the air, but I chose to deal in certainty. I had a wife and child. I had a home and crops. I didn't need anything else. If it turned out that someone was stupid enough to fuck with my family, that person would learn the cost of their asininity.

The autumn was uneventful. The start of winter much the same. Thanksgiving and Christmas came and went. A low-key New Year's Eve followed. Juan attempted to stay awake but only made it to eleven thirty. Angie and I listened to the festivities at Morales Bar from the comfort of our couch, our sleeping kid between us. The live music from across the street boomed loud and late. The trumpeter still played when I woke up at eight the next morning. And I swear he played the same tune that I fell asleep to. It was like traveling in time.

I had learned a number of important life skills growing up on a farm, not the least of which were work ethic, the enjoyment of my own company, and most importantly, patience. As much a survival skill as a defense mechanism, patience is second nature to any farmer. Show me an impatient farmer, and I'll show you someone who is dressed in overalls and a straw hat for Halloween.

We made every effort to keep things normal, but the impact of the events in Mexico and the potential threat of Fernando Palomera hung over our heads. While Angie and I hadn't become full paranoids, we rarely let Juan out of our sights unless he was at school or under the supervision of another parent. Otherwise we kept him close.

As another precaution, Angie and I now carried firearms whenever we left the house. There were helicopter parents, and there were the two of us. We were the Blue Thunder and Airwolf versions, hovering nearby and fully armed for battle.

By February, our diligence waned. It was like standing guard for sixty hours straight. If nothing happened, any guard would start to zone out or get tired. We started to embrace the possibility that Palomera had no interest in Juan. At least no interest in making any effort to get him. That it had been knee-jerk back in Mexico but too much hassle now that we were a thousand miles and a border away.

Tomás had promised me that he would do his best to monitor Palomera's activity and warn me if anything seemed impending, but Tomás's crimebossing kept him busy. The last few times that I had checked in, the most I got were a few responses of "It's fine" and "If anything happens, you'll know." I got the impression that he was dealing with his own problems. Tomás didn't fluster easily, but I could hear the tension in his voice.

During one short conversation, he vaguely expressed that his interests in Sinaloa had gotten increasingly complicated and had started to spill over into Mexicali. Our Mexican adventure had shaken up a can of snakes, spilling them out in all directions. One of the main reasons why it's rarely a good idea to purchase a can of snakes. Although to be fair, from the outside most of them look like a can of mixed nuts. Damn you, nut snakes.

When the Holtville Carrot Festival rolled around in February, Angie and I decided to loosen the tether. Keeping Juan cooped up when he knew there were rides, games, cotton candy, and a parade bordered on criminal. The unpredictability of crowds concerned me, but Juan needed to be a kid. Hindsight would tell me if it was a good idea.

In the classic Warner Brothers cartoon "Bully for Bugs," Bugs Bunny ends up in a bullring on his way to the Coachella Valley and "the big carrot festival therein." Contrary to popular belief, relying on a cartoon character for accuracy when it comes to regional events is a mistake. Bugs Bunny is not a credible source. If you take a wrong turn in Albuquerque, you won't end up in Timbuktu. That's science fact. And duck season and rabbit season are concurrent, so Elmer Fudd should have shot both Bugs and Daffy.

The carrot festival is not in the Coachella Valley, but in my hometown of Holtville, California, in the Imperial Valley. Holtville is the self-proclaimed carrot capital of the world. Every winter for the last seventy years, there had been the carrot festival, which included a parade, a carnival, cooking contests, a 5K run, a rib cook-off, and a whole bunch more small town awesomeness. It's an all-week event culminating in one of the best parades on the planet. They always get the coolest people to act as grand marshal. Quaint and fun and enthusiastic and full of charm. Not flashy, but real. I couldn't imagine missing it and couldn't let Juan miss it either.

Juan was scheduled to ride with the other Cub Scouts on the fire engine. He'd been looking forward to it for months. I usually rode on Bobby's float, which was just a tractor hauling a trailer with a few bales of hay on it and a sign that said, "The So You Want to Be on a Float Float." It was exactly that. Anybody who wanted to be on a float could jump aboard. Usually a hodgepodge of kids and their parents singing along to one of Bobby's mixtapes. Which meant they better like Warrant and Whitesnake, because that's mostly what would be playing.

I had my sights set on entering my carrot latkes in the cooking contest. My "Carrot Surprise" the previous year had been a dumpster fire of a meal, an unmitigated disaster. Apparently, the "surprise" was that other people found the combination of hot dogs and carrots disgusting. My friends still gave me a hard time about it. The most common was someone saying the word "Surprise" while they pretended to vomit. It hurt.

But if I let embarrassing failure stop me from doing things, I wouldn't get out of bed. And I definitely wouldn't have invented the Napeau, a hat with a pillow attached.

I had been experimenting with flavor combinations for the last three months in an effort to redeem myself. For those keeping score, I settled on a spice base of paprika, cumin, and a touch of chili powder. Doris Vessey was going down.

Friday night was the best night of the festival. The carnival was in full swing. A great crew got together to work on Bobby's float. "Working on Bobby's float" translated as playing Wa-Shoos and drinking beer in Dusty Odermatt's backyard into the wee hours.

Most of the actual work on the float got done in a fevered half hour right before the parade started on Saturday morning.

Angie and Juan hit the carnival midway. I would meet up with them after the cook-off. Full of anticipation, I took my Saran Wrapped platter of latkes to the auditorium. While the sequestered judges tasted the fare and made their decisions, two very nervous and very adorable young ladies earned 4-H points by giving an expository presentation on how water travels through the Imperial Valley.

An hour later the verdict was read. I came in third place. Redemption from last year, but still disappointing. Doris Vessey won every year, so it was no surprise that she had won again. I suspected chicanery, but there was no regulatory body for me to contest her victory. Seriously, how good could carrot sushi be?

With my small trophy in hand, I hit the short midway looking for Angie and Juan. I walked past the Ring Toss, Punk Pitch, Dime Toss, and all the other pocket-draining short cons. I considered throwing darts at balloons. But I knew that even if I hit all three, I wasn't winning the giant stuffed bee. I would end up with a crappy plastic squirt gun or some piece of shit pencil sharpener. This wasn't my first carnival. Fool me once, shame on you. Fool me eight times, I'm an asshole.

I found Angie and Juan waiting in line for the Hammer, one of the more terrifying rides in the park. The spinning upside down two different ways wasn't the terrifying part. It was the slipshod, rickety look of the thing. When it really got going, the entire mechanism shook and made terrible metal noises. Like two trains crashing into each other over and over again. Loud enough to drown out "Once Bitten, Twice Shy" playing on repeat. There was no way I was going on the Hammer.

"Pop," Juan said, "are you going to ride with me?"

"Of course he is," Angie said, putting Juan's hand in mine. "I've got to find the ladies' room."

I gave Angie a death stare. She gave me a smirk. I fake-smiled down at Juan. "This is going to be fun."

"Did you win the cooking prize?" Juan asked.

"Third place."

"Is that the trophy?"

I nodded, showing him the small trophy.

"I want a trophy."

"Well, you have to win something," I said. "I'm sure you will."

"Mrs. Vessey won, hunh?"

"You know it," I said. "She's a machine. She's like a carrot-cooking Terminator."

"Those are the worst kinds."

There were only three people in front of us. Three people separating me from what could be the instrument of my untimely demise or at the very least my unfortunate maiming. I wondered how long it would take to learn to eat with my feet.

Then I saw something that scared me more than the Hammer.

Two men stood in front of the Tilt-A-Whirl, their arms crossed. There were hundreds of other people at the carnival, so there was no reason for them to raise any hackles. Plenty of other tough-looking Mexicans as well. The difference was that these two guys stared directly at Juan. Their eyes locked on him.

If it had been one man, I might have brushed it off as someone zoning out or a run-of-the-mill weirdo. Two men staring with intent was too much to ignore. The one covered in tattoos had on a tank top to show them off. The other guy went full-on vato: baggy Dickies, crisp tee, top button flannel, hairnet, head tilt. Far too serious for a carnival. Hell, they were too serious for a funeral. How much effort would it have been to buy a balloon or a giant foam finger for the sake of camouflage?

Usually the carnies were the scariest people at a carnival. That's stiff competition. These men weren't working for the carnival, but they were definitely working.

I took a step in their direction, but Juan pulled at my hand and yelled, "It's our turn! It's our turn!"

"One second," I said, turning to Juan. When I turned back, the two men were gone. I scanned the crowd but couldn't find them.

"You getting on, chief?" the carny asked. "There's a line, you know."

Juan kept pulling on me. I gave one last look and then got on the ride, still distracted. Maybe from a higher vantage point I'd be able to see the two men.

"You're going to want to double-check that safety belt," the carny said. "We've been having some bad luck with a couple of them."

"Are you kidding me?" I said as he slammed and locked the door of the cage we were now inside. I pulled at the door, but apparently the door that locked from the outside was working just fine.

The mechanism groaned into gear. What was essentially a human rock tumbler chirred into motion. Metal scraped metal. A few weird pings and we were turning. There was no sound the machine made that didn't make my butthole pucker.

"It's moving," Juan said, full of glee. "Hold on, Pop."

I tried to distract myself from the ride by looking for the two men. The mesh cage obscured my view, and once we were upside down, it was impossible. At first we rocked back and forth. No big deal. It didn't take long, though, before the ride leveled up into full chaos mode.

I've never been good with rides that spin me in circles inside of circles. My inner ear wasn't built for that bullshit. The biggest, scariest roller coasters are cake, but as I might have mentioned before, the Teacups—a.k.a. the Mad Tea Party ride—at Disneyland turned me into a puke howitzer. The Day Ruiner is what that ride should be called.

Juan screamed in delight as he slid around under his loose seat belt. I held my arm across his chest and gripped the door handle tightly with my other hand. Through gritted teeth and spun bowels, I made it through the first couple loops. My sunglasses fell from my shirt pocket and pinballed around the cage as we gained speed.

I. Fucking. Hated. Every. Fucking. Second. Of. The. Fucking. Hammer. Ride.

Four agonizing minutes later, when the torture of supposed family fun finally ended, I walked out of the contraption a changed man. I knew what Neil Armstrong had felt like when he had returned from space. My legs wobbled on my return to earth. My head pounded, but the air smelled sweeter than it ever had. The sweet smell ended up being the cotton candy machine ten yards away.

Juan took off running toward what would most likely be the next skull-splitting experience of the night. Distracted by my elation over not being on the ride anymore, I had temporarily forgotten about the two men. Then the panic kicked in.

In the brief moment when I lost sight of Juan, I felt a deep sinking feeling. Every parent's greatest fear. Juan darted through the thick crowd back into view, turned a corner, and headed toward the midway out of view.

"No, no, no," I said. "Juan!"

I rushed in the direction Juan had headed, searching the crowd. The throng grew denser as I approached the midway. I squeezed through, hopped, and used my height to look over the mob. I felt like a salmon swimming upstream. Every time I yelled Juan's name, a few Mexican men turned to see what I wanted.

"Not you," I said. "Have you seen a kid?"

Everyone shrugged at the stupid question. Of course they had seen a kid. We were at a carnival.

"Juan!" I yelled again.

Angie grabbed my arm. "What's going on?"

As I started to explain my parental failure, I spotted Juan leaning on a counter watching a game that involved fishing poles and plastic frogs on plastic lily pads.

"Nothing. Everything's okay. Just lost sight of him for a second."

Angie gave me a look but didn't say anything. We walked to Juan.

"Hey, Pop. Hey, Mom," he said, oblivious to my concern. "I don't think this game is possible to win. The frog mouths look smaller than the hooks."

I got down on one knee to look Juan in the eye. "I need you to listen to me right now, Juan."

He looked worried, reacting to my tone.

"You cannot run off like that," I said. "Don't ever take off without me knowing where you're going. Okay?"

Juan looked scared. His eyes got wet. "I'm sorry. I didn't mean to."

I gave him a big hug. "You're not in trouble, kiddo. You just scared me."

"I'm sorry," Juan repeated.

"You almost gave your old man a heart attack."

Angie shook her head. "Way more likely the twenty pounds of barbecue ribs you ate this afternoon would cause an infarction."

I scanned the crowd again to see if I could spot the two men, to see how close I came to losing my son. I didn't see them. Maybe I was just paranoid.

"You two should go on the Hammer again," Angie said. And in one sentence she let Juan off the hook and punished me.

"I want to help you, Jimmy," Ceja said. "Honest, I do. But there's like a hundred reasons I can't. And if I could, I wouldn't know how."

On Monday after the parade weekend, I had come to talk to Holtville's finest. The two men at the carnival had spooked me. I wanted to see if the Holtville Police Department could help keep my family safe.

Ceja Carneros put aside his busy schedule of watching porn on the city's dime to talk to me. "You can't even say for certain if those two men were after Juan."

"I told you what happened in Mexico," I said. "This Palomera guy. He might try to abduct my son."

"You know that most people don't piss off a drug cartel on their Mexican honeymoon, right?" Ceja shook his head. "The worst most people end up with is a sunburn or dysentery or, God forbid, a timeshare."

"This is about Juan, man. I need your help. Any kind of help."

"Sorry," Ceja said. "Didn't mean to joke, but there's nothing I can do."

"I know I live way outside the city limits, which makes it a county thing, but I'm a Holtville guy. This is my town."

Ceja stood from his desk and went to the mini-fridge. He grabbed two Cokes, tossing me one. "You been back months and nothing's happened, right? You don't know if the dudes this weekend were bad dudes. Could've just been some mean-looking dudes. We got plenty of those down here. You gringos are prone to finding us brown folk scary. You got no idea how many calls I get for suspicious-looking Mexicans. One time I got a call and the caller was talking about me. They were calling me and looking across the street at me talking to them. Do I look suspicious?"

"It's the one eyebrow," I said.

Ceja sat back down, putting his feet up on the desk.

"I'm supposed to wait until someone tries to grab my son?" I asked.

"It's not a jurisdiction thing," Ceja said. "I could care less about that shit. There's just nothing to do. You got no idea if something is even going to happen. Let alone when or by who."

"What if I told you that an assassin was hired to kill me? What would happen in that scenario?"

"Fuck if I know. Protective custody, maybe. It's not the kind of thing the HPD deals with. "We're more of a locked-your-keys-in-your-car outfit. Besides, you wouldn't want Juan in protective custody for who knows how long. That don't make no sense."

"Someone's going to try to take him. I know it. This Palomera, he ain't going to let it go."

"We're the police. We don't prevent crimes. We show up after they're all done. We clean up the mess and arrest the bad guy. Actually someone else cleans up the mess, but we arrest the bad guy. If we can find them. Like half the time. A little less than half. Mostly we give people tickets."

"None of that really describes protecting or serving."

"You can hire some bodyguards or security."

"With all my millions? We're scraping as it is. I haven't slept more than a few hours a night in months. I thought money problems were stressful. This is worse."

"As a sworn officer of the law, I can't officially help you," Ceja said, "but we're friends. If you need a hand, I'll come and sit on the porch with a shotgun on my off days."

"Thanks, buddy." I gave him a slap on the shoulder. "You just keep your eyes peeled for any suspicious characters that aren't you."

FOURTEEN

Two weeks passed. No sign of large staring men. No kidnappers in the cornfield. No ninjas in the fridge. No nothing.

I watched Juan carefully paint his Pinewood Derby car, his tongue sticking out the corner of his mouth. Paint fumes filled the dining room turned woodshop. Stained newspaper covered the table. The clump of wood Juan painted looked vaguely car shaped, more Fred Flintstone than John DeLorean. But Juan had made it himself. Sawing, planing, sanding—he had done everything. I sat back as consultant, showing him how to use the tools, giving sage advice. His car would definitely be the funkiest one on the ramp, but it was honest. He could take pride that he did the work and had learned some skills.

Juan had enjoyed working with the wood so much that he already had his next project scoped out. A homemade yo-yo. He had brought up trying to make a bow and some arrows, but I told him to talk to his mom about that.

"Are those racing stripes?" I asked him.

"Yeah, like the ones on Uncle Bobbiola's truck," Juan said. "They make it go faster."

"Well, they make it go oranger," I said. "And a Ranchero is a car, not a truck."

Juan laughed. "Uncle Bobbiola said that it is a truck and only doodoo-heads call it a car."

"That sounds like Bobby. Next time you see him, call his car an El Camino. It's a fun game we like to play."

Juan held the car at arm's length and squinted at it. "More stickers," he said, and added additional numbers to the side of the car.

"Good call," I said, heading into the kitchen. I took a quick look back at my son before I left the room. I hadn't planned to ever be a parent, but now I couldn't imagine not being one. Not having someone in my life that I cared about—worried about—that much. And I was definitely worried.

"The car's looking pretty good," I said to Angie, taking the sponge out of her hand and taking over at the sink on the remaining dishes. "It's got character. Some of Juan's personality."

"It still feels like something is going to happen," Angie said, no interest in talking about Pinewood anything. "Is that crazy?"

"Maybe those two guys were just two guys, and I put that fear back in play. We've been on edge since Mexico. It was probably my imagination. Nothing's really happened. That's a good thing."

"It feels overdue," she said. "You don't think Palomera will let this go either."

"Yeah," I said. "I know he won't."

"How do we do this? Go about our lives pretending like nothing is going to happen?"

"We could board up the windows, buy provisions for a year, and watch Netflix until we wish it away."

"We could take Juan to my cousins in LA."

"We can't protect him from two hundred miles away."

"It's like living in a war zone," Angie said. "Bombs dropping, people shooting all around you, but people still go to work. Because what else can they do?"

"Yeah, like that," I said, "but without the bombs and the shooting."

"You know what I mean."

"A couple scary dudes looked at him wrong. Do you know how many people give me the hairy eyeball on a daily basis? I have one of those faces. We're careful and diligent and all that shit, but we can't stop Juan from doing kid things. I don't want to mess him up."

"If you're wrong," she said, not bothering to finish the thought.

"Look at it from Palomera's perspective," I said. "If he wants his grandson by his side in Mexico, his best option would be legal means. He is Juan's grandfather. The two of them are blood relatives. He'd at least have a case."

"That doesn't make me feel better. All you're telling me is that he has more than one option for taking our son away from us." Angie took the sponge from my hand. "You're doing it wrong. That's crystal."

I stepped away, hands in the air. "I know it sounds like I'm being cavalier with his safety, but until the threat is real, we can't bury ourselves underground and bring him into the bunker with us."

"You broke it," she said, holding the wineglass to the light. She opened the cabinet underneath the sink and tossed it in the bin.

"I'll get Bobby to go with me tonight. As backup. Feel a little better?"

Angie nodded. "Try not to get into any trouble."

"Define 'trouble.'"

Most nights since getting back from Mexico, I woke up at four o'clock in the morning. The same time every night. The consequence of some nightmare that I never remembered. My heart raced. Anxiety took over my body, making my skin vibrate. Apnea was wishful thinking. This was dread, the same spinning thoughts careening through the brain. I stared at the ceiling and questioned every decision I'd ever made, but chiefly the most recent ones.

In those spinning thoughts, I found myself regretting not killing a man. Things had to be seriously fucked up for not committing murder to be a regret. But that's the decision that hounded me.

Tomás and Mr. Morales had been right. Killing Fernando Palomera would have ended the threat to Juan. It would most certainly have brought another one, but that threat would be pointed in my direction, not my son's.

As I replayed and second-guessed, it rarely changed my decision. If I had a second chance, I wouldn't have done anything different. The theoretical murder of another human being and the actual execution of another human being existed on two different planes. Palomera wasn't running at us with a knife. I had to believe in right and wrong. And even if someone else was capable of the wrong thing, that didn't mean that I shouldn't do the right thing.

None of those thoughts or ideas helped me fall asleep.

"No problemo," Bobby said when I asked him if he could come along to Juan's Cub Scout meeting to ease Angie's mind.

Bobby would never have told me if it was a problemo. That's the kind of friend he was. The same was true for Mr. Morales,

Buck Buck, Snout, Joaquin, and all my other pals. Since I'd been back in the Imperial Valley, I'd lost count of the number of times people had been willing to drop everything when it came to helping me. In small towns, friends are family.

I suspected that Bobby had an ulterior motive revolving around his skewed concept of redemption.

Since we'd been back from Mexico, it took less than five minutes in any conversation for Bobby to begin a lament about his lack of participation in the violence down south. He had been threatened, kidnapped, and shot at, yet Bobby didn't get to hit, shoot, or bludgeon anyone. He had hit a guy with a bottle. But for some reason that only Bobby's internal logic could explain, that didn't count. The unfairness of it all. In Bobby's mind, that was not a proper Mavescapade by any standard. He had remained a bystander through most of the adventure. Like going to Six Flags and only standing in line. Or reading magazines in the lobby of a whorehouse. Bobby was still waiting to get his number called.

If there was a slim chance that some violent shit might go down, Bobby was sure as hell going to be there. If a single punch was thrown and he heard about it the next day, he'd kick himself for not getting the chance to kick someone else. That's the class of regret that haunted a man like Bobby Maves.

Juan and I drove in my truck. Bobby followed in his Ranchero. Juan wore his Cub Scout uniform and had his Pinewood Derby car in his lap. He turned the wheels, a final inspection on the car's axle.

"It's a good car," I told him. "I'm proud of you."

"What if I don't win?" Juan asked. "It took me hours and days."

"Then you don't win. No big deal. Doesn't change that you made it. That you did your best."

"But I want a trophy."

"Remember, so does everyone else. You may win. You may lose. The only thing that you can do is put your everything into it. You tried your hardest, didn't you?"

"Yeah."

"You can't put in more than a hundred percent."

"I put in two hundred percent."

"I stand corrected," I said. "I'm not as good at math as you."

I didn't have the heart to tell Juan that sometimes your best isn't good enough. That sometimes the repercussions of losing are so great that it doesn't matter what you put into a thing. It only matters that you lost. That nobody cares if you tried, only that you failed.

But that's a huge bummer, and I'm a decent-enough father to not poison my son with my mind's pessimism.

We didn't pass any other cars on the ten-mile drive into town. Dark fields and a few owls. None of the owls looked too suspicious. When victory was nothing happening, I knew my world was messed up.

The competitive air was palpable in the Finley Elementary School cafeteria. Among the parents, not the children. Most of the kids ran around, screamed, and made fart sounds with their mouths and/or armpits. Meanwhile, a group of grown-ass men argued about the slope of the toy car ramp.

Juan joined a group of more sedate kids playing at one of the tables. Juan showed them his car. The others would have shown theirs, but the fathers kept them guarded until race time. Juan had named his racer the Flame Fire, the name painted on the side, the letters growing progressively smaller as he ran out of space, the final *E* just above the *R* in "Fire." A big orange flame adorned the hood.

I greeted a couple of the moms and dads. Handshakes and how-you-doings. I knew everyone in the cafeteria but wasn't exactly close to any of them, including a second cousin. Didn't like a few of them, including a second cousin. PTA pals and Cub Scout cronies. Bobby said hello to a few folks, then pulled me aside.

"I feel creepy being here without a kid," Bobby said. "It's weird, right?"

"It's a little weird," I said.

"I'm going to walk the perimeter," Bobby said. "Check to see if everything's five by five. Look for any chupacabras. Make sure no one's stirring up some evil shit in the bushes."

"You got beer in your car, don't you?"

"No. I don't have beer in my car."

I stared at him.

"I have beer in my *truck*." Bobby gave me a hard slap on the ass and walked out the door. I asked myself for the millionth time why we were friends, but at the same time I considered slipping out and grabbing one of those beers. Competitive fathers weren't my favorite thing. I dreaded Little League, Pop Warner, and every other competitive sport in my son's future.

Dan Reschert gave me a nod and walked over. "Buck Buck was talking. Said you might have some trouble coming your way. Said there might be a fight. I'm down for a fight."

I played football in high school with Dan and his brothers. Didn't know them that well, but the Rescherts were good people. Always ready to help out in a pinch.

"Was Buck Buck drinking?" I asked.

"What do you think?"

"Right now things are good." I shrugged. "Appreciate the offer, though."

"Just putting it out there. You need a hand. A fist. An extra gun. You let me know. You don't fuck with Holtville."

"Thanks."

You don't fuck with Holtville. That psalm had been recited after many a violent victory. Bleeding challengers on the ground in the parking lot outside the bar wondering why they fucked with Holtville. When you fight the heat and the desert and hardship every damn day, a three-hundred-pound drunk with a chip on his shoulder wasn't nothing but a nuisance.

I hadn't lived in any other place where the people had my back like they did in the Imperial Valley. It was more than just local pride. It was a common loyalty within the community. Dan didn't need to know the details, only that help was needed.

Or maybe the people of the Imperial Valley didn't actually care about helping. Maybe they were itching for a fight. Any fight. Some leisure violence. I didn't really care. When the thing you're fighting for has weight and the people fighting are on your side, motivation doesn't matter.

The Pinewood Derby went according to plan. That is, if Juan's plan had been for two of the wheels to fly off in the first race, only to have the car slide down the slope sideways and miraculously cross the finish line first. Veeders never win pretty.

The look on some of the other fathers' faces, losing to a misshapen chunk of wood, was priceless. Jeb Ayers muttered something about disqualification because the whole car didn't cross the finish line, the wheels ending up halfway across the room. Jeb had always been a bit of a whiner.

After a pit stop and some quick repairs on the Flame Fire, Juan was ready for the second race. The wheels stayed on, but the car finished third. Maybe it was meant to only have two working wheels.

When the derby was over, some other kids won, but everyone got a trophy. I personally wouldn't have taken a hell of a lot of pride in a trophy that had "Participant" etched on it, but Juan seemed happy with the outcome. That was all I gave a shit about.

Juan walked out of the cafeteria with his first trophy. He couldn't stop staring at it and smiling. Bobby waited for us by his Ranchero. He downed the rest of the can of beer in his hand and tossed the empty in the bed of his car.

"That's a pretty badass trophy you got there, Juanito," Bobby said.

"There were bigger ones, but this one is good, too," Juan said. "It's bigger than the one Pop got for his carrot hash browns."

"They were latkes," I said.

"Like either of us care," Bobby said. He leaned in so that Juan could show him the trophy. "Participant. That's awesome. You totally participated. Let me see that car. Those are some sick racing stripes."

After grabbing a victory chocolate-dipped cone at Arnold's, we headed home. No moon, country dark, the only light came from the stars and the orange glow of Mexicali on the southern horizon.

We passed Hunt Road, halfway home. Bobby honked, and I saw him take the turn toward his place in the rearview mirror. Only a couple more miles and no other cars on the road. It seemed overly cautious for him to follow us all the way back home. Even though we had been taught to wait until your date was inside before you drove away.

As I neared McCabe Road, I watched a car pull out from behind a long stack of hay bales. Maybe a hundred yards ahead. The car's high beams blinded me when they kicked on. I tapped the brakes. It could've been an irrigator, but the timing was more than suspicious.

Driving toward us, the car hit the emergency brake and slid to a stop perpendicular to the road about thirty yards in front of me. Nope, not an irrigator. I had three options and no time to choose. I could stop my truck, ram the other car, or attempt to go around.

"Hold on," I said to Juan as casually as I could. He didn't look concerned, focused on polishing his trophy. He buffed the shit out of the thing with the bottom of his shirt.

There was a ditch on the left, but I couldn't remember if there was one on the right. If there was, it was going to be a tight squeeze or a short chase. I jerked the wheel, just missing the car and fishtailing in the hardpack. I turned the wheel left and right, trying to regain control. I somehow managed to get past the car and back on the road.

Another set of headlights approached from a quarter mile away, a truck with KCs on top. Could be another bad guy or just a field worker. I wasn't going to risk it. It was time to show these assholes that not only did I know these back roads, but I had watched a shit-ton of *Dukes of Hazzard* in my youth. And by "my youth," I meant three episodes in the last ten days. Yee-haw, motherfuckers.

First chance, I turned off the road and headed up a narrow ditch bank, invisible unless a person knew it was there. The wrong speed or angle of approach and the car behind me would be in the ditch or lettuce field.

I had spent my teenagerhood playing car tag on these roads. The challenge was in the fact that all the fields made a grid and it was flat as hell. Without trees, there weren't places to hide. You couldn't lose someone using the geography. The way to lose someone in the country was to put distance between you and them or make them crash. See *Smokey and the Bandit*, *High-Ballin'*, and the rest of the Jerry Reed canon for reference.

The first maneuver any self-respecting, reckless youth learned was how to drive at night without headlights. That's day one for country teenagers. On the road, you could use the power lines that ran parallel as a guide to stay straight. If there weren't any power lines, you had to use the field rows, which was harder.

There was limited practical function for the skill, other than to sneak past the deputies that broke up one's country bonfire. At the moment, I felt justified knowing that one of the many useless skills I had taught myself might save my son. I wasn't going to lose the other car by catching grapes in my mouth or belching the alphabet.

I kept my headlights on for the moment as I barreled down the ditch bank. The blueprint for my less-than-intricate plan formed quickly.

"How you doing?" I asked Juan, keeping my voice steady.

He glanced out the window. "Where are we?"

"Have to check the fields," I said.

He shrugged and went back to his trophy.

I pulled out my phone and called Bobby. A glance in my rearview told me that the car was a good quarter mile back. I couldn't tell if the truck with the KCs had joined the chase. Bobby answered on the second ring.

"Hey," Bobby said.

In the calmest voice I could muster, I said, "I got a car chasing me. Get to the house. Check on Angie. Call her first. Then call Gris."

"Where you at?" Bobby said. "You want me to come to you?"

"No, get to Angie. To the house. I got this. I'm past Bowker."

"Just flipped a u-ey," Bobby said. "I'm on my way. You should head out to the Rubins' eighty. The one where we shot that horror movie when we were fourteen."

"Way ahead of you."

"What was the name of that movie?"

"*Out of the Darkness*," I said.

"We blew the shit out of some stuff for the big finale."

"A stake to the heart isn't the only way to kill a vampire. Explosives and shotguns work, too. Hold on a sec."

I zigged the truck across the road and zagged onto another dirt road, just missing a long row of hay bales.

"I probably got the VHS somewhere," Bobby said. "I'm going to dig that shit up."

"I got to get back to driving."

"A fucking car chase and I'm missing it. Show Buford T. Justice what for, and I'll see you back at the house."

I turned onto Heber Road and headed back east. I got up to sixty but kept it there. The car had lost a few seconds on that last turn. I needed the right distance between us and them. I saw the car turn behind me and gun it. When the car was about a hundred yards back, the turn appeared ahead of me.

I slowed to almost a stop and turned onto a dirt road that bisected a carrot field. I needed the other car to make the same turn. I headed north, swerving here and there to kick up as much dust as I could. The road washboarded in the center, bouncing us in our seats and vibrating my whole body.

"Pop?" Juan said.

"It's okay, son," I said. "Just playing a driving game."

"The bumps are making me have to pee."

"Can you hold it?" I asked, glancing at the rearview and seeing the headlights peeking through the dust. Perfect position.

"I'll try," he said. "But I really got to go. It's bouncy."

"I'm on it." With one hand on the wheel, I dug around under my seat. I found a half-full Gatorade bottle that was probably a year old. I handed the bottle to Juan.

"Only if you really have to," I said.

It wouldn't be the first time Juan had pissed in a bottle. Angie had never approved of my laissez-faire approach to vehicular urination, but my truck, my rules. I hated stopping for anything other than beef jerky when I was on a long road trip. No trucker bombs, though. I never just chucked it out the window. I had class, after all.

The dirt road formed a T up ahead. If I kept straight, I would drive right into the Ash Canal. Not a cement ditch, but a wide dirt canal. No guardrails, no fence. No sign or warning. If you didn't know it was there, you'd better be able to swim. I was betting that the car behind me didn't know it was there.

For my plan to work, I had to give the driver behind me no time to brake. I had to drive toward a deep canal with my son in the car and no headlights. If I had another option, I would have taken it. Sometimes the only option is the stupidest one.

The timing had to be stainless. It had been years, but not only had Bobby and I blown up a mannequin in the name of cinematic art out here, but I had irrigated this field from my freshman year in high school until graduation. I knew every bump on this road. I had spent more time out on this eighty-acre patch than in my own backyard.

I heard a strange sound, a low rumble. A tire? My engine? Had I hit a rock? None of the above. I turned to see my son urinating into the Gatorade bottle.

I couldn't see the canal, but I knew where it was. I cut the headlights, counted to three, braked, and turned sharply. I should have warned Juan, because he lost his grip on the bottle. It hit me in the head, splashing a warm Arnold Palmer of piss and Gatorade on the side of my face. I barely noticed, more concerned with the truck's back tire dipping over the edge of the canal. I gunned the engine and held my breath until the truck righted itself and we were headed down the ditch bank.

I stopped the truck and turned in my seat. The car behind us braked. Not in time. It slid sideways into the Ash. Water splashed in the full canal. The car's headlights quickly submerged, the scene falling back into darkness. I looked around for the other truck before I popped the headlights back on.

"Sorry, Pop," Juan said. "I dropped the bottle and peed all over the place."

The dashboard in front of him dripped with urine. I was olfactorily reminded that we had eaten asparagus for dinner.

"We've all been there, kiddo," I said. "Not your fault. It's on me."

"It is," he said. "It's all over you."

Never had getting covered by whiz been funnier. And getting covered by whiz was pretty damn funny to begin with. We laughed as I put the truck in gear and headed back to the house.

FIFTEEN

Bobby sat on the short front wall with a shotgun across his knees. He hopped off when I pulled my truck into the driveway, eyes on the road.

Rufus and Joaquin sat outside Joaquin's Airstream trailer. Joaquin smiled, waved, and held up his shotgun to tell me that he was ready for anything. Rufus barked once and then went back to licking his junk.

Juan ran past Bobby into the house. "Hey, Uncle Bobbiola."

"How's Angie?" I asked him.

He shook his head. "You smell like cat piss."

"Son piss."

"You go inside," Bobby said. "I'm going to stick around out here. Grab a beer with Joaquin. Play some charades."

Walking into the house, I got a long stare from Angie. Not angry, but concerned. It was her I-told-you-someone-was-going-to-try-something stare.

Juan went straight back to his bedroom with the Flame Fire and his trophy, seemingly unaware of the recent danger. He usually noticed grown-up things, but being around me and Bobby had inured him to certain activities. That wasn't Juan's first back road car chase.

I gave Angie a big hug. "We're safe. He's safe."

She gave me a sniff and a wince but didn't let go. "For how long?"

"For now. That's the best we can do. Also, our son's covered in urine."

Griselda showed up later, coming straight from the scene at the canal. Angie, Bobby, Griselda, and I sat around the dining room table. They nursed their first beer. I was already three beers in. I needed the extra help. When it had finally hit me what had just happened, the shakes hit my hands and legs. Calm in a crisis, a mess afterward.

In one sense, I won the parenting award for bringing Juan home safe and keeping him in the dark about his grandfather attempting to abduct him. I subsequently lost the parenting award for driving recklessly at night without headlights and almost sinking into a canal with my kid in the truck. The parenting award was a very fickle award.

"The car in the canal was empty," Griselda said. "No driver. I would've stayed, but I couldn't watch the dumbfuckery anymore. Ten deputies staring at a canal with their hands on their hips. IID guy pissed he had to come out so late. Arguments about who did what next. You know how often people drive into ditches? Nobody ever wants to do the work. They managed to run the plates. Stolen from the Costco lot in Calexico."

"You literally ditched him," Bobby said, looking around for some acknowledgment of his wordplay. He got none. "You guys suck."

"They found the car," I said. "That means that they'll have to believe my story, take this situation seriously. What happens now?"

Griselda shook her head. "Official investigation, but I wouldn't expect much to come of it."

"What do you mean? We need protection."

"It's complicated," Griselda said. "We didn't file anything with the Mexican authorities when we got back, because we didn't know if Palomera would try anything. There was no reason to unnecessarily rile him."

"Now we know," I said. "There's got to be something we can do."

"They got a stolen car in a ditch and your story," she said. "Even with me corroborating, the most they'll do is file some files. I'll bring it to the Feds, but I'm not optimistic. They'd want something out of it. An arrest, a case, information. We don't know who we're looking for. We know who's behind it, but not who's here in the US."

"Damn it," I said. "If Juan wasn't with me, I would've pulled the driver out of the water. Couldn't risk it with the possibility of that other truck out there."

"Keeping Juan safe was the right thing to do," Angie said. "I mean, not the reckless driving with your kid in the car. That was the wrong thing to do. That aside, you did mostly the right thing."

"I'm sure some of me and Jimmy's car chases were way more dangerous," Bobby said.

"What car chases?" Angie asked.

"You're not helping," I said, kicking Bobby under the table.

"Can't the Sheriff's do something?" Angie asked. "You were in Mexico with us, Gris. Can't you convince your people that if they tried something once, they'll try again?"

"I keep trying," Griselda said. "They gave me the same boilerplate answer. No resources for twenty-four-hour protection. Best they could offer is to drive by once in a while. Way out in the country like you are, they'd do twice in a day, tops. Don't see that helping."

"I ain't that worried about when we're here," I said. "We're loaded for bear. Got Joaquin and Rufus. Mr. Morales is better than neighborhood watch across the street. We can see three miles in every direction. Anyone stupid enough to come after Juan here will get a poke in the eye."

"Bringing Juan to LA is still an option," Angie said.

I shook my head. "He's safer here. People got our back. Besides, unless we shipped him off permanent, he'd be coming back to what he left. Palomera can afford to be patient."

"He's proved that," Bobby said. "Took until now to try something."

"Palomera doesn't get to win anything," I said. "We're not going to change shit because of him. I got crops. You got work. Juan needs to go to school. I don't mind pulling him out for a week, even two, but we ain't living on the run. Couldn't if we wanted to."

"Everything is easier when you got money," Angie said. "Even being the target of a drug cartel."

"Fucking fuck fuck," Bobby said loudly, pounding his fist on the table. "This is fucking bullshit. We know who the fuck it is that's doing everything. We know what the fuck he wants. And we know he's going to have some assholes try it again. We got all the whos and whys and whatevers, and there ain't shit we can do about it."

"Yeah," I said. "'Fucking fuck fuck' about covers it."

"It's like trying to punch smoke or a ghost," Bobby said. "There are fucking rules and shit. It's like the Geneva Convention don't mean anything to these fucks."

"I don't think that's what the Geneva—" I began to explain.

"Great," Angie said, interrupting. "It sucks. Okay. We know that. We still got to figure out what we're going to do. Next. What happens tonight? Tomorrow? We need a goddamn plan."

"You and your plans," Bobby said.

"We're going to protect our son," I said. "That's the plan."

"Oh, for Christ's—this isn't a fucking movie trailer, Jimmy," Angie said. "This is our lives, and that's nothing but a bullshit pile of words. Past the macho crap, it means jackshit. We need to know what actually happens next."

We sat around for another half hour, nothing left to say. None of us could come up with a plan. Not even the start of one. We had no idea what we were going to do. Instead, we drank beer in silence, resigned to the fact that we were destined to make it up as we went. That was the sad state of affairs. I was too poor and too stupid and just too damn tired to find a better way to protect my son than wait for them to try it again.

"We could drive to Mexico," Bobby said. "Back to that town, Coatepec. Put the fear of God in Palomera. Stomp a mudhole in his ass and show him who he's fucking with. Wouldn't take more than fifteen or twenty hours if I floored it."

We both leaned against Bobby's Ranchero, eyeing a lone passing car on the road. It didn't stop.

"Hear me out," Bobby said. "We'd have the element of surprise. And my big bag of guns. We'd fuck some shit up. Walk through his fucking house and Bickle whoever stood in our way. Scare the son of a bitch. Show him that we're not fucking around. That we can get to him anytime we want."

"Your plan might be overly optimistic," I said. "Let's call it plan G."

"We got to bring the fight to him," Bobby said. "Or else we're like a dove in a field of milo. Waiting for the hunters to come and shoot our delicious asses."

"Is that the Imperial Valley version of a sitting duck?"

"He's firing rounds through the border fence at us. He thinks that fence keeps him safe."

"If it had just been you back in Mexico," I said, "would you have killed him?"

"Let's just say I wouldn't have not killed him."

"I can't get my head around the idea of killing Juan's grandfather. Hell, killing anyone. It's wrong."

Bobby put his shotgun back in the rack behind the seat. "I'm going to feel like a dick for bringing this up. I know you're touchy like a girl. But isn't this the same deal as Alejandro? Wasn't that preemptive, not emptive? That's a word, right?"

I could feel my face flush. My mouth got dry. I reflexively looked over my shoulder. "Alejandro was different. He wasn't just a threat to Juan. He was a murderer. He had to pay for that."

"I'd be pretty shocked if Palomera hadn't dropped a few bodies in his past," Bobby said. "You don't get a nickname like El Loco by being the guy that sweeps up the spilled cocaine at the end of the day. 'El Loco' means 'The Crazy.' I don't know if you knew that."

"There's a solution that isn't murder," I said.

"Is there?" Bobby asked.

"There has to be," I said. "I just can't figure out what it is. I was hoping Gris or Angie had something. They're smarter."

"You want me to stay? I got my sleeping bag."

"We'll be okay tonight," I said, "but I'm going to have to figure out something for the long haul."

"Juan is my family, too. You know that, right? You and me—we're brothers. We might not be real blood, but we're chose blood. I ain't going to let anything happen to him. To you. To Angie. Neither is Gris. That's how we do."

"Thanks, Bobby."

"Alls you got to do is keep fighting. Even if it's swinging fists in the dark like we used to do when we boxed in the darkroom in high school. Most of the time you're missing, but eventually you hit a fucker. Knock him the fuck out."

I gave Bobby an uncharacteristic hug.

He hugged me back, crushing my ribs. "We got this, brother. I'll call you tomorrow."

I watched Bobby drive away, feeling Rufus sidle up next to me. I hadn't heard him or Joaquin, who was now also standing beside me. Rufus made me feel both nervous and safe at the same time. His heavy dog breaths were the only sound in the night.

Joaquin held his hand low, indicating Juan's height, and then gave a thumbs up. Juan was going to be okay. And then he pointed his finger in a long arc across the horizon, pointed at him and Rufus, and ran his finger across his throat. Anyone out there was going to have to go through him and the giant wolf-dog, and it would not end well for them.

"Thank you," I said, with my fist on my heart. "Gracias." True loyalty was a rare and beautiful thing. I only hoped it would be enough.

Angie found me sitting outside with my back against the front door. I couldn't sleep, didn't feel like reading or watching a movie, so I sat outside and cried. The frustration had finally gotten too big. I felt defeated, like I had failed my son and family. I had pushed it down, but I was lost and it all came out in tears.

She didn't say anything, sitting next to me and putting her hand on my back. She softly ran her fingers up and down my spine.

I wiped the tears from my cheeks and found my breath. "I tried to do the right thing. But doing the right thing don't mean a situation ain't going to explodc into a shit-cyclone and blast-fuck feces all over you."

She laughed. "That was probably the first draft of 'The road to hell is paved with good intentions.' The version that was covered in poop."

"We're not in hell," I said, letting out a little laugh. "We're in shit. So my analogy works."

"Did you say 'blast-fuck'? What does that even mean?"

"It's self-explanatory. All in the poetic poetry of the word."

"You're going to have to talk to Juan," Angie said. "Don't tell him people are after him—that would give him nightmares. I can't see that helping. But things have changed. He can't do some of the things he's used to doing."

I kissed Angie on the forehead. "I'll do it tomorrow."

"You want to come in now?"

"Give me another ten minutes. It's peaceful out here."

"Okay," she said. "And after you talk to Juan tomorrow, head into town and buy more ammo."

Five years earlier, a man named Alejandro had abducted Juan and tried to use him as leverage in a much different fight. He threatened Juan's life. Bobby and I got him back. That's the day Juan became my son.

I killed Alejandro and left his body to be consumed by the Algodones Dunes east of Holtville. I'd lived with that decision—questioned it—from the moment I'd fired that shotgun. I didn't know if I would or could make the same choice today. It might sound stupid and obvious, but killing a person was hard.

I could never be certain that I had made the right decision that day. If I didn't question it, I wouldn't be human and I'm not sure it would be real to me anymore. Some of our choices need to haunt us.

Juan was three years old when that happened. If he remembered being abducted, it didn't show in his personality. But I knew that was not exactly how the brain handled trauma. Whether he could recall it or not, that abduction sat back there in his head. In that place where bad memories got stored to mess you up later.

It hurt to remember how scared he had been then. How confused. I never wanted Juan to be that frightened again. But I had to be honest with him, too. I wasn't going to give him details—how do you tell a kid that he was the target of kidnappers?—but he needed to know that things might get nutty.

"Hey, Juan. What're you up to?" I asked, walking into his room the next morning.

One wall of his bedroom was adorned with posters of Marvel and DC superheroes, the other wall with a growing collection of lucha posters, courtesy of Mr. Morales. Juan didn't see any distinction between Batman and El Santo but still kept them separate. American superheroes and Mexican superheroes.

I was operating on very little sleep. Angie and I had talked ad nauseam about the situation, until we got bored with the repetition of our impotence to stop Palomera. Hence the "nauseam." We briefly discussed having sex, but neither of us could muster the energy. Eventually I got an hour or two of restless shut-eye, but the anxiety dreams made me more tired. I could only dream about losing my car keys inside a giant turtle so many times before it was no longer funny.

"Drawing drawings for my yo-yo," Juan said. He had sheets of paper and colored pencils scattered around him. The current drawing looked like a circle on fire. With his Pinewood Derby car and the yo-yo both sporting flame motifs, I hoped I didn't have a future pyro on my hands.

"Is that yo-yo on fire?"

"Yeah, but not really," he said, which I'm sure made sense to him.

"Does your yo-yo have a name?"

"The Fast Flash." The kid seemed to like alliteration with *F*s. Who could blame him? I said f-words more than any other words, for sure. "It's not really on fire. It's just so fast that the air burns up from how fast it is. That's how fast it is. Fire fast."

"That's really fast."

"Yeah," he said, adding more red to the tips of the flames.

"I need to talk to you about something important," I said. "Can you stop drawing for just a couple minutes?"

"Sure, Pop." Juan set the colored pencil down. "It's mostly done anyway."

I had rehearsed with Angie a little beforehand, but now that he was sitting there with expectant eyes, I found it difficult to start.

"Things might get a little weird around here," I said.

"They're already pretty weird."

"Yeah, but a more serious weird. You know how we taught you about stranger danger and not trusting people you don't know and not getting into cars—but especially vans, except Buck Buck's van, but even then, because they don't have seat belts—and not taking free candy and all that stuff."

"Uh. Yeah," Juan said. "I haven't done none of those things, Pop. Honest."

I laughed. "You're not in trouble. I know you haven't done anything. The reason we keep telling you to be careful is because we love you and we don't want anything to happen to you. But there are bad people out there."

"I know about bad people," Juan said. "Like the ones that the Blue Demon fights, but in real life."

"Exactly, but not vampires and aliens. Regular people that do bad things."

"Okay," Juan said, "I'll be careful. I won't go in no vans or cars or nothing."

"That's good, but we're going to be extra careful, okay? We might even pull you out of school for a little while."

"Awesome."

"You'll still have to do all your schoolwork."

Juan's expression told me that he didn't consider that news nearly as awesome.

"If you see anything or anyone that doesn't look right to you, tell someone you know. Me, Mom, your teacher. There might be some bad guys around."

"Is that why that other car chased us last night?" Juan said. "Was that a bad guy?"

I stared at my son for a moment. I thought I had gotten away with my subterfuge. He noticed more than I gave him credit for. Although a backwoods car chase was arguably hard to miss.

"Yes, that was a bad man."

"I knew it. When you and Uncle Bobbiola chase around, you don't sweat as much. You smile and laugh more. He wanted to hurt us?"

"That's what bad guys do. If you knew he was a bad guy, why weren't you more scared?"

Juan looked at me like I was stupid. "Because I was with you."

The waiting game was a shitty game. Worse than the *E.T.* video game for the Atari 2600, which ended up getting buried in a landfill. The waiting game sucked that bad.

For the next week, nothing happened. I wasn't stupid enough to believe that whoever was out there had learned their lesson from the car chase and hightailed it back to Mexico. They were somewhere. Not knowing when or what was coming next was insanely frustrating.

It looked like Palomera's plan was to ice the kicker. To let us stew and wait. To bore us into letting down our guard. I had always thought it was a stupid ploy in football, but the plan was definitely proving to be an effective tactic in psychological warfare.

With each day, the imminent threat became more abstract, a monster on the horizon. I could hear the beast's breathing, but I couldn't see it. My defenses were at 100 percent, but I was more tense and paranoid not knowing when the hammer could come down.

Angie and I kept Juan at the house after the car chase. We talked to his teachers to make sure that he didn't get behind. A week went by. Juan hadn't left the house, not even to play in the yard. He started having the occasional meltdown, angry and confused and feeling like he was the one that had done something wrong.

It wasn't fair to him, and as a strategy, it was weak. We couldn't keep our son a prisoner. In an effort to balance it out, I took Juan out with me in the daytime as I did my work and ran errands. We would keep to crowds, and when I could, I would bring one of the Fun Bunch with me. The Fun Bunch consisted of Bobby, Griselda, Buck Buck, Snout, and Mr. Morales.

Juan went back to school after that week. It wasn't working. Open-ended incarceration wasn't a plan. School was the only place where he was out of our sight, but we laid down some protective ground rules. He wasn't allowed to play in the playground with the other kids during lunch and recess. We told Ms. Singh that it was a punishment, rather than the truth that a cadre of Mexican kidnappers might try to take him by force. Juan took it in stride, more sad than angry. Luckily he was a reader, so he entertained himself easily.

Three weeks after the car chase, Juan and I headed to the mall after school without any backup from the Fun Bunch. We had kept close to the house and school, but fuck any fucking kidnappers. I could protect my own damn son. It was the middle of the day in a well-trafficked public place.

I should have waited, but my kid needed pants.

Juan had a special gift for tearing the knees and ass off a pair of pants, and then tearing off the patches. He was a tree-climbing, grass-staining, and rolling-in-the-mud brand of child. At that moment he was down to a pair of white corduroys that had a big red Kool-Aid stain on the crotch that made it look like he accidentally pissed blood and some pajama bottoms with cross-eyed pigs on them saying "Pig Say Oink" that were definitely made in Asia. If we sent him to school in either of those two leg-covering options, our next visit would not be from kidnappers but the Imperial Child Protective Services. They were both that awful.

I would have picked up the pants myself, but the kid had grown an inch in the last month and showed no signs of stopping. I didn't want to keep going back until I got the size right. He was going to try them on. One trip to the mall was one too many but all I was going to make.

On a normal day the mall in El Centro was enough to make me want to punch someone in the face with my foot. (I know that most people call that kicking. Quit interrupting.) Walking through the air-conditioned structure, I found it strange that El Centro had an indoor mall. It had been there a few years by then but still felt like a betrayal.

In my youth, downtown El Centro had been the shopping district, but it had become a ghost town, shuttered businesses and thrift stores. The independent, locally owned businesses had gone bust a while back. You could now hit the mall and eat at fucking Olive Garden or shop at Macy's. What kind of asshole goes to El Torito with the best Mexican food in the world right around the corner? An asshole kind of asshole, that's who.

Juan got a concise series of instructions in the truck before heading into hell's maw—I mean, the mall. Stay close. Hold my hand. Don't run off. Don't talk to anyone. Head down. Get the pants and get out of there. He listened and nodded seriously. We were on a mission. Like spies or samurai or luchadors.

Juan and I marched to the Marshalls with his small hand in mine. We didn't dick around, finding three pairs of pants that looked like they would last at least a month. Where were the Toughskins when you needed them?

I went in the changing room with him mostly to check the fit, but also to keep him in my sights. I'd seen enough movies to know that the moment you looked away, that's when something happened. The fitting was uneventful. If you're keeping a box score, two of the pants fit, the other was slightly too small. Two pairs would have to do. We were going to buy these and get the fuck out of Dodge.

When I walked out of the changing room, the door next to ours swung open. A hulking, bald Mexican guy with a tattoo reading "Chingón" in gothic letters on his neck walked out and blocked our path. I jumped back a step.

"Pop?" Juan said, worry in his voice. The guy was huge, muscles bulging out of his tank top.

I pushed Juan behind me, squared up, and yelled, "Back the fuck off, fucko! I will fuck you up."

He turned to look behind him at the opening that led out of the dressing room area.

"Hey, *American Me*," I said, fists raised. "Get the fuck out of our way."

"Easy, ese," he said. "I ain't going to fight you."

"Me hitting you," I said. "You hitting the floor."

He shook his head. "That don't make sense, homes, unless you say the first part. The two-hits part. Have you been drinking?"

"Tell Palomera that he's never fucking getting Juan."

"I don't know what you're talking about. And you're saying 'fuck' around your kid way too much. I came here for some dress shirts. They were on sale."

That's when I realized that he was just a guy. A regular guy in a regular changing room trying on regular shirts that were on sale. Big and imposing, Mexican and tattooed. But just a guy. I put my hands down.

"Sorry, man," I said. "I'm on edge. Someone's been threatening my boy."

"That's messed up." He nodded like I had a legit excuse. "I got two girls. Anyone looked at them wrong, I would bust them up serious."

"I just racially profiled you. That's what I did, but that's not me."

"I know what I look like. Let me give you some truth, though. You keep up that weak-ass tough guy stuff, you're going to get yourself hurt. Like a serious beatdown." He nodded like he was teaching me a lesson. In a way he was.

"Thanks, man. I really am sorry."

"Take care of your kid," he said. "And wear baggy pants if you're going to go to the mall strapped. I can see your cuete on your ankle."

I looked down. Sure enough, my pistol was in plain view. I had to get my shit together.

"Pop?" Juan said as we walked back through the mall to the truck.

"Yeah," I said, "back there? I lost my cool. I judged that man by how he looked. You shouldn't do that. Although I told you to tell me if you saw suspicious people. It's confusing, I know. And scary. But we're okay. I hope you're not traumatized. You're not traumatized, are you?"

"I don't know what that word means," he said. "You said the f-word a lot. I mean, a lot."

"What your mom doesn't know won't hurt me."

"She doesn't need to know about the ice cream either."

"What ice cream?" I asked, then got it. "Seriously? Extortion? You're blackmailing me?"

"You said the f-word like fifty times. Maybe a hundred. That's two scoops' worth."

"More like ten times," I said. "One scoop."

"In a waffle cone."

"Deal," I said, worried that I had created an effective blackmailer. Or worse, a future politician.

SIXTEEN

The Baskin-Robbins had closed in El Centro ten years earlier. In a rare turn, the national chain was replaced by a local business. Not a particularly good one, but the ice cream void needed to be filled. In a cost-cutting effort, the people that took over the business modified the existing signage. A common practice in El Centro and the valley. Case in point, the Buick Restaurant where the old car lot had been and the Enny's where the Denny's once was. It always bugged me that Enny's hadn't ponied up the extra dough for an *L* or a *K*. Enny wasn't even a name.

The Baskin-Robbins was now 13 Flavors. By inverting the numbers, they had saved money on not only the sign, but the inventory. Much more fitting to the city's station. El Centro wasn't a town that flaunted a decadent thirty-one different flavors. That was eighteen flavors more than desert folk needed. Cookie Jar Mashup, Rock 'n Pop Swirl, and S'More the Merrier were for people more highfalutin than the regularfalutin residents of the Imperial Valley.

The bored teenage girl that worked the counter had a crazy fan of blow-dried hair standing at attention over her forehead.

No paper hat for this pachuca. Dark eye makeup, bright red lips, and chola eyebrows completed the package.

Juan checked out the flavor selection—all thirteen of them—his hands and face up against the glass, sliding back and forth across the length of the display. He read each name softly to himself, mesmerized.

"Vanilla, Rocky Road, Very Cherry Swirl, Butter Brickle." He turned to me. "Pop? What's a brickle?"

"About two dollars," I said reflexively.

"Ugh," he said, having heard that joke a thousand times in his short life.

I smiled at the teenager. She stared at me, squeezing the ice cream scoop's handle in time to her gum popping. The ice cream at 13 Flavors cost money, but the attitude was free. No matter what I said to this girl, she was going to roll her eyes. I would bet my balls on it.

"Bubblegum," Juan said decisively.

"Are you sure?" I said. "It's a good one, but you wanted a waffle cone. And bubblegum is more of a cup situation. The gum gets gross when you're chewing it at the same time as the cone."

"I'll chew the gum on one side of my mouth and the cone on the other."

I stared at Juan. He had just blown my mind. I had seriously never thought of that as an option. If he was right—if that could actually work—it opened up ice cream possibilities that I had long considered dead. The dawning of a new cold dessert era.

"Can we get two bubblegum waffle cones?" I said to the girl.

She rolled her eyes. All I had done was order. And she rolled her eyes.

The girl dug the scoop into the tub of pink ice cream. When she looked back up, her eyes went from bored to engaged. Big and round and focused on something behind me, all tough-chick facade gone. She dropped the ice cream scoop and booked out the door behind her.

I felt a little pee trickle out when I turned and looked outside the front glass. In the parking lot, three armed Mexican men were climbing out of a white SUV and rushing toward the front door.

I picked up Juan and set him on the other side of the counter. One last look behind me and I jumped the counter myself. The men ran in, the bell on the door jangling behind me as I pulled Juan into the storeroom and slammed the door shut.

I locked the door. It was surprisingly heavy for an ice cream storeroom. I pushed over a metal rack, knocking it in front of the door as well.

"Pop, I'm scared," Juan said.

"I got you," I said, finding the back door. I pulled the snub-nose from my ankle holster, grabbed Juan's hand, and rushed outside.

The alley behind the ice cream parlor was empty, but we were now on foot and in the open. In a word, we were fucked. We could be spotted at any moment, completely exposed.

"Piggyback," I said, leaning down and patting my back. Juan jumped onto my back and wrapped his arms around my neck.

"Hold on," I said. I climbed the chain link fence that ran next to the building, a skill I had learned from years of breaking into abandoned amusement parks. "Whatever you do, don't let go." Juan's grip tightened around my neck, choking me.

I got to the top of the fence in a couple seconds. It abutted the roof, and I was able to scoonch myself and Juan from the fence onto the roof. I awkwardly swung my feet away from the edge at the same moment I heard the back door of the ice cream parlor crash open. Voices shouted in Spanish below us.

Juan had played enough hide-and-seek to understand what to do next. We both got as flat as we could on the pebbly roof. I held my finger to my lips. He nodded.

I didn't think they saw us come up there. I hoped they didn't. My grip tightened on the pistol. I closed my eyes and listened.

"¡Mierda!"

"¿A dónde fueron?"

"¡Chingada!"

I opened my eyes. Juan stared back at me, our faces close. He didn't blink. He looked scared, in shock. I winked to try to calm him. Gave him a weak smile. It didn't work. He wasn't stupid.

A few more Spanish expletives, followed by barked orders. Their footsteps headed in both directions, up and down the alley. Sirens rose in the distance. I owed that teenage girl a huge tip for calling the cops.

I hated that my son was scared. I hated that he was in danger. It made me sick to my stomach. In that moment, it made me wish I had killed his grandfather. Which made me sick all over again. I was going to name my ulcer Fernando in homage to Palomera.

I had to give the sons of bitches credit. I hadn't expected a coordinated daytime attempt on my son. Especially while trying to buy a fucking ice cream cone. Palomera's men were some seriously evil bastards to attempt to grab a kid while getting a bubblegum ice cream waffle cone.

Once we got off that roof, I needed to get my son to a safe place. And then I needed to get him the ice cream cone that I had promised to him. A double scoop this time. He had earned it. Hell, I might have to go full banana split to even things out after this bullshit.

We stayed on the roof until the police arrived. I whispered softly to Juan, comforting him and even making him laugh once when I made a fart joke. Don't ever underestimate the power of "Pull my finger."

When I caught sight of the police car beacons, I manufactured the courage to peek over the edge of the roof. Two police cars had pulled into the parking lot. Officers with their guns out slowly walked to the entrance. The SUV was gone.

"The police are here," I said to Juan. "It's safe. We're safe."

The pistol in my hand was one that I had borrowed from Bobby. Having no clue about its provenance, I wiped off my prints and hid it in an empty paint can that sat among some wood and other cans on the alley-side corner of the roof. I would have to come back and get it later.

"Hey!" I shouted down to the two police officers standing in the alley next to their car. "Me and my kid are up here. We were hiding. We're coming down."

"Okay, but don't move too fast," one of the officers said, his gun drawn but pointed at the ground. "I got no idea what's going on. What's going on?"

"A shitload of bad shit," I said.

Two hours later, I was still at 13 Flavors, answering the same questions. After the tenth retelling, I don't even think they were listening. They sure as hell didn't believe my story. I started to wonder why I kept repeating it.

Juan sat on the ground with his back to the wall a few feet from me. Even surrounded by a half dozen police officers, I kept him close. He looked bored, but I'd take boredom over fear all day. Considering the ordeal he had just gone through, boredom was positive.

"These three men were hired to abduct my son by a man in Mexico named Fernando Palomera. A dangerous man known as El Loco by the cartels." I really had no idea why I bothered with the truth. It hadn't done me dick so far. I should've clammed up and told them that I was getting a cone and didn't know what the hell happened. El Centro PD couldn't help us, and Juan and I would have been home by now.

The police officer nodded and wrote something down. From my angle it looked like he was just drawing concentric circles on his pad. I was pretty sure they were boobs.

"I'm serious," I said. "They were after my kid. What would be my reason for making any of that up? Why would I do that?"

"I don't try to guess why people do things."

"You should. You're a cop. That's literally what cops are supposed to do."

"We have no evidence that corroborates any part of your story."

"What evidence would there be?"

"I don't know. A ransom note?"

"Ransom notes are sent after people are abducted," I said.

"There just ain't no evidence to back up your story."

"Three men," I said. "An SUV. An Explorer, I think. They didn't steal anything, did they?"

"The reason they didn't steal anything has to do with our lightning-quick response time," the officer said, a little too dickishly. "They heard the sirens and hightailed it."

"It takes three men to rob an ice cream parlor?" I asked. "And who robs an ice cream parlor? Does it have a lot of black market value? Ice cream is fucking perishable. It melts."

"I doubt they were here to steal iced cream," he said.

"Then what?"

"Think about it. This place has been here like eight or ten years. They only got a dozen flavors."

"A baker's dozen," I said.

"The iced cream sucks. Like generic boxed at best. Nobody ever buys iced cream here. Yet it's still open for business. How is that?"

His insistence on using the phrase "iced cream" grated like nails on a chalkboard. Rather than correct him, I chose to enunciate the word.

"I buy *ice* cream here," I said. "What are you implying?"

"13 Flavors is a known drug front used to launder money and distribute illegal drugs, among other things."

As if the two men had timed it, a police officer walked out of the back door of 13 Flavors holding up two very large baggies of marijuana.

"There it is," the police officer said. "What you just witnessed was an attempted robbery on a drug stash. You and your son were unfortunate bystanders. There's probably cash in there, too."

"They were after my kid," I said. "The pot is the coincidence."

"You see that marijuana? That's evidence. We have evidence. You don't have evidence."

"Finding the pot doesn't help find the men in the SUV. That just fucks over this place. It doesn't help catch the bad guys, which is the whole reason you're here."

"We're here because a crime was committed," he said. "A crime is a crime. We got some very dangerous drugs off the streets."

"Pot isn't dangerous."

"You're one of those?" he said. "Were you really here to buy iced cream?"

"It's pronounced 'ice cream.' *Ice* cream, not *iced* cream. Fuck."

The officer stared at me and shrugged. Police work appeared to be no different than any other job. The story that created the least amount of work or effort was the story he was going to go with. Truth, justice, and the mediocrity way.

"What we need is a midget," Bobby said. "A Mexican midget."

When the cops finally released us, I had called a summit to figure out some kind of game plan. Bobby, Griselda, Angie, and I were back around the dining room table. This time we were joined by Mr. Morales. There had now been two attempts made to abduct my son, and none of the authorities in the area gave two fat shits. Either they didn't believe me or didn't have the resources to help me. We were on our own.

"I'm not really in the mood for jokes, Bobby," I said. "I still got the pebble pattern from that roof on the side of my face."

"Who's joking? We got to draw these sons of bitches out, but we can't do it without putting Juan in danger. He's the target, so they go where he goes. If we had a decoy or two, like stunt doubles, we could go toe to toe with them. Trap them."

"And where do you propose we get a Mexican midget?" I asked, having no idea why I asked.

Angie and Griselda silently stood up from the table and walked into the other room. Grown-ups tired of sitting at the kids' table. No shake of the head or eye roll necessary. I couldn't blame them, but it didn't dissuade me from continuing to participate in our inane discussion.

"Or dwarf. Or gnome. Or whatever they're called."

"Little person," I said, "but I don't think the nomenclature is the issue."

"I just don't want to offend the little fellas," Bobby said. "The circus in Mexicali is swarming with Mexican midget people. We went, remember? One of them was a clown that kept running around and getting hit with a pan by a bigger clown. And then there was an even-littler guy that took tickets. Which seemed like a waste of his talents."

"Being small isn't really a talent."

"Tell that to Ant-Man."

"I can't tell that to Ant-Man," I said. "He's not a real person."

"Midgets can't be that expensive to rent."

"You mean hire. You don't rent people."

"Do you want to hear this plan or not?"

"Not really."

"Then shut up," he said. "We bring the midget back here, throw a ball cap on his head, make sure he's clean-shaven, the works. And then we take him to the park to play catch or Frisbee or marbles. At some point, the bad guys show up, and *BAM!*"

"Bam?"

"Not bam, unenthusiastic and shit. But, *BAM!* With some oomph."

"Is that the part of the plan where we fuck the fucking fuckers up?"

Bobby nodded solemnly. "That's implied in '*BAM!*'"

I turned and jealously watched Griselda and Angie talking in the living room. My guess was that they weren't talking about circus midgets playing Frisbee in the park and then bam.

"It doesn't matter if we stop whoever Palomera sends," I said.

"Whomever," Bobby corrected me.

"Are you fucking kidding me right now?"

"Yeah, sorry," he said. "I honestly got no idea when to use 'whom' anyway. I just think it's funny to do that."

I took a deep breath. "When there's a threat, we got to repel it, but it's a stopgap. That shit's going to keep happening. Palomera will keep sending people. He can do it forever. All it takes is money. He can keep throwing fuckers at us from a thousand miles away."

Mr. Morales cleared his throat. I had forgotten he was there. He nodded toward the doorway. Angie and Griselda stood with their hands on their hips.

"Are you two idiots done talking about elves?" Angie said.

"Yeah," I said. "We're done."

"You're not going to tell her our plan?" Bobby said.

"It's not my plan," I said.

"We heard the beginning," Griselda said. "That was enough, honey."

Bobby shrugged at the dismissal, but he looked a little hurt. I was surprised that he wasn't used to it by now.

"Griselda and I talked about it," Angie said. "We think we have the solution."

"There's more to talk about, decide if we can even do it," Griselda said. "If we should. But I think we all know that there's only one way to make this nightmare end."

"Leave it to the women to man up," Mr. Morales said. "They're right."

I didn't say anything. I didn't have to. I already knew what they were thinking. I had pretty much come to the same conclusion on the roof of the ice cream parlor. My wife was just the one with the balls to finally say it out loud.

"We didn't know what was going to happen," Angie said. "We couldn't. Now we do. We have to do what we didn't do in Mexico. We have to kill Fernando Palomera. Until he is out of the picture, Juan will never be safe. His men will keep coming."

"If he was trying to hurt Juan," I said, "it would be different."

"If he brings Juan to Mexico," Angie said, "Juan's life will be ruined. He would be a part of a world that would change him. It would hurt his future more than any physical threat."

Bobby held his hand out with his thumb pointed down. "The old man's got to go."

"We tried," Angie said, "but I can't think of any other way."

"I hate it, but he's forced the choice." Griselda's eyes were wet and red, but her voice was strong. "It's the only way. Goddammit."

"It's the solution," I said, "but we're talking about killing a man. Or having him killed."

"Sometimes the world is a better place without certain people in it," Mr. Morales said.

I instinctively looked over my shoulder, but I knew Juan was asleep in his room. "He's Juan's grandfather. Juan's blood. The only person we've found from that side of his family."

Angie put her hand on mine. She didn't say anything, but looking at her reminded me what I was fighting for. It was my job to keep Juan safe. Hard decisions had to be made in war.

"Okay." I nodded. "Fernando Palomera needs to die."

With that, we sat in silence, letting the idea sink in all the way. It wasn't every day that five people made the unanimous decision to take a man's life. It wasn't something to celebrate. There was nothing good about the feeling.

I had always tried to do the right thing, even when I seemed to consistently make things worse. Now it was time to do the wrong thing. I hoped that worked out better.

"Before you suggest it, Jimmy, you aren't going back down to Mexico," Angie said. "If I have my way, you're never setting foot in that country again."

Griselda turned quickly to Bobby. "Same goes for you, stupid."

"He's the one that gets in trouble down there," Bobby said. "I'm like an innocent bystander."

"You have never been innocent in your life," she said.

"It'd be a hell of a thing to sneak down there," Bobby said. "The ultimate Mavescapade. We'd drive down. Smuggle guns in. Get to Coatepec undetected. Full-on black ops."

"Despite your violence boner," Griselda said, "it's not happening."

"I do have a little bit of a chub."

"You both need to be here to protect Juan," Angie said. "Not in Mexico. If they're going to keep coming, we're going to be prepared. Tomorrow, we fortify the shit out of this place. I'm talking zombie apocalypse precautions. Board windows and electric fences. We can't control outside, but nobody is getting in here. No more fucking around."

"I can't say that I feel good about doing something from a distance that I couldn't do up close," I said. "It doesn't feel right. It feels cowardly."

"We're pulling from his playbook," Griselda said. "He's lobbing mortars at us. We hit him with the howitzer."

"How do we do it?" Angie asked. "We never got around to talking about that. Kind of a big part of the plan."

"It makes me sad to say this," Mr. Morales said, "but there's only one person that can help you. The murderer in our lives."

"He's right," I said, "but I know how you feel about asking Mexican crime lords for favors, Angie."

"Call the son of a bitch," Angie said. "Send the devil to stop the devil, or whatever that fucking expression is. Tomás Morales is the one that got us in this mess. It's time he fixed what he broke."

SEVENTEEN

The day after I had vowed to never go back to Mexico, I was back in Mexico.

I drove my truck over the border, Bobby riding shotgun. Taking the first left turn after the border crossing, I headed east. With the border fence on my left and the city of Mexicali on my right, I attempted to dip my toe into the country. The address that Tomás had given me was two miles down the road. A residential neighborhood, one of the newer expansions along the border on the east side of the city. The maquiladoras had taken over the west side development, but the east continued to grow.

As much as I trusted Angie to protect Juan, I had left reinforcements back at the house. Buck Buck and Snout were playing Lego with Juan. They didn't make a special trip. They had a standing Lego date on Sundays with my son. Even when Juan wasn't available, they played Lego at my house without him there.

Joaquin and Rufus maintained their patrol outside the house. Better than any alarm system on the market, they were our ghostlike sentries working around the clock. I couldn't imagine anyone or anything sneaking past them.

I trusted them, but I still didn't feel good about being gone. Not even for a few hours. The attack at 13 Flavors had spooked me good. An SUV full of armed men hell-bent on snatching your kid was known to have that effect.

I wished there was such a thing as a vault that I could put my child inside. The Child Safe—patent pending—something that protected my kid from the outside world. Large enough to run around in. One with air holes that wouldn't suffocate him. Admittedly, I hadn't figured out the engineering logistics of the Child Safe—patent pending—yet, but the child would definitely have to be able to breathe inside.

I turned my truck onto the working class residential street and parked in front of the modest ranch house. A new development, there appeared to be three styles that alternated, all painted the same salmon color. The border fence stood only two blocks away. Calexico didn't extend nearly as far to the east. Across the fence was the All-American Canal, and behind that, farmland with a few scattered farmhouses.

"The last time we showed up at one of Tomás's houses," Bobby said, "he was shooting a porno movie inside. It ruined porno for me. Porno was an important part of my life. I seriously haven't watched one since."

"Do people still say 'porno'?" I asked. "I think they just call it porn."

"They're wrong," Bobby said. "Sounds too harsh. Porno is fun. Porn is mean."

"I find it hard to believe that you haven't watched any porn in the last five years."

"Sure, with two ladies in them, but that's like art. Admiring the feminine form. Other than my own hammer of the gods, I ain't seen a dude slam his wang in a whisker biscuit since."

"That's what happens when you learn how the sausage is made."

"I know how sausage is made," Bobby said. "I have literally killed an animal, butchered it, ground the meat, spiced it, filled a casing, cooked it, and eaten the sausage. Porno isn't sausage. Porno was special. You'll never understand."

"Are you crying?"

"Shut up."

Little Piwi opened the door as I was raising my hand to knock. I glanced for the cameras that alerted him to our presence. Or he could have looked out the window. That would have worked, too.

"Hey, L. P.," I said. "Can you not talk my ear off today?"

He stared blankly. A common reaction to my jokes. We followed him into the house. The living room and dining room looked like Ikea showrooms. Modern and tasteful, but antiseptic and unused. Like walking through a catalogue. The same was true about the kitchen. Modern appliances, all polished and spotless.

Tomás Morales sat on a stool at the breakfast nook with a cup of coffee and a Red Bull in front of him. If I didn't know Tomás, I would have guessed that he was a new dad or an adult student in the middle of finals week. Dark rings circled his eyes. He appeared sleep-deprived and anxious. His shoulders slumped, as if the weight of his body was difficult to carry. I had never seen Tomás show any signs of weakness. Haggard was new territory.

"Hey, Tommy," I said. "Thanks for meeting."

"You look like shit," Bobby said.

Tomás grinned. "I've never liked you, Maves. Not even when we were kids. You were an asshole. One of those fuckups that thought being a fuckup was charming."

"The ladies love it," Bobby said.

"I need your help," I said. "It's for something that I'm not comfortable asking."

"Before you ask anything, you got to know how things are—where they're at. I'm in this fucking kitchen because some motherfuckers came at me. At my place in Villafontana. Straight up Tony Montana–style. Surrounded the house and then hit from all sides like fucking Waco and I'm Koresh."

"Who?" I asked. "The cartel?"

"Who the fuck else?" Tomás said. "The Mormons? Been fighting almost a week. Mostly street-level stuff. Business to business. I thought I could handle it. Territory battles, but bodies been piling. They already took over some of my shit, scared my connects, and turned a few of my crews against me. That shit took them four, five fucking days. Caught me with my pants at my ankles and my dick in my hand. Years for me to build, days for them to tear it down. I'm trying to negotiate a deal—keep what I got. They ain't budging."

"I thought you had Mexicali tied up," I said. "Some agreement or truce. I don't know how that shit works. You must be protected by the police or government or something."

"Police are rented, not owned. The lease can run out. Bosses never stay bosses forever. We're like gunslingers in the Old West. Eventually some new kid is faster. It's the nature of the business."

"How could they take over so quickly?"

"Because they're the fucking cartel. They used money and guns and power. The big three fuck-yous. One of my own men tried to stab me while I was getting a massage. I was all relaxed and shit."

"That must have thrown off your chi," Bobby said.

"Fuck you," Tomás said. "Cabrón should have shot me. They've completely infiltrated my operation."

Bobby looked over to Little Piwi, who stood in the doorway. "No offense, big guy," he said, then turned back to Tomás, "but can Piwi be trusted?"

We all looked at Little Piwi. His expression didn't change.

"I trust the Piwis like you trust each other," Tomás said.

"Good enough for me," I said. "Can't you fight them?"

I wasn't completely sure why I was encouraging one criminal to fight another criminal, but I knew that Tomás in charge of Mexicali was better than a drug cartel in charge, even if they were running identical businesses.

"Fighting isn't working, but there are other ways to end a war," Tomás said. "You said they tried to take your kid again?"

"Three men. At 13 Flavors in El Centro."

"That pinche place is still there?" he said. "You know that's only a front for some low-rent pot dealers, right? They buy the ice cream from Safeway."

"I do now," I said.

"Three men was probably all they could spare," Tomás said. "They've got everyone focused on me right now. But if they lock up Mexicali, they'll throw their whole army at you. You should run."

"I ain't running from my home," I said. "I can't. That's why I need your help."

"I can't help you," Tomás said. "I got my own fight. I am not some magic genie that you get wishes from."

"You got us in this mess, Tommy," I said.

"I had no reason to believe that I needed to vet your son's grandfather."

"Sending those two other guys—that was your idea. That made everyone think we were with you. Put us on the cartel's fucking radar."

"I'll give you that," Tomás said. "That was a miscalculation. I don't want to talk bad about the dead, but those two vatos were fucking idiots. You have no idea how hard it is to find good muscle."

"Have you tried Craigslist?" Bobby said. "Look in the 'Hoods and Flunkies' category."

"Those two weren't even supposed to follow you. They got the whole thing wrong. Fucking idiots." Tomás stood up and walked out of the kitchen. Bobby and I followed him. We stopped at the front door.

"You came to ask me to kill Fernando Palomera, right?" Tomás said.

I had no response, a little stunned that he had figured that out so easily.

"It's your only play," Tomás said.

"He totally called it," Bobby said. "Still hate your guts, Tommy, but I got to give you that one."

"Is this an 'I told you so'?" I said. "Is that what you're going to do?"

"I told you to kill him," Tomás said. "I told you this would happen."

"Totally an 'I told you so,'" Bobby said. "Two, in fact."

"At the time, between killing my son's grandfather and not killing my son's grandfather, I thought it was important to err on the side of not murder."

"You think too much," Tomás said. "Murder is always an option. Murder solves problems permanently. It's in the Bible a lot. One of the primary problem-solving tactics. Motherfuckers are killing other motherfuckers all over the place in the good book. That's got to tell you something about the effectiveness of murder and maybe question your black-and-white point of view about it."

"I've read the Bible," I said. "There's also a commandment in there that says not to kill. It's specific about that."

"There are always loopholes."

"I didn't come here to talk theology," I said.

"No, you came here to ask one criminal to kill another criminal. Arguing about ethics is hypocritical, if not downright rude."

Little Piwi walked to us, holding a thick padded envelope. He held it out to Tomás, who took it and handed it to me.

"What's this?" I said.

"Money," Tomás said. "Twenty-five thousand dollars."

"With the what now?" I said.

Bobby whistled. "Fuck with ten *u*'s."

"I can't help you right now," Tomás said. "I don't have the resources for two fronts. But I have plenty of money. Money can help you. That is money."

"I don't know," I said.

"Bro, shut up and take it," Bobby said.

"Not enough to start a new life somewhere else," Tomás said, "but you can use it to hire six, maybe eight guys to run a security detail. I'd give you a list of names, but I'm not comfortable supplying recommendations. I don't know who I can trust anymore."

"I'm not going to surround my eight-year-old son with a bunch of Mexican gangsters. He'll end up as the only third grader with a teardrop tattoo and spiderweb elbows. Besides, the last bodyguards you sent to protect me are not only dead, but in your words, 'fucking idiots.'"

"Get men, get out of town, or get some big guns," Tomás said. "However you want to play it. Money can win a fight that fists can't."

"I'll pay you back," I said, putting the envelope in my pocket.

I opened the front door to the sight of twenty or thirty Mexican police officers pulling up onto the street. Some men were already out of their cars, guns drawn, cautiously approaching.

"The fuck?" Bobby said behind me.

More police jumped out of their cars and headed toward the house. Some in tactical gear, others in short-sleeve shirts.

Behind the row of police cars, I recognized the only man that was not an officer, confidently leaning against the fender of a Hummer, a different one than he had driven in Mexico. Polo Shirt looked at me, took a pull from his vape pen, and smiled through a cloud. He wasn't wearing a polo shirt at the moment, but if I called him Button-Up Shirt in midstride, the story would get confusing. For the record, the pastel-green shirt he wore was equally as douchey as the polo.

A meaty hand grabbed my shoulder and pulled me back into the house. Little Piwi pushed me behind him and threw the door closed.

"Follow me," Tomás said, walking quickly toward the garage.

"Are you about to get arrested?" I asked.

"You forget what country you're in? I'm about to get killed."

"The US ain't much different, if you're brown," Bobby said.

The first gunshot shattered a window and pinged around the house.

"Fuck this," Bobby said, ducking down and crabwalking.

Little Piwi followed Tomás into the garage. Bobby and I were right behind them. A home gym had been set up: Nautilus equipment, a heavy bag hanging from the ceiling, a treadmill, and racks of free weights. Little Piwi put his shoulder to the treadmill and pushed it across the concrete floor. It made a scraping noise that sent chills through my body.

"That's not how you use that piece of equipment," Bobby said.

After Little Piwi had pushed the treadmill eight feet, he walked back to where it had been, reached down, and pulled open a trapdoor in the ground. Under the hatch was a small hole, a ladder visible at the top.

"I bet I know where that goes," Bobby said. "And it ain't Wonderland."

Tomás climbed into the hole and descended the ladder. He disappeared into the darkness.

"Are we supposed to follow him?" I asked.

More gunfire erupted from inside the house. And what sounded like an explosion. Maybe a concussion grenade.

"Yes, we are supposed to follow him, you fucking dumbass," Bobby said, giving me a shove.

I got down on my knees and lowered myself into the dark hole, Bobby right behind me.

The ladder kept going, at least thirty rungs. I had gone down two stories, maybe more. When I reached the bottom, I couldn't see a thing. The only light came from the small hole above. Bobby's foot kicked my head.

"Hey!" I shouted.

"Move!" he shouted back.

I moved to the side to give Bobby room. The trapdoor closed, and the scraping noise returned from above. In seconds we were in total and complete darkness. I literally held my hand in front of my face and saw nothing but black. It made me dizzy.

"This is fucking great," Bobby said, bumping into me.

Dull popping sounds came from above.

"Is Little Piwi still up there?" I asked.

"Where the fuck else would he be?" Bobby said.

Lights turned on, illuminating the space around us. I might have screamed. It was that shocking to go from dark to light so abruptly. We were in a small open area that led to a long, well-lit tunnel. Better than a compass, I knew exactly what direction due north was.

Tomás stood by a series of electrical plugs at the mouth of the tunnel. A string of lights ran along each ceiling corner. The tunnel was shored up every eight feet with six-by-sixes. I had to duck my head a little, but Tomás and Bobby could walk upright. We headed down the passage. All in all, it was a quality tunnel. There was a little water on the ground, but they had somehow managed to avoid the flooding that I got in my concrete basement. The Imperial Valley had tons of groundwater from all the irrigating.

"It's about a quarter mile," Tomás said. "They'll find the opening eventually, but they won't follow. Too afraid it's booby-trapped. Nobody isn't afraid of getting buried alive."

"This goes under the All-American Canal?" I asked.

"That was the tricky part," Tomás said, "but I hired top engineers."

"Is it booby-trapped?" I asked.

"What do you think?" Tomás said, clearly not answering my question. "They'll want to keep the tunnel for their own use anyway. These things are expensive to build."

"How much?" Bobby asked.

"A few hundred thousand."

"Pesos?"

Tomás shook his head.

"Fuck me," Bobby said. "You should've spent the extra fifty grand and put a Starbucks down here, too. Really trick it out."

"I never thought of you as a smuggler," I said.

"I've never used it before," Tomás said. "I built it in case I needed a tunnel. I knew it would eventually be something that I would need."

"Of course," Bobby said. "That's normal."

"If I needed a border tunnel and didn't have one, I'd've been upset with myself for poor planning. They take a long time to build."

"You built a tunnel from the US to Mexico just in case?" I asked.

"No," Tomás said. "I built three tunnels between the US and Mexico just in case."

"I'm not even going to try to deny how fucking badass that is," Bobby said. He might not have liked Tomás, but Bobby admired an ambitious outlaw.

It took fifteen minutes to reach the other end. Another ladder led up. Tomás climbed first. In a couple minutes, the three of us were in a corrugated tin barn. Farm equipment, hay bales, a large pile of miscellaneous rust in the corner. Out of place was the spotless Mercedes parked inside.

"What about Little Piwi?" I asked.

"Someone had to close the door on the other side," Tomás said. "He will do whatever he has to do."

"That's cold, Tommy."

"That's business," Tomás said. "I wouldn't expect to get your truck back this time, but you can use some of the cash to fix that."

I felt the bulge in my pocket that I'd forgotten I'd been carrying. It only takes a little bit of gunfire to forget twenty-five grand.

We drove out of the barn onto a dirt road just east of Calexico. Tomás stopped at the first intersection. We all looked back at Mexicali through the fence. I spotted a few police cars, but the house was out of view. Black smoke rose from where the house was. It looked like television footage of the aftermath of a bombing. Tomás turned right, and we headed north.

"I saw the guy that was in Mexico," I said. "The juiced cartel guy from the fields. He was with the Mexican cops back there. Like he was in charge."

"Polo Shirt?" Bobby said. "Yeah. I thought I saw him, too."

"His name is Porfirio Díaz," Tomás said. "The cartel sent him to Mexicali to be my replacement. To take over my businesses. He's the one been coming after me."

"Someone's mother was a fan of Mexican history," I said.

I heard Bobby exhale loudly in the backseat, a frustrated sigh. "Go ahead. Teach us some stupid piece of trivia that you know because your brain is so good."

"History isn't trivia," I said. "Porfirio Díaz was the president of fucking Mexico for like twenty-five years. Sue me for knowing shit about our neighbor to the south."

"Polo Shirt reminded me of you, Tommy," Bobby said. "Like a swole-up version. You have any long-lost cousins in Sinaloa?"

"He's dangerous but surmountable," Tomás said. "Third-generation cartel. Which means he knows the business, but not the struggle. Like a millionaire's kid. Grew up outside the country. He's only lived in that bubble of power. That makes him a bully and a punk."

"You're surprisingly calm considering they just stormed your safe house," I said.

"I'm always calm," Tomás said.

"It was the federales. How can you fight them?" I asked.

"They're not the problem. Hired help with fancy badges. They can be rehired. In chess terms, they took my rook, but I still have enough pieces to win or push."

"Can you put that in Hungry Hungry Hippos terms so I can understand?" Bobby asked.

"What the fuck am I thinking?" I said. "What about Radical and Pepe?"

"I see where you're going," Bobby said. "They were with us in Coatepec. Seemed down for anything. You thinking maybe they could finish the job? You know, the Palomera thing."

Tomás nodded. "That could work. I'll reach out to Radical. He might be able to arrange something with Pepe, but I don't know how long it would take."

"We can hold down the fort," I said, "so long as we know there's an end in sight."

Tomás pulled into the dirt patch in front of Morales Bar. He turned to me. "This is not something that there can be any miscommunication on. Everything has to be clear. It might sound like ceremony, but I need you to tell me out loud that you want Fernando Palomera, the current mayor of Coatepec, dead. That you're asking me to contact Pepe, 'El Bárbaro,' to kill him."

"Pepe's nickname is 'The Barbarian'?" Bobby asked. "Color me jealous. We should've hung out more."

I thought about my son. That was the only thing I wanted to be thinking about at that moment. I wanted to be sure of what I was about to do. And why. I wanted the motivations to be powerful enough for the action. That's how it is when you decide to do the wrong thing for the right reasons.

"I want him dead," I said. "I want Fernando Palomera dead."

"I'll make the call," Tomás said. "Be ready. Díaz's men are busy with me, but he could hire out or turn their attention in your direction at any time. Put people around you that you're sure about. Use the money. Don't trust anyone in a uniform if you don't know them personally. Like Christmas-card-list know them. American cops aren't that different than their Mexican counterparts. They're underpaid and underappreciated. They would be the first people I'd hire. If you call them for help, you might be calling in reinforcements for Díaz."

"We'll be ready," I said.

After Tomás dropped us off, Bobby decided that running from gunfire had made him thirsty. He went to Morales Bar to drink all the beers and brief Mr. Morales on what was going on. I walked across the road to my house. Rufus sat under the shade of one of the tangerine trees, alert and ready. I was sure Joaquin had eyes on me, but I didn't see him.

Angie walked out the front door and met me in the driveway. She had probably been keeping watch from one of the windows.

All the curtains were closed. A few of them had already been boarded up, and a stack of lumber sat next to the house. I held the padded envelope in my hand.

"Where's your truck?" she asked.

"Mexico."

"What's in the envelope?"

"A shit-ton of money."

"From Tomás?"

"Who else?"

"Why'd he give you money?"

"Because."

"Are we ready for this?"

"We have to be."

EIGHTEEN

I'd been broke my whole life. Occasionally I would come into a little bit of money. For a few days, I would be a multi-thousandaire ready to go ascot shopping, but it never lasted. I always ended up blowing it. I could never help myself when it came to books and DVDs.

I had learned from my many pecuniary mistakes and did the smart thing with the wad of cash that Tomás had given me. I gave it to Angie and put her in charge of the money. At the very least, she wouldn't spend it all on beer and candy and hard-to-find Hammer horror DVDs.

My cousin Mike loaned me a truck from his farm fleet. He didn't ask what happened to mine, only how he could help. People like that really do exist. The Ford F-150 was bigger and manlier than my Mazda, but I still missed my little POS. It was the truck I drove when I moved back to the Imperial Valley.

Angie gave me a stack of hundos and sent me to Costco with a list. I was ordered not to deviate from that list. Luckily it did not look like I would be forced to lie to my wife, as she had included both beer and ice cream sandwiches.

While we waited to hear from Tomás about the plan in Mexico, our domestic strategy was to be prepared for any and all kinds of threat. To keep Juan at the house and to make the house impenetrable. A hurricane or a sharknado or a panzer full of Nazi zombies, it didn't matter. We would be ready for anything.

The work on the house had begun. Windows got boarded, equipped with small holes to see or shoot from. Doors got reinforced with metal and wood braces. As a second line of defense, we even reinforced some interior doors.

I got the sump pump working and unflooded the basement, bagged up the frogs that lived there, and aired it out. If things got really bad, that would be the safest place for Juan. Not the Child Safe—patent pending—but away from any errant gunfire, at least. I gave Angie some shit about my bomb shelter / man cave plans that she had ixnayed a year earlier. It would have come in handy about now, and it would have had a pool table and stand-up *BurgerTime* arcade game in it.

Buck Buck, Snout, Bobby, and Joaquin worked on the upgrades to the exterior. The house already had a seven-foot-high stucco wall around the backyard and a short wall around the front, but there were weak points that might need booby traps, barbwire, or some other pieces of nastiness to keep unwanteds out.

I felt like Noah building the ark. Everyone that drove past must have thought us insane, but I had faith that the flood was coming.

Before I left to get provisions, I brought a six-pack out to the boys. Buck Buck, Snout, and Bobby had been working for hours in the backyard. I handed each of them a beer.

"Don't you worry, Jimmy," Snout said. "We'll make it like the Alamo."

"Don't be a dumbass," Buck Buck corrected him. "John Wayne dies in that one. This is more like *Rio Bravo* or *El Dorado.* One of the ones where the Duke lives."

"You know the Alamo is a real place, right?" Bobby said. "It really happened."

"Yeah, right," Buck Buck said. "This is like when you tried to convince me there's a place in Europe called Brittany. I'm not a gullible. That's like naming a city Ginger Lynn."

"The Alamo movie has Davy Crockett in it," Snout said. "Learn your history. Was Paul Bunyan there, too? Did Johnny Appleseed fight Mexicans with him?"

Bobby looked like his head was going to explode. "Are you kidding me? It's history. The Alamo, the building, is in Texas. You can go inside. I've been there. That's why people say, 'Remember the Alamo.'"

"I've never heard anyone say that," Snout said.

"They're talking about the movie," Buck Buck said. "Like when people say, '*Remember the Titans.*'"

"No, it's not like that," Bobby said. "That's the name of a movie." He dropped his hammer on the ground and walked away. "You're fucking idiots."

"Good meeting," I said, and headed out to do my shopping.

I roamed the canned goods aisle, putting flats of chili and soup into my oversized cart. While I stood mesmerized by the Chef

Boyardee selection, my phone rang. I didn't recognize the number, but the country code told me that the call was coming from Mexico. That could mean a range of things. I answered with appropriate trepidation. Not a lot of good news had come from Mexico lately.

"Hello," I said. "Hola."

"Is this Jimmy?"

"This is Jimmy."

"It is Radical. In Mazatlán."

"Yeah, I only know one Radical." I looked up the aisle to see if anyone could hear me. I kept my voice low.

"Tomás Morales told me to call you."

"Thanks."

"He told me what you need done. He offered an appropriate amount of money."

"And?" I said. "Is that the kind of thing you can do?"

"It should have been done that day. When we were there. It would have been easier. For you. For me."

"What is it with everyone telling me, 'I told you so'?"

"Did you think it would be over so simply?"

I was tired of people second-guessing me. I picked up a can of mini raviolis and glanced at the nutritional information on the back. Fuck, that was a ton of sodium.

I dropped my voice even lower, double-checking the empty aisle. "I didn't know that my biggest mistake—my biggest regret—would be not killing a guy. I thought I'd go back home a thousand fucking miles away in another fucking country and nobody'd be crazy enough to do nothing. I didn't know he would pull this shit. I didn't know it would matter that much to him. I don't know what I fucking thought."

"They call him El Loco," Radical said.

"I didn't learn that tidbit until later," I said. "Can you do it?"

"No. I cannot."

"Fuck. What the fuck am I going to do now?"

"No, no, no," Radical said. "I cannot do it, but Pepe can. And will. He's enthusiastic."

"Why did you make me think—never mind. Why are you calling me and not him?"

"Pepe does not use telephones. He does not trust them."

"Afraid people will listen in. Smart man."

"No, he believes that his soul is weakened by words. The more people talk, the more scarred their beings become. That silence is man's true state. And its healthiest. He could explain, but he doesn't like to talk. It is complicated."

"Uh-hunh. Yeah. I got nothing. I have literally nothing to add to that. How does this work? When can he do it?"

"You would have to ask him.

"Is he there?"

"No."

"How do I talk to him?"

"I don't know," Radical said. "He does not use the phone."

"Who the fuck are you? Chico Marx?"

"Who is that? I do not know him."

"Never mind. What happens next?"

"Pepe will contact me tomorrow to confirm. With these things it's best to confirm two, three times. Then Pepe is on his own. You will not hear anything until it's done. When he has news, he will contact me and I will contact you. Until then, silence."

"It is man's true state."

"Exactly," Radical said. "A week. Maybe less. Pepe is efficient."

"He's done this kind of thing before?"

"His specialty in Ejército Mexicano. Now it is part-time. For fun."

"Why don't I ever meet normal people?"

"Because they do not exist."

"What if I change my mind?"

"You can, but it won't change what happens," Radical said. "Once Pepe gets the order, he will carry it through to the end."

Surrounded by people buying bulk toilet paper and sampling trays of hard salami, I found it difficult to accept that I had just given the confirmation for the death order of Fernando Palomera: the mayor of Coatepec, the former narco known as El Loco, and Juan's grandfather. Life didn't get stranger than that.

I grabbed a couple pounds of teriyaki beef jerky from the shelf, threw it in my basket, and continued my shopping.

I would process the decision over time, not in the moment. It should have been profound, but I felt neutral to the idea. It had been as easy as saying yes, both impersonal and surreal. I wasn't even the one paying for it. I could see how presidents or generals sent men to fight in wars. I gave the order and then went about my day like nothing happened. While miles away, a man was sentenced to death.

And then I thought, fuck Fernando Palomera. He had threatened my son's safety. And that was all I cared about. If that meant getting rid of a man that I had met once and who had only given me grief and pain, threats and violence, then fuck him.

By the time the checker scanned my siege provisions, I was surprisingly good with the decision. Feeling not just acceptance, but excitement. Time would tell if that feeling would stick, but the thought of this nightmare being over made me damn near giddy.

Fernando Palomera might have been Juan's blood, but blood only confused the idea of family. Just because someone was blood related didn't mean I had to like them, give a crap about them, or even try. It's the same as throwing random people into a room and demanding they care for each other. There were assholes in the world, and all of them had relatives. My real family consisted of the people who I chose to put around me, some blood and some not. I would take those reprobates any day of the week.

I grabbed a bag of M&M's, a Butterfingers, and some Rolos from the impulse-buy shelf. Angie didn't need to know about my new candy stash. I had earned it.

The second-to-last person I expected to see in the parking lot of the El Centro Costco was Porfirio Díaz, a.k.a. Polo Shirt. (The last person I expected to see was Don Knotts, but that was only because he was dead.) Back in his namesake casual wear, Díaz looked surprisingly well suited to the surroundings. I could've easily mistaken him for a soccer dad buying treats for the team and not a Mexican narco. He even had the collar popped up like the douchebag he was.

Slowing my pace to an amble, I took out my phone and quickly texted Angie with one hand. "Shields up. Polo Shirt is here. Be ready for anything."

Díaz leaned against my borrowed truck, talking on the phone. He hung up and put the phone in his pocket as I approached. He glanced around the parking lot. I looked behind me to see if I was about to get jumped. I should have run, but my knees weren't built for quick movement.

"You need a hand with those groceries?" he asked, grabbing a flat of Chef Boyardee cans out of the cart and setting them in the truck bed. "You shouldn't eat this garbage. Have you seen the sodium content? You'll get hypertension."

"My blood pressure is already through the roof from stress," I said. I regretted not wearing the shoulder holster that Bobby recommended, sticking with an ankle gun. The shoulder getup would have meant wearing a jacket, and it was already getting in the nineties outside.

"Even more reason to eat healthier. That stuff will kill you. Artificial colors and flavors. You're a farmer. You should know better."

"From your casualness, I'm assuming that someone or someones are pointing a gun at me right now. I'm going to move slow to be on the safe side."

"That would be the wisest move."

I scanned the lot for any men that had me in their sights but didn't see anyone. I couldn't imagine that this guy traveled without muscle. He would pick a fight, but only if there were ten guys standing right behind him to step in if his hair got mussed.

"What do you want, asshole?" I asked.

"You know what I want," Díaz said. "I want what Mr. Palomera wants. He's become fixated on the idea of being reunited with his grandson."

"United, not reunited. And I ain't never letting that happen. Never. He's my son."

"Is he?"

"Fuck you."

"You act like Mr. Palomera is going to hurt the child. He's an old man who wants to know his only remaining heir. The child isn't your possession. He is Mr. Palomera's family. You're denying them both."

"I would never see him again."

"Then it is about you. Not the child."

"Juan is not going to have people like you and Palomera in his life."

"'People like you?'" Díaz repeated in mock outrage.

"He's growing up normal. He's not growing up around criminals. Look how you turned out."

"Fucking rednecks," Díaz said. "I don't care about the kid or you or this desert shit-hole. My people put their trust in me—told me to accommodate Mr. Palomera's wishes. It's going to get done. I am judged on my results, not my understanding of familial relationships."

I considered telling him that I had just ordered Fernando Palomera's death, making the abduction of Juan moot and unnecessary. But that would have given the plan away. He would warn Palomera. It would simultaneously thwart the plan and put Pepe in danger.

"I thought you guys were all business," I said. "All this trouble because El Loco has a notion? A lot of money and resources for something this stupid."

"Loyalty is important," he said, scanning the parking lot. "Mr. Palomera made sacrifices in the past. Those sacrifices hold meaning. He helped people rise to the position they're in. It doesn't matter what I think. It's my job to do what is asked of me."

"And you came here expecting me to hand over my son?" I asked. "Pretty stupid."

"It would certainly make things easier for both of us."

"Has bullshit like this worked for you before?"

"Your ángel de la guarda, Tomás Morales, is done in Mexicali. Once I have finished things there, I will take your son."

"Why did you say 'guardian angel' in Spanish?"

"It sounds better," he said.

"I don't need Tomás or anyone to protect me and my family," I said, dropping the flat of bottled water that I had in my hands. A few broke, but mostly they just smacked against the ground.

I leaned down to pick up the loose water bottles. My body was squeezed between two cars, the best cover I was going to get from any potential shooters. I pulled the pistol from my ankle holster, stayed low, and pointed it at Díaz.

"You made one mistake," I said.

He smiled. He fucking smiled. "What's that?"

"You think that I consider myself the good guy. That I have some moral code or ethos or something that forces me to play by some set of rules. You couldn't be more wrong. I am not a good guy. Not even close. I've killed people, and I would enjoy killing you."

I hadn't planned past that point. I was definitely capable of shooting him but wasn't convinced that would change anything. It would be satisfying, but unproductive. The cartel doesn't take kindly to their employees getting killed. Maybe I could shoot him in the leg or fuck up a toe or two.

I was also very aware that when I moved from the cover of the two cars, I could be shot. I had no idea where his men were positioned.

"Consider this," Díaz said, raising one hand in the air. Almost a heil, but more like he was hailing a cab. "If you hand over the child now, he gets both a father and grandfather. If you continue to resist, he ends up with only a grandfather. It's hard for any child to grow up without a father. I know."

"Boo fucking hoo for you."

"Your boy is not in any danger. Hurting him would be antithetical to my mandate," Díaz said. "The same isn't true for

Angela, Robert Maves, Griselda Villareal, Nestor Morales, and anyone that you care about. I could kill them all."

"'Antithetical to your mandate?'" I said. "I got your mandate right here."

"Easy or hard. It's all the same to me." Díaz looked behind him. "I've always enjoyed the hard way more."

I pulled the hammer of the revolver back.

"My ride is here." Porfirio Díaz walked two steps away and then turned back to me. "If you try to run, we will hit you on the road. If you ask for help, those people will pay for their loyalty. If you call the police—well, give that a try."

"None of that surprises me."

"You can't win," Díaz said. "I'm going to take your kid back to Mexico. And now you've pulled a gun on me? That pisses me off. I'm going to enjoy killing you."

"Fuck you. I've been threatened before!" I shouted, feeling my finger tense on the trigger. It was about fifty-fifty that I would shoot the son of a bitch. I didn't know myself.

"Put the gun down," a voice said sternly over a loudspeaker. I knew a cop voice when I heard it.

I turned my head, the gun still pointed at Díaz. An El Centro PD squad car sat parked a few cars down, an officer pointing a gun at me from behind his open door. It must have been a fucking Prius, because I didn't hear the damn thing pull up. Either that or the Ginger Baker pounding of my rapid heartbeat drowned it out.

"It's not me," I said. "He's the one threatening me."

"You're the one with the gun," the officer said.

"Fuck me." I slowly leaned down and set the pistol onto the asphalt.

"Put your hands where I can see them," the police officer said.

A small crowd had gathered at the front entrance of the Costco. They watched with interest, most of them filming it on their phones. I was going to make the fucking news.

"See you soon," Díaz said, smiling and turning. A white SUV pulled up next to him. He climbed inside. I recognized the SUV from 13 Flavors. Díaz had the fucking nerve to give me a wave before the SUV took off and headed south.

"He's leaving? You're just going to let him go?" I asked. "What the fuck is that?"

"Hands on the tailgate," the officer said. "Move very slowly."

I followed his orders. He came out from behind his car, picked up the gun, grabbed my arm, and twisted it behind my back. Then the other one. He handcuffed me efficiently but more aggressively than necessary.

"Great work, Officer Krupke," I said. "The guy you let go is a member of a Mexican drug cartel."

"Mr. Díaz was the victim," the officer said.

I'm not the sharpest tool, but I am definitely a tool. It took me until that moment to figure out what was going on.

"All these people, they're witnesses. If you take me out to the desert, there will be an investigation."

"If I was going to shoot you, I would have done it when you had the gun in your hand, dumbass."

"How much did he pay you?"

I had never been tased before. I wouldn't recommend it. My body went rigid, and then I collapsed. It hurt like hell, an intense pain throughout my entire body. It hurt worse than pissing on an electric fence, and that hit you square in the dick.

"You have the right to remain silent," he began. It was a good thing that I knew the rest by heart, because I was definitely not listening to him. I contemplated whether it was sweat or urine that was making my underwear feel so damp.

NINETEEN

The police officer brought me down to the station. He led me through the building and into a stark, almost-empty room. Not really an interrogation room or holding cell—I'd been in both before—more like an unused office. The officer didn't take a statement or get my fingerprints. He didn't even ask me my name. No phone call or lawyer. No nothing.

I alternated between sitting and pacing. Every fifteen minutes I gave a knock or pound on the door to make sure they knew I was alive.

My biggest fear was that Díaz was using my absence to try something back at the house. I hoped that Angie had gotten my text. I sat in the corner and meditated on all the ways I was going to hurt Díaz. After three hours, the officer that had brought me in returned. He never made eye contact.

"You're free to go." He said it like a movie cop. A bad actor's line reading.

"What the fuck was the point of all this?" I asked.

"I'm not charging you, letting you off with a warning."

"I guess arresting me would be as much trouble as shooting me," I said. "You fuckers sure do hate paperwork. Or in this case, a paper trail."

"Are you arguing about not being arrested? Get the fuck out of here before I change my mind." This guy needed a better screenwriter.

"Is someone going to give me a ride back to my truck?" I asked.

"Not my problem."

"How about my gun?"

He shook his head.

"Then I suppose it'd be out of the question to be reimbursed for any food stolen out of the back of my truck and the ice cream sandwiches that have definitely melted by now. Two dozen FatBoys down the shitter."

The moment I got my phone back, I called Angie and started my four-mile walk back to Costco. She answered on the first ring.

"Jimmy?" she said immediately. "Where are you?"

"Are you okay? What's going on?"

"We can't both ask questions," Angie said. "Everything is fine here. We handled it. Not really a thing. What did you mean, 'Polo Shirt is here'?"

"Polo Shirt. The asshole down in Mexico. He was in the fucking Costco parking lot. What do you mean, 'We handled it'?"

"Two women from child services showed up. Wanted to know why Juan wasn't in school. Even though we already took care of that. They had ID and paperwork, seemed legit, but I got the willies."

"Might even be their real job, but the timing is suspicious as shit," I said. "Is Juan okay?"

"I'm not stupid. I told them to come back. That Juan was out with you. They seemed to know that wasn't true."

"Someone's probably been watching the house."

"They really wanted to get a look inside. Kept trying to invite themselves in. I called bullshit on that."

"Good."

"The weirdest thing was that they never commented on the windows being boarded up or the other preparations we've done. Like it wasn't strange at all. They eventually left. Rufus gave them a growl. I'm pretty sure they shit themselves a little."

"Díaz is going to throw everything at us."

"Then we throw it back at him," she said. "Where have you been?"

"Police station. Kind of arrested but not really. I'll tell you everything when I get home," I said. "I'm walking back to the truck and need to pick up more ice cream sandwiches."

Angie met me at the truck as I pulled into the driveway. She had on a pair of work gloves, but her arms were still scratched up, covered with small red lines and scabs.

"So what the fuck happened?" replaced "Hello" as a greeting. Not angry, but matter-of-fact. It was a common greeting in our household.

"Polo Shirt—Porfirio Díaz is his name—threatened me, threatened you, threatened everyone. I got pissed. Pulled a gun on him. The cops—or rather, a cop—showed up, was already there. He took me in. He was on loan to Díaz. Not an official arrest."

Angie took off the gloves and wiped the sweat and grit from her forehead with the bottom of her shirt, giving me a brief glimpse of midriff and bra.

"You pulled a gun on him. The cop witnessed that. Was it one of Bobby's guns?"

"Yeah."

"So not a gun registered to you. I don't understand why he would let you go. Wouldn't it be better for them for you to be in jail? Out of the way."

"I don't think having me arrested was Díaz's plan," I said. "If the cop shoots me or arrests me, it becomes official. An investigation, a trial. All that shit. Díaz doesn't want to be a part of that. He wanted to show me that the cops couldn't help and that he was more powerful than me."

"Most fights aren't fair."

"No shit. I long for the days that I got to fight one-on-one instead of a bunch of fuckers."

"You have to tell Griselda," Angie said. "If there's a cop taking money from that son of a bitch, she should know."

I surveyed the front of the house. "It looks like you got more done."

"The windows are done. Doors reinforced. Buck Buck, Snout, and me have been running barbwire along the top of the back wall." She grabbed two of the bags out of the back of the truck. "They brought over a fuckton of guns to add to Bobby's pile. I swear I saw land mines in the bunch. I made them leave the dynamite in their van."

I picked up a couple flats of cans, and we headed into the house.

"I'll double-check to make sure they haven't buried any land mines," I said. "They're idiot enough to want to use them."

"It would take a tank to get inside the house," Angie said. "It feels secure. I thought all the people would bug me, but it actually feels good."

"It's only for a short while," I said, then lowered my voice. "Radical called me. Palomera is . . . It's being taken care of. Don't know how long, but soon. We just have to wait it out. Once he's gone, Juan is safe."

"I can't believe we went through with it." Angie stopped and looked south. It was a strange thing to do, but it made sense to me. She couldn't see what was going to happen, but she knew where it was happening.

"How's Juan doing with all this? With having everyone around? With all the changes? He's got to know something's up."

"He was a little freaked out at first, but he likes hanging out with grown-ups. Or at least people grown-up age, considering your man-child friends. All the activity is exciting. Mr. Morales has been entertaining him. I saw them both laughing."

"Mr. Morales doesn't laugh."

"I swear," Angie said. "That old man knows a lot of dirty jokes. A lot. I mean, filthy ones. I tried to stop him but gave up. I'd rather see Juan laughing. We'll figure out how to unteach him everything when this bullshit is over."

"Write down the officer's name, badge number, whatever you got." Griselda shook her head in disbelief. "We got good police down here, but the temptation is strong. Some just can't help it. City cops, sheriffs, border patrol, Homeland, whoever. All it takes is looking the other way and you can make good money. In his defense, you were pointing a gun at someone."

Bobby and Griselda were cleaning and sorting an array of firearms laid out on the dining room table. Between Bobby's stash and the Buckleys' private reserve, it was a sizeable arsenal.

Even though I grew up with guns, I rarely thought of them as anything more than a tool. I had been brought up to respect guns, just like I was raising Juan to do. I couldn't think of not owning them, but I didn't fetishize them the way some people did. Too loud. Too destructive. Too many people that I hated loved them. Mostly unnecessary, until they were necessary.

For all the reservations about having them around, I had always loved the smell of gun oil. It reminded me of hunting with Pop.

"The cop didn't give me the gun back either. Sorry, Bobby. I didn't want to press my luck on it. I guess it's his new throwdown."

"Do you carry a throwdown, baby?" Bobby asked Griselda.

She slapped his arm, which I'm going to assume was a no.

"I forgot to tell you," I said to Bobby. "I left that other gun of yours on the roof of 13 Flavors. It's in an empty paint can."

"What are you, Johnny Gunseed?" Griselda said to me, and then turned to Bobby. "I thought we talked about distributing guns willy-nilly."

"I gave them to Jimmy, not Willy," Bobby said. "That Nilly fellow can't be trusted." He smiled at his stupid joke.

"Why do you make loving you a challenge?" she said.

"I'm like Everest," Bobby said. "It's because I'm there. Remember, you're the one who asked me to bring these over here." Bobby waved his arm over the weapons on the dining room table.

"Can you find out if Porfirio Díaz is wanted in the US for something?" I asked. "If his documents are in order? If he's here legally or not? Can we get Interpol on it?"

"I'm sure I'm supposed to know what Interpol does," Griselda said, "but other than art forgery, I got no clue."

"He's a criminal," I said. "We know that."

"I'll check," she said, "but my guess is he's clean. Here and in Mexico. The cartels are deep into their second, third generations. They're Mexico's largest exporter. With the kind of money they make, they're educating the youth. This guy probably went to an American college. Or maybe in Europe."

"Pop, Pop, Pop," Juan said, running into the room. He held his arms out to his side in a look-at-me pose.

"Hey, Juano. What's up?"

"I got a riddle," Juan said. "Why can't you play Uno with a Mexican?"

"Oh, hell no," I said. "Where's Mr. Morales?"

"Why can't you play Uno with a Mexican?" Juan repeated, now laughing to himself.

Mr. Morales walked in from the kitchen. He put a hand on Juan's head, giving his hair a shake.

"Are you telling Juan racist jokes?" I said.

"No," Mr. Morales said. "Only jokes about Mexicans. I didn't tell him none about coloreds or Orientals. I'm Mexican. He's Mexican. How can that be racist?"

I stared at Mr. Morales, at a loss as to where to start. I turned to Juan instead. "We don't tell jokes making fun of other people's race or religion or nationality or gender. Okay?"

"That cannot include Polish jokes," Mr. Morales said.

"I have to agree with Mr. Morales on that," Bobby said.

I ignored both of them, still looking at Juan. "Do you understand, Juan?"

Juan nodded and scrunched up his face. "How about jokes with poo-poo and pee-pee in them?"

"Those are fine," I said, feeling like I'd made a valid parental compromise. "But not around your mother."

"I got another riddle," Juan said. "What's brown and smelly and behind a wall?"

"I don't know, Juan. What's brown and smelly and behind a wall?" Bobby fed him perfectly.

"Humpty's dump," Juan said. He laughed so hard that I thought he would hurt himself. Performance over, he ran out of the room as if he was late for an appointment. Mr. Morales shrugged and followed him.

"That's my boy," I said. "The budding comedian."

I turned my attention back to the table, examining the weapons. Griselda returned to the job of cleaning the gun in her hand.

"What are you people, barbarians?" Bobby blurted out.

I stopped what I was doing and turned to him. "What's wrong now?"

"Because they steal all the green cards," he said. "That's why you can't play Uno with a Mexican. You can't let a joke get half told. No matter how racist it is. It's against the laws of nature. If you tell the first half, you need to tell the second half. It's like a Gypsy curse if you don't. What kind of lessons are you teaching your kid?"

I went into the backyard to check on the progress. Buck Buck and Snout were busy pounding on something that looked like a catapult. I didn't ask what they were building, because I knew the answer would be a catapult. I wasn't up for that conversation.

"Where do you keep your gunpowder?" Snout asked. "We couldn't find it anywhere. You should really keep it in the fridge to maintain its potency."

"I don't have any gunpowder," I said. "And I don't think refrigerating it does shit."

They looked at me like I was made out of insanity.

"If you don't have any gunpowder, what do you make your shotgun shells with?" Snout asked.

"I don't make shotgun shells."

"Seriously, Jimmy," Buck Buck said. "I worry about you."

"If you make your own, you can fill them with whatever," Snout said. "I blew the shit out of a pumpkin with a shell full of dimes. I filled one with gummi bears, but they melted in the air and made the gun barrel gooey. You should see my bandolier. It's like Green Arrow's quiver, but shootier."

"The blinds looks good," I said, pointing to the two deer blinds they had built on the roof. Essentially treehouse construction to act as lookouts. Redneck turrets.

"Maybe you can talk some sense into Buck Buck," Snout said. "I've been telling him we should put a bunch of rattlesnakes back here. There's tons of sidewinders out at Heber Beach. We get a net and catch the suckers. Don't matter who you are, you ain't going to try to trek through a lawn of rattlers."

Buck Buck shook his head. "I told him it was crazy."

"Thanks for being the voice of reason," I said.

"Anyone that's seen *Raiders* knows that all you need is fire to repel snakes. Besides, they would slither out too easily. If we're going to do it, we would need to dig a pit first."

I squeezed the bridge of my nose. All of a sudden I felt a headache coming on. "I'm not putting rattlesnakes in the backyard."

"I'm just spitballing," Snout said. "Wasps or bees would just fly away, obviously. You could use scorpions, but you'd need a whole mess of them."

"We already shitcanned scorpions," Buck Buck said. "A good pair of boots is all you'd need to get past them. How about a mountain lion? That's gangster."

Something blocked the sun for a moment. A shadow flashed across the lawn. Like a bird flying overhead, but its movement was unnatural. Maybe it had a bad wing. I looked up, trying to catch sight of the hawk or owl. I loved watching the red-tailed hawks mouse-hunt over the fields. We called them "country eagles" when I was growing up.

It wasn't a bird. It wasn't a plane. And it sure as shit wasn't Superman.

"Are you fucking kidding me?" I said.

"What the hell?" Buck Buck said. "Is that what I think it is?"

"Yeah," I said. "It's a fucking drone."

A four-propeller drone hovered over the backyard about one hundred feet in the air. When I squinted, I was pretty sure I could see a camera at its center, the lens reflecting the sun's glare.

"These sons of bitches got all the cool toys," Snout said. "Why don't we got drones?"

"It's for reconnaissance," Buck Buck said. "They're gathering intel. Seeing what we got back here."

"What do we do?" Snout asked.

The blast of a shotgun and the disintegration of the drone answered his question.

Plastic and metal shards fell to the earth just on the other side of the backyard wall. When something got shot, I wanted fire and smoke, but it was just parts. Kind of disappointing.

I couldn't climb the seven-foot stucco wall because of the fresh barbwire that had been secured to the top. My own defenses used against me. I was forced to walk through the house and go around.

"What the fuck was that?" Bobby said as I walked through the dining room. He looked through the small viewing hole in the wood that boarded the window. He held revolvers in each hand.

Griselda stood behind him, a shotgun pointed to the ground.

"A drone," I said, walking past him to the front door. "It was flying over the backyard."

In the field next to the house, Joaquin stood over the fallen fuselage of the drone. He pushed at the shattered plastic with the barrel of his shotgun. Rufus sniffed at it but walked away disinterested when it didn't appear to be edible.

We all stood around the busted thing, hands on hips. I had never seen a drone up close. I couldn't figure out what the big deal was. It was a remote control helicopter as far as I could tell. They'd been around for years.

"Going to see more and more of these," Griselda said. "They use them to smuggle, too. Depending on how much they can carry, you can fly any contraband you want over the border fence."

I leaned down and examined what was left of the drone. Both the camera and its body had taken a direct hit from the birdshot.

"Nice shot, Joaquin!" I yelled, pantomiming shooting a rifle and giving him a thumbs up.

He gave me his gummy smile, mimed the drone exploding in the sky, and walked back to the side of the house. Just another day at the office, shooting shit out of the sky.

TWENTY

"Do you understand what's going on?" I asked Juan. "Why everyone's here? Why we're making the changes to the house?"

The two of us sat on Juan's bed. Another in a string of serious conversations between me and my son. I couldn't wait to get back to more standard father/son conversations, like why boobies made his pants feel funny.

"I think so," Juan said. "Mom explained it. There's people mad at you. They might come here and try to hurt you. So Uncle Bobbiola and Uncle Buck Buck and the Snouter are here to not let them. To make sure you don't get hurt."

"To make sure none of us get hurt," I said.

There was no good reason to tell Juan that he was the target. He needed to know that there was danger, but it wasn't fair to terrify him. That would have been a lot for an adult to absorb, let alone an eight-year-old. The most important thing was that he understood that we weren't playing a game.

The debate on what and how to tell Juan had grown over the last week. That's what happens when you spend your day sitting around waiting to be attacked and nobody attacks you. We had completed the improvements on the house. Created a rotating schedule. No word from Radical. I had tried Tomás several times but got no response from him. We lived in our bubble, eating way too much canned chili. I would have given a hundred dollars for a special quesadilla from Camacho's.

"I've got good friends, don't I?" I said to Juan.

"Mr. More-Or-Less's jokes are funny. He knows more good ones than even you. But not more than Uncle Bobbiola. He knows all of the jokes."

"Hold on there. I know more jokes than Bobby."

Juan shook his head. "I don't think so."

I almost started arguing with my eight-year-old son about who knew more jokes, but as the adult in the room I stopped myself. I had grown over the last few years. Besides, I knew that I knew more jokes than Bobby. There was no reason to get het up over a child's ridiculous wrongness.

"It's like a slumber party," Juan said, "but for grown-ups."

"I'm sorry you can't play outside. It's only for a short time."

Griselda poked her head in the room. "You need to come and listen to this."

Neither her tone of voice nor her insistence sounded good. Things were about to get suck.

I turned on the lights as I walked in the room. The sun had set twenty minutes earlier. Red and orange light streaked across everyone's faces from the gaps in the boarded windows. Bobby and Angie sat around the coffee table. Griselda and I joined them. We all focused our attention on the object at the center of the table, Griselda's police scanner.

The squawk of numbers and codes and voices made little sense to me. It sounded frantic and even a little panicked, but I had nothing to compare it to. Maybe it was always like that. More than a dozen voices spoke, carrying on multiple conversations. I would pick up something every tenth sentence, but it was mostly gibberish to my ears.

"I can't make head or tail of this," I said.

"Yeah, I'm only getting pieces," Bobby said.

"Sounds like a lot happening all at once," Angie said.

"I'll translate," Griselda said, "but that's the gist of it. A lot is happening. Too much all at once. Nothing normal about it."

She picked up the scanner, put it on her lap, closed her eyes, and listened.

Griselda translated the copspeak for us. "There's a hay fire off Dogwood. Sounds big. You know those storage barns near the fertilizer plant?"

"Terry Pruitt's place," Bobby said.

"Sanchez Jewelry in Calexico got held up at closing time," Griselda said. "One person shot in the leg. Huge bar brawl at Portagee Joe's in Holtville. A group of Mexicans started some shit with some farmers. It spilled out to the street. Shots fired."

"That ain't too strange," Bobby said. "Maybe a little early for a brawl. I usually like to end the night with a wind-down."

"There's more," Griselda said. "Truck explosion at the border crossing in Calexico. Another fire out past Bonds Corner Road. Abandoned house."

"Do you think Díaz is behind all this?" I asked.

"No way to know, but it would makes sense," Griselda said. "If I had a map, I could show you why. If you wanted to spread out every agency that works the border, then this would be the best way to do it. Everyone on duty will be at one of these calls."

"This is it," I said. "He's going to make his move."

"Fucking shit," Angie said, for all of us. It's what we had prepared for, but that didn't mean we were ready for it to happen.

"Where are Buck Buck and Snout?" I asked.

"Across the street," Bobby said. "It was their beer break."

"We have beer here."

"Beer tastes different in a bar," Bobby said.

"I'll get them." I turned to Angie. "Get Juan to the basement. Get set up. Stay with him."

"I can fight," Angie said. "I want to fight."

"I know you can," I said. "But Juan is going to need one of us with him. One of his parents. You're his mom. You're the last line of defense."

"Is this really happening?" Angie said.

"As crazy as it sounds," Griselda said, "I think it is. We need to start making calls. Get any help we can get. Law enforcement, friends, family, anyone who will come out. Anyone who will fight."

"Make sure they know what they're risking," I said. "What they're up against."

"I don't want this to sound like I'm taking any of this shit lightly. But." Bobby yee-hawed loudly to the sky. "I've been waiting my whole life for a fight like this. Finally. It's finally time to fuck some fuckers the fuck up. Let's get Nolan Ryan on their Robin Venturas."

"Not everyone gets your references," Griselda said.

"I did," I said. "It means we're going to make them pay for thinking they could fight us."

"Google it, Gris," Bobby said. "Or YouTube. Is Ask Jeeves still a thing? There are no excuses anymore for not understanding a reference."

Joaquin and Rufus stood guard in the front of the house, where they had patrolled every night since we'd gotten back from Mexico. Joaquin offered me a drink from his Tecate. I took a pull and handed it back. I pointed to the horizon, pointed toward myself multiple times, and then held up my weapon. My best sign language to indicate that they were coming, even if I didn't exactly know what "they" meant. I pointed to him and the house, that he should go inside.

Joaquin smiled and shook his head. He lifted up his shotgun and kissed the barrel. Rufus barked once. It made me jump.

I had no idea what was coming, but Díaz had the money to hire men. Outside the short walled-in front yard and tall walls of the backyard, there was little safety. A few trees to hide behind. The Airstream parked on the side of the house was the opposite of impenetrable.

Díaz was trying to abduct Juan, which handcuffed him in terms of his violence selections. He couldn't use firearms or explosives for fear of hurting Juan. That was true for attacking the house but wasn't true outside the walls. Joaquin could get hurt.

I took no pride in my son being our human shield, but that gave us a clear advantage. We could shoot out, but they would be hesitant to shoot in.

I pointed at Joaquin and then the house again. Joaquin laughed silently, shook his head, slapped my back, and walked away. Rufus gave me one of those sideways dog looks and followed Joaquin, casually pissing on a sapling along the way.

Buck Buck and Snout were the only customers in Morales Bar. Mr. Morales leaned against the bar, playing checkers with Snout.

Buck Buck whispered in Snout's ear, pointing at the board. Snout swatted him away.

"You want a beer, Jimmy?" Mr. Morales asked.

"Díaz is making his move," I said. "It's time. The crime rate just jumped throughout the county, and Griselda thinks it's to keep the cops busy. Whatever they got planned, they put a lot of effort into making it happen tonight."

Mr. Morales pulled his axe handle and shotgun from behind the bar. Buck Buck and Snout chugged their beers and put the unopened cans in their pants pockets.

"Don't put the checkers away," Snout said. "We'll finish the game later. I was going to win this one."

"No, you weren't," Mr. Morales said. "You boys ready to fight hard?"

"We don't know no other way," Buck Buck said. "Do we, Snout?"

"Nope," Snout said.

We all left the bar together. Mr. Morales went to his car and grabbed a big rucksack. We crossed the street to my house. It wasn't dark yet, but it was getting there. From the road I couldn't see most of the changes we had made to the house unless I really looked. The windows were boarded from the inside, so you had to squint to notice.

"Jimmy," Buck Buck said, pointing south.

A mile away on Heber Road, a line of cars. Like a parade, all the same speed. Slow. "The Duke Arrives" from *Escape from New York* played in my head. The lead car turned onto Orchard Road, its headlights shining in our direction.

"How many do you see?" I said, picking up my pace toward the house.

"Eight or ten, give or take one or two," Snout said. "Plus those."

He pointed north, where another half dozen cars approached.

"A dang army," Buck Buck said. "This is going to be a helluva battle."

"There's still time for the two of you to get out of here," I said. "You, too, Mr. Morales."

"And let you have all the fun?" Snout said. "You're hilarious."

Buck Buck and Snout laughed all the way to the front door of the house.

"Juan will be okay," Mr. Morales said. "I won't let anything happen to your boy."

"He's your boy, too," I said. "You're more of a grandfather to Juan than that bastard."

"Blood is just blood," Mr. Morales said. "It ain't nothing more."

"I have no idea what's going to happen," I said. "I don't know how this is going to end. I wish I had time for some big speech, but I don't."

"Good," Bobby said. "Because you ain't no Herb Brooks."

"Another sports reference?" Griselda asked.

"Yeah, baby," Bobby said.

"You two don't got to be here, but you are," I said. "That means something big to me. To me and to Angie. That's all I got to say. Thanks."

At the kitchen door, Griselda and Bobby held hands. Angie was already settled in the basement with Juan. Buck Buck and Snout were outside, getting into position in the deer blinds on the roof. Mr. Morales said he had a plan of his own. I had no idea what that meant, and I didn't ask.

"I called it in," Griselda said. "Talked to a few men I trusted. They said the most they can send out is two cars, and it might be a while. Can't spare more. It's chaos all over the valley. Until a shot is fired, something happens, the other scenes are the priority."

"I talked to Ceja," Bobby said. "He's dealing with the bar brawl but said he'd do his best to round up some folks, head out himself. Doesn't know how long, though."

"We got to assume it's just us," I said.

"That's all we've ever needed before, bro," Bobby said.

We had equipped all the boards on the windows with small viewing holes. I peered out the window near the front door. It gavc me a good view of the front yard, circular driveway, and one side of the house. Not expansive, I still had some blind spots, but I had another set of eyes on the roof.

Over a dozen cars sat parked in front of the house. The cars blocked the road in either direction. Two drove up either side of the driveway. Another two drove down the dirt road on the side of the house.

This war would be fought on three fronts: the north and south sides of the backyard and the front of the house. The back was accessible, but not practical. A large-enough canal behind the house acted as a natural barrier. It was definitely possible that a person could move through the cornfield and swim across the canal, but they'd still just be at the wall. To make matters worse for anyone willing, Rufus patrolled the space between the canal and the wall. I had more faith in that wolf-dog than I did in any of us.

A steady stream of chatter continued over the walkie-talkies, Buck Buck doing play-by-play for the people that were positioned in places where the front yard wasn't as visible.

"They're just sitting out there," Buck Buck said. "I figured it out. This isn't a John Wayne movie at all. This is definitely *The Magnificent Seven.* The real one, the Yul Brynner one."

"Most of them die in that one, too," Bobby said.

"How about the sequels?" Snout said. "*Return, Guns, Ride*?"

"Apparently there were a lot of magnificent cowboys willing to be cannon fodder," Bobby said. "Tell Snout when you want him to play my mixtape, Jimmy."

"You made a mixtape for a battle?" I said.

"Of course," Bobby said. "Bobby Maves' Fightin' Music for Fightin'."

"I'm assuming it's just a fuckton of Warrant."

"Don't be an idiot," Bobby said. "Warrant is exclusively for partying. I take fighting seriously."

"No, you don't."

"You're right," Bobby said, "but I take mixtapes seriously."

"Fair enough."

"Something's happening," Buck Buck interrupted.

I focused on the front yard. All the men exited the cars, trucks, and SUVs at once. The timing was so crisp, it looked like a choreographed flash mob made up of men who did not do flash mobs and did not know what flash mobs were.

Tough guys came in all different varieties. Bars are filled with silent, unassuming men that could kill you efficiently. While at the same time, you can find bodybuilder types that cry at a hard pinch. Someone needs to write a field guide. Looking tough and being tough have little to do with each other, but subtle signs reveal the truth. It's all about the way a man carries himself.

The men that exited the cars were from a number of different breeds. This wasn't an army of Mexican drug cartel soldiers. It looked more like a bestiary of people pulled out of bars in the afternoon. There were as many white guys as Mexicans. Some looked genuinely hard, while the others tried to keep pace, without the same confidence. These men looked like they were on loan from Thugs"R"Us.

"You getting the same vibe as me?" I said. "These men don't read as cartel."

"Why would Díaz risk his own soldiers on a farmer and his friends?" Griselda said. "It would probably be insulting to ask."

"I forgot," Buck Buck said. "Are we shooting to kill, maim, or is it more of a strafe-the-ground-at-their-feet, *A-Team* type of situation?"

"No killing," Griselda said. "Only if there is no other option. We talked about this."

"Yeah," Snout said, "but we weren't listening."

After his men had arranged themselves into position, Porfirio Díaz got out of the lead car in the driveway. He scanned the house and pointed to the roof. He looked left and right, squinting into the darkness at the side of the house. The car headlights cast the only light, most of them pointed at us.

"I can take him out right now," Bobby said. "Just say the word."

Díaz pointed to the sides. Two men got back in their cars and drove onto the lawn to cast more light into those areas. Díaz didn't appear to be in any hurry, confident no one was coming to help. He pulled out his phone.

My phone rang.

"Get the fuck off my land," I said. "And tell the fucks who just drove onto my lawn that I'm sending them the bill for fresh sod."

"It looks like you prepared," Díaz said. "You couldn't have prepared for this many."

"A couple dozen punk-asses don't scare me. I suggest you leave before the cops show up."

"You're on your own," Díaz said. "I made sure of that."

"That's not how it works here in the valley," I said. "There's always help. We take care of our own."

"How very American," Díaz said. He looked at the roof again. "Are the men on the roof wearing lucha masks?"

Fucking Buck Buck and Snout. Only they could manage to embarrass me at my own siege.

"You're damn right they are," I said. "All part of our plan."

"Have you talked to Tomás Morales recently?" Díaz asked.

"I told you. I don't need Tomás to protect my family."

"You are a farmer," he said. "You are all farmers. You think you can fight me—us. If I don't get what I want today, I come back tomorrow. The next day. The day after. There is no way to stop me."

"Walk out in the open a little more, and I'll stop you."

"I gave you a choice."

"Remind me to tell you the joke 'Death or Ugu,'" I said. "That's the choice you gave me."

Díaz turned to the man standing at the back door of his SUV, pointed to the door, and waved forward. The man opened the door and pulled out a hooded figure. The figure's body language read as tired or half-conscious. His legs held but looked wobbly. Head sinking down to his chest. Díaz's man walked the hooded man up next to his boss. Díaz stared forward and pulled off the hood. It felt self-conscious and posed, like a magician revealing a dole of white doves.

"Oh, fuck," Bobby said over the walkie-talkie.

"What?" Griselda said.

Tomás Morales stood with his hands tied behind his back. He was backlit by the headlights, but I could see him enough to see the damage. Blood covered his swollen face and matted his hair. One eye looked completely closed. It was hard to tell from a distance, but it looked like he might have been missing an ear.

"Motherfucker," I said, barely remembering that I was still on the phone.

Díaz kicked the back of Tomás's legs, forcing him onto his knees.

"He has Tommy," Bobby said on the walkie. "I have mixed feelings about this."

Díaz reached a hand back to the man who had retrieved Tomás. The man put a pistol in Díaz's hand. Of course he didn't lower himself to carrying his own gun. This guy was all about theatricality. He'd probably seen more gangster movies than me but liked the remake of *Get Carter* better than the original. You know, your basic asshole.

"What do we do, boss?" Buck Buck said.

"He shoots Tommy," Bobby answered, "you shoot him."

"That doesn't really help Tomás," Griselda said.

"I told you I had mixed feelings," Bobby said.

I tried to ignore them, staring out at Díaz's smug face. The phone still held to his ear. I felt like Tomás's life was in my hands.

"I'm not going to trade Juan for Tomás," I said. "I can't do that. You have to know that I'd never do that."

"That's not what's happening," Díaz said. "I'm not asking for an exchange. This is more a demonstration. I wanted to show you that nobody is untouchable. That I can kill whoever I want."

"Whomever," I said, just to be a dick. Bobby was right. It was fun to correct people.

Díaz ignored my grammar lesson and placed the gun to the back of Tomás's head.

Tomás laughed like the funniest joke in the world had just been told. He spit some blood to the side, but continued laughing.

"You're about to die, chicalon," Díaz said to Tomás, his voice away from the phone but audible.

I could only make out some of Tomás's reply. "Killing people makes . . . powerful. I answer to no one. You are an employee . . . take orders . . . not even a soldier . . . an errand boy . . . a bitch. That isn't power."

"Are you watching, Veeder?" Díaz said. "I want you to watch."

I was watching.

Just in time to see an arrow hit Porfirio Díaz high in the chest, knocking him backward. I pulled my ear away from the phone, his screams filling my head.

"What the heck?" Buck Buck said.

"A fucking arrow?" Bobby said. "Nobody told me we could bring arrows."

TWENTY-ONE

The moment the arrow struck Porfirio Díaz, everything went south quickly. It went so far south, we were heading north again. Not only did hell break loose, but jahannam, naraka, and xibalba broke loose. All the hells broke loose. If I was telling this story in person in a bar—where all good stories are told—I would be standing on a table shouting in three-word sentences, gesturing wildly with my hands, splashing beer foam from the top of my glass.

What had once been a siege mutated into a clusterfuck of elephantine proportions, filled with swearing and running and blood and gunfire. And fucking arrows. If there was any question that country boys and Mexican thugs knew how to party, the lid had been put on that debate.

The arrow had hit Díaz just below his collarbone. He fell back as much by the shock of getting arrowed as the force of the arrow, screaming the whole way down. Not a manly *aargh* either, but more of a high-pitched *waa.* Any facade of toughness had disappeared. There's nothing quite like seeing a sadist get his violence cherry popped and feel some real pain. It was in those moments that I loved violence as much as a child loved candy.

Before Díaz hit the ground, Tomás was on his feet running awkwardly toward the front door. Whether he had been playing possum or survival adrenaline kicked in, he sprinted like an Olympian. Although an Olympian with his hands tied behind his back. He stumbled forward, skidding on the walk just in front of the gate.

"Cover fire!" I shouted into the walkie. "He needs cover fire."

"Finally," Bobby said.

Buck Buck and Snout opened fire from the roof. Bobby fired from the bedroom window. Griselda let loose from the second floor office. They blasted out windshields and tires. The bullets and shot kicked dirt at the feet of Díaz's men. They ducked for cover. Two men dragged Díaz behind a car. He screamed the whole way.

I threw open the door and ran to the front gate, Tomás just on the other side. A couple of Díaz's men attempted to flank me from the side of the house, sneaking around the tangerine trees. Bobby spotted them and fired in their direction as they ducked for cover.

"Go!" Bobby shouted.

With my back against the low wall, I opened the gate and reached out my hand. Tomás crawled toward me and grabbed it. I dragged him the rest of the way. In my peripheral vision, I saw Mr. Morales at the corner of the house nock another arrow into his bow. Mystery solved. That old man was full of surprises. I ducked back and kicked the gate closed. Tomás and I put our backs against the low wall.

"Who shot that arrow?" Tomás asked.

"Your grandfather," I said.

"Well, I'll be damned."

"Can you make it to the door?"

Tomás nodded.

"Stay low."

Díaz's men returned fire. The bullets striking the plaster and wood of the house thumped like heavy bass.

Tomás and I crawled toward the door. Once Tomás was safely inside, I rose into a crouch to get a second look at their setup. Smart move, dingus. Something stung my arm. I looked down. A graze along my bicep. Served me right. I fired a couple random shots, slammed the door shut, and locked it.

Angie rushed into the room. "What the hell happened? Why is he here? Are you shot? This is fucking nuts."

"It's just a graze," I said, clutching the wound. "You need to be with Juan."

"I'll go right back down," she said. "I needed to know what was happening."

"It's going to get uglier," I said.

Angie pulled my hand away and examined the wound. "Barely made it through your shirt. I'll kiss it later."

"I still got shot," I said. "It counts."

Angie moved to check on Tomás. He leaned against the front door and sat with his eyes closed.

"I'm not shot," Tomás said, gently pushing Angie away. "This is from an earlier disagreement with Señor Díaz."

"Your ear," she said, brushing his hair away.

I had been right. Most of Tomás's right ear was gone, a scabbed hole left on the side of his head. Ragged skin and red pulp.

"Fucking hell," I said. Which is what you say when you see something fucked up. The pope would say "Fucking hell" if he saw something as fucked up as Tomás's not-ear. It was that fucked up.

"I haven't looked in a mirror yet," Tomás said. "It'll hurt more then."

"You're surprisingly calm about it," Angie said.

"One of the perks of being in my chosen vocation is that I know a plastic surgeon who specializes in ear reconstruction."

"Is there a need?" Angie said.

"Most of his patients are former kidnap victims. Sending ears in the mail is very Mexican. Dr. Proctor capitalized on the niche market. He'll knock out a new ear for me, no problem. That is, if I survive to the end of the day."

"Most of the bleeding has stopped," Angie said, "but this needs to be cleaned and bandaged." She left the room and came back with her medical bag.

The gunfire continued outside, but like popcorn in a microwave, the time between shots grew further apart.

I peered out the slit in the plywood that covered the big living room window. Díaz's men appeared to be in a huddle deciding their next move. It was difficult to see past the glare of the headlights.

I took the walkie off my belt. "Buck Buck, how the two of you doing?"

"We're good. You?"

"I got shot, but not enough to stop me."

"Cool," Snout said. "You'll have to show me later."

"What happens now, boss?" Buck Buck asked.

"Don't know," I said. "It's their move. We're on defense."

"Yeah, I guess we ain't going nowhere," Buck Buck said. "Over and out."

I moved away from the window and sat on the couch. I had quit smoking a year earlier. I had never wanted a cigarette more than at that moment.

"Do either of you have any gum?" I asked.

Angie stopped bandaging Tomás's head and turned to me like I was a crazy person. Tomás reached into his pocket and tossed me a pack of Juicy Fruit. That guy was ready for anything.

"What happened?" I asked Tomás. "How did they get you?"

"You know, I considered cashing out. Letting them take over. Retiring. Thought about Europe, Argentina, maybe Asia. I've always wanted to see Angkor Wat."

"It's amazing," I said.

"I'd just be back. I know myself well enough to know that I don't take losing well. It really came down to how difficult a fight I wanted to be in. I went back to Mexicali to get mine back. Ow!"

"Hold still," Angie said.

"Little Piwi gave me up," he said.

"Little Piwi?" I said. "That sucks."

"It's on me. I put him in a corner and shouldn't have put him in that position. I would have done the same thing to survive. It was his only play."

"He handed you over to Díaz?"

"It was terrifically anticlimactic."

"I'm sorry, man," I said. "I know the Piwis were like family."

"I had thought that, but I was wrong," Tomás said. "You don't pay family to protect you. These people here helping you, they are family. You're family."

Although I wasn't sure if Tomás had said "Your family" or "You're family," I heard the latter.

Griselda's voice came from the walkie. "Before these dicks get their shit together, someone should get to Mr. Morales and get him the hell inside. He either lost his walkie-talkie or it's not working or he's kamikazing it. He's in the Airstream. Once they realize it, our Mexican Robin Hood is going to be exposed."

"I'm closest," I said. "I'll get him. You all keep an eye out. Tell me if they make another move."

"You know it, brother," Bobby said.

"I'll get back down with Juan," Angie said. "Tell me this is all going to work out."

"This is all going to work out," I said.

Angie ran back down the hall to the basement to be with our son. I racked a shell into the chamber and headed for the side door to get Mr. Morales.

"Stay here," Tomás said, rising slowly to his feet. "Stay close to your boy. My abuelito needs help, I'm the one to help him."

"You up for it?"

"I need to be," Tomás said. "Where are the guns and explosives?"

Armed with a pistol and a pistol-grip shotgun, Tomás limped out the side door. He looked rocky, but adrenaline worked magic. Getting on the other side of the wall wasn't a problem. We had built hidden escape routes at three points in case we had to make a run for it.

From the viewing hole in the window, I watched Tomás lift a board and shimmy into the low hole that ran under the wall. He would end up behind a row of sawgrass, out of view. That pampas was going to cut him up, but it made good cover. I was glad that I had put off chucking those hateful plants for the last two years. Laziness had its merits.

I clipped the walkie-talkie to my belt and ran to the basement to check on Angie and Juan. I knocked the secret knock. Shave and a haircut. Angie opened the door.

We had made the basement as comfortable as possible, while at the same time safe. The small window was covered with a bolted-in piece of sheet metal. It was as close to a Child Safe as we could build.

Juan listened to my old Power Records forty-fives with a pair of headphones. Each side of the record was a different superhero adventure. They were corny and not particularly well written or produced, but I wanted to slowly introduce Juan to the joy of radio drama. Power Records were the gateway.

"I heard guns," Juan said, taking off the headphones. He looked scared, but not terrified. I'd take it. My concern was for his safety. We'd deal with the mental health issues later.

"You're going to hear more guns, kiddo, but it's okay," I said. "How do you like those records?"

"They're like movies without pictures. When I close my eyes, I can see the story. Metamorpho just used science to beat Fumo the Fire Giant."

"That's a good one."

"I'm scared, Pop."

"I know. It's scary. But you're with your mom, and there ain't no safer place in the world than with her. When we're done, I'm going to have Mr. More-Or-Less show you how to make a bow and arrow."

"Uh, I'm not so sure," Angie said, but didn't fight it further than that.

"After I make my yo-yo," Juan said. "I made drawings for all sorts of arrows. I need a boxing glove."

"That sounds awesome," I said. "Show me later, okay?"

"Okay," Juan said. His mood shifted, not drastically but in the right direction.

Buck Buck's voice squawked from the walkie. "Round two, boys and girls. Grab your socks."

"Got to go," I said. "I love you. Both of you."

"Love you, too, Pop," Juan said.

I ran up the stairs. Angie followed me and stood at the basement door.

"Be careful, stupid." She closed the door. I heard the locks click and her footsteps recede back down the stairs.

Bobby gave the next report. "They're spreading out. A few in my blind spot. Looks like they're going to blitzkrieg."

"All four sides," Buck Buck said.

"Three sides," Snout said. "A couple dudes tried to sneak through the back. Waded the canal, but Joaquin and that wolf made short work of them. That dog's in the process of literally tearing one of the guys a new asshole. The other dude's running from Joaquin, who has a hatchet. We should have totally videoed this."

"They'll be careful about shooting at the house," I said. "You ain't as protected, Buck Buck, or you, Snout. They might take some shots in your direction."

"Can we quit pretending," Bobby said, "and admit that we're going to have to shoot a couple of these jabronis? In the leg or arm or something. They got to hurt a little. It's the only way to take the fight out of them. Else they forget they're in danger."

"Only if you have to," Griselda said.

"Oh, I have to, baby," Bobby said.

"Where you at, Bobby?" I asked.

"Living room."

"Here they come!" Buck Buck shouted. "Thunderdome, bitches."

Gunfire erupted outside, no way to tell from what direction. If it was ours or theirs.

Over the gunfire, the opening guitar riff from "Modern Day Cowboy" by Tesla blared out from some serious speakers. The first track on Bobby's mixtape. I would never tell Bobby, but he might have been right. This batshit-crazy scenario needed a soundtrack.

I headed down the hall. Passing Juan's bedroom, I saw one of the boards on the window shaking. Someone was trying to get inside, attempting to pry a corner loose. I rushed into the room, talking quickly into the walkie.

"How many in front?" I asked. "Can anyone get a visual?"

"I'm kind of fighting people right now," Buck Buck said. Gunfire and guitar made his voice barely audible. "Four, maybe five dudes. Some of them are up to the wall of the house. Can't see them no more."

Bobby was right about the whole let's-not-shoot-anyone bullshit. It was inevitable that we would be firing back at them. I would do whatever was necessary and deal with the aftermath. That was the way I'd always done things. Blow the shit out of a thing and then try to put the tiny pieces back together.

"Fuck it," I said, and fired my pistol at the plywood. Three shots, random grouping.

I told myself that if I hit the person behind it, the wood would have slowed down the bullet considerably. Rationalization 101. If I could rationalize eating a bar of chocolate because of the antioxidants, I could sure as hell rationalize shooting someone. The whole point of rationalizations was to make mistakes into good decisions. How could that be a bad thing? Rationalizing was awesome.

A splintered hole formed in the wood. I hadn't heard the gunshot because of the Tesla and all the other gunfire. A puff of plaster appeared in the wall behind me. Another unheard shot.

Either this guy didn't get the "Don't shoot inside the house, there's a kid in there" memo or it was a knee-jerk instinct to fire back when someone shoots at you. A pry bar jammed through a corner of the board. It started to buckle at the bottom. I rushed forward and pressed my body against the board, grabbed the pry bar, and yanked it into the room with me. I heard swearing in Spanish, and another gunshot followed. The hole appeared about four inches from my head, a splinter scratching my cheek.

"A little help," I said into the walkie. "They're almost in the bedroom. I can't hold them for long."

"On it," Bobby said. "It's about time I went Mexicutioner on these motherfuckers."

"Don't do anything stupid," Griselda said.

"Sorry, babe," Bobby said. "You know that's not how I roll."

It felt like another person had joined the first guy, the pressure on the board doubling. From behind the wood outside, I heard a familiar yee-haw and then a whole bunch of sounds. Not gunfire, but thuds and whacks. The force on the board stopped. I tried to look through one of the bullet holes but couldn't see a thing.

Luckily I stepped back just before the board collapsed into the bedroom. That's what happened when a body was thrown against it. Bobby stood bent over in the front yard, pounding the hell out of some desert bro's face. An unconscious Mexican guy lay facedown on the ground next to them.

"Make sure the guy inside is out of the fight," he said, literally not missing a beat. "Tie him up or something."

The guy's feet were still on the windowsill. I dragged him the rest of the way into the house, disarmed him, and tied his wrists behind his back with an extension cord.

"Get in here," I said to Bobby. "You're too exposed."

Bobby stood over the two unconscious and bloody men, panting. I pointed to a couple guys running toward him from the driveway. I could just make out Díaz's silhouette, farther in the background. He sat on the ground, the arrow still in his shoulder.

The Tesla song ended, and "Hair of the Dog" by Nazareth kicked in. Bobby had really put some thought into the mix.

Bobby pulled something from his pocket and tossed it in the direction of the charging men. He jumped in the open window, quickly scrambling to his feet. He grabbed the board off the ground.

"Grab the other end!" he shouted.

We both lifted the board back in place over the window.

"Tell me that wasn't a grenade," I said.

"That wasn't a grenade." He winked.

"You asshole," I said.

A loud bang echoed from outside, but I didn't feel any push on the plywood. When I say loud, I mean Motörhead-live loud. My ears rang. My head thumped.

I found a five-pound dumbbell on the ground. That's the kind of thing you'd find on the ground in my house. Angie and I were slobs. I used it as a hammer to nail the board back in place as quickly as I could. In a pinch, everything is a hammer.

"What the fuck was that?" Griselda said. "What exploded?"

"It was me, baby," Bobby said into the walkie. "Flashbang." He turned to me. "Stun grenade. It's all Griselda would give me from the cop arsenal. Did you know cops had bombs?"

"Yeah, the cops bombed the shit out of Philadelphia in the eighties."

"You're making that shit up," Bobby said.

I pulled the walkie from my belt. "What's going on? What do you see?"

"When I get my hearing back, I'll tell you," Buck Buck said. "Thanks for the warning, you dickshits."

Snout laughed. "He's always been sensitive. They're backing off this side of the house. Seems like the end of their first salvo."

"Did you just say 'salvo'?" I asked.

"Boggle," he answered.

"It really is a great game," I said. "Can you see the Airstream from there?"

"Not real good," Snout said. "Griselda?"

"Most of it," Griselda said. "Some of his men are shifting to that area."

"Mr. Morales and Tommy are in the Airstream," I said. "They're going to need cover."

"They need to get their butts out of there," Snout said.

Bobby nodded at me. We headed to the other side of the house.

At the side door, my phone rang. I looked at the number. Mexico. I knew who it was. I hoped this was the news I had been waiting to hear.

"Radical?" I said as a greeting.

"It's done," he said. "I saw Pepe. The business is done. Is that gunfire?"

"Díaz is here," I said. "Is there anything else I need to know?"

"It won't come back to you," Radical said. "Fernando Palomera died in a tragic accident. Kill Díaz if you get the chance."

I was about to thank him, but he had already hung up. Nothing else to chat about. Message delivered.

Hearing that the man that I had requested to be killed had been killed was a little more real than I had expected the news to be. I thought I would be relieved, but I had already begun to question the decision.

"What? What is it?" Bobby asked. "We got to get to Mr. Morales."

"Fernando Palomera is dead," I said. "Pepe did it."

"Fucking A," Bobby said. "Good news, right?"

"It means it's over," I said. "We just have to wait for Díaz to hear the news. Then he should call off his men."

"Call him and tell him."

"He has to hear it on his own. Or else I'm admitting that I was involved. It has to be an accident. We got Palomera off our back. We don't want the cartel looking for revenge. This is our chance to end it."

The gunfire died down outside. From a barrage to stray shots. My phone rang again. I looked at the number.

"That didn't take long," I said. "It's Díaz."

Bobby nodded toward the phone. I answered it.

"You calling to surrender?" I said.

"Fernando Palomera is dead," Díaz said. "He choked on a shrimp."

Pepe was more creative than I would have given him credit for. Death by shellfish sounds like a cozy mystery title. Apparently nuance was one of the weapons in El Bárbaro's arsenal.

"Tragic news," I said. "I'll light a candle in church on Sunday."

"The timing is suspicious," he said. "Men like Palomera do not die that way."

"Nobody is immune to choking," I said. "What happens now? We're done, right? With Palomera dead, there's no reason for you to be here. No reason for you to try to get my son. I'm willing to call it a draw. Head our separate ways."

Porfirio Díaz laughed. He laughed until he started coughing uncontrollably.

Fuck.

TWENTY-TWO

Porfirio Díaz hawked a loogie after a coughing fit that lasted a half minute. Chuckles bubbled out of his heavy breathing, then a few groans of pain. I should have hung up on him, but I listened to his whole mad scientist impersonation.

"It's good to laugh," he said, catching a breath. "The job can be so serious. I miss laughing."

"Like I give a shit," I said. "It's time for you to pack up and head back to Mexico. You got no more business here."

"El Loco is dead, but that doesn't mean that I'm done."

"Juan was your target," I said. "Palomera wanted him. What could you possibly want from me and my family?"

"I'd been holding these men back because of the child. Now that that no longer matters, I'm going to crush you."

"That doesn't make sense," I said. "There's no upside for you."

"You made it personal."

"I made it—what the fuck are you talking about?"

"You shot me with an arrow," he said.

"Rub some butter on it."

"I'm going to be a barrio legend for this shit. In a month or two, they'll say I got shot with ten arrows. Men will sing corridos about me."

"Then I did you a favor," I said. "A regular Saint Sebastian."

"I can't let you shoot me with an arrow and live," he said. "That would be ridiculous. I'm going to kill you. I'm going to kill your wife. And your kid. I'm going to kill Tomás Morales. And everyone in that house. I'm going to burn your house to the ground and piss on the ashes."

I felt my face get hot enough to make my cheeks hurt. My jaw clenched. My hands shook. I had no idea how to respond to that direct a threat to everyone I cared about.

Bobby's face was near mine, doing his best to listen. "Fuck this guy. The time for talking is done. It's time to kick ass," he said, and pointed upward as "Pure Rock Fury" by Clutch blasted from above. Like the song seconded his motion.

I took a breath, attempting to release some of my rage. The best way to lose a fight was to get angry. Reason. I would try reason. Fighting was on the table, but diplomacy was always the first option.

"Murdering an American family is the kind of thing that would be frowned upon by your bosses. Cartel violence on Americans always brings the hammer down from DEA and Feds. That couldn't be good for you."

"You're right," he said. "Send your friends and family out. I'll let them go untouched. This is between you and me. And me and Tomás Morales."

He didn't even try to make his lie sound like anything but a lie. I covered the phone with my hand and turned to Bobby. "Get on the walkie. Tell Buck Buck, Snout, and Griselda that we ain't playing anymore. Anyone makes a move toward the house, shoot the fucker. Shoot them dead."

"They're about to see how we wage war in the Imperial Valley," Bobby said, and headed into the other room to relay the message.

I put the phone back to my ear. "You promise that you'll let them through?"

"Scout's honor."

"My kid's in the Scouts. He has more honor than you, and he's eight," I said. "I know you're lying."

"Most definitely." He laughed. "I thought it would be funny. To see your reaction."

"You're about as funny as Carrot Top on a—"

A loud crash interrupted me—which was for the best, because I had no punch line for the end of that sentence.

I pocketed the phone and rushed back toward the living room, where I heard a loud thud and shattered glass. Bobby got there at the same time.

The front half of a black SUV protruded into the living room through the large picture window. The plywood boards had been thrown halfway across the room. The car would have driven straight through the room into the kitchen if the back axle hadn't gotten caught on the planter beds and the lip of the window.

"Eat lead," Bobby said, and fired two shots from his shotgun.

The windshield pebbled but didn't shatter. It made visibility inside the vehicle impossible. I held up a hand. Bobby nodded but didn't lower his shotgun, finger staying on the trigger.

"I always wanted to say that," Bobby said. "It felt pretty good."

Cautiously approaching the vehicle from the passenger side, I held my pistol tightly in two hands like the movie cops taught me to do. Bobby approached from the driver's side. I mouthed "one, two"—we opened the doors simultaneously, guns poised.

The SUV was empty. I took a quick look into the backseat. Nothing. Bobby reached inside and turned off the ignition.

Through the back windshield, I saw three men rushing at our position. I fired a couple shots in their general direction, not bothering to aim. One dove to the ground. The other two scattered out of sight.

"Fucking shit, Jimmy!" Bobby shouted, backing out of the car with a hand to his ear. "Never shoot a gun in a car. I can't hear shit now."

"Sorry," I said, my ears ringing. "I missed the *Afterschool Special* that taught that lesson."

Buck Buck's voice rose from the walkie-talkie. "Holy shit. It's like *Saving Private Ryan* out here."

Gunfire erupted outside. A lot of gunfire. It was impossible to tell where it was coming from. It sounded like it was coming from everywhere.

"Get low," Buck Buck said. "Get down. They're shooting everything at us."

"They're trying to kill the house," Snout added.

"They must have watched *The Gauntlet* recently," Bobby said.

"Classic," Snout said. "Over and out."

The funny thing was that if Buck Buck hadn't told me, I would have had no idea that anyone was shooting at the house. I wasn't standing in some shitbox made in three weeks out of drywall and aluminum studs. My grandfather might not have known what he was doing when he built this house, but that just meant that he overdid it. When you don't know how to tie a knot, you just keep knotting. They could shoot all day at the thick plaster and stucco walls. It would take a howitzer to make a dent. Like trying to dig a hole in the sidewalk with a shovel. The plaster swallowed bullets. When this was over, a little Spackle and paint and the house would be like new.

"We're fucking standing around," Bobby said. "We need to get in this scrap." He talked into his walkie. "Gris. Where do Jimmy and I need to be?"

"Mr. Morales is still exposed. We need to get him in the house."

"Can you see Tommy?" I asked. "Is Mr. Morales still in the Airstream?"

"I don't know," she said. "I'm mostly shooting at people. I've lost track. If they light up that trailer, they'll turn the aluminum into swiss cheese."

"What about Joaquin and Rufus?"

"Don't know about the dog, but Joaquin crossed the canal. He's in the cornfield fighting from the perimeter."

"I'll get Mr. Morales," I said.

"The hell," Bobby said. "Go and be with your family. I'll do it."

"Mr. Morales is family, too," I said. "That fucking car created the only way into the house. They're going to try to use the opening. You need to be here to shoot every fucker that tries."

"That's still waiting," Bobby said. "Outside is fighting. I hate waiting. I want fighting."

"You won't be waiting long," I said. "We can't let them inside. You're our best fighter. This is where you need to be."

"You're right," Bobby said. "I am our best fighter."

Bobby held the shotgun to the SUV, waiting for the first unlucky son of a bitch to try to climb through. I booked toward the side of the house. The shotgun blast behind me told me that Bobby didn't have to wait long.

Stepping outside through the side door into the backyard, I immediately felt exposed. Being outside meant that a bullet could come from any angle. And the gunfire was ten times louder. It was like taking off headphones and realizing that I was in a battlefield.

I considered running back inside. I wanted to be with Angie and Juan, but everyone that was helping me was here out of no other obligation than friendship. Mr. Morales was risking his life to fight at my side. I owed him the same.

I got down on my hands and knees and slid through the small opening under the wall. The sharp edges scraped my back, but I kept moving. On the other side, I sat jammed up against the root base of a giant tussock of pampas grass. The sharp blades of the plant sliced my arms, papercutting the shit out of me. I bit the inside of my cheek to avoid squealing.

With my body folded in an awkward position, I readjusted as best I could. Using my face as leverage against the plant, I pushed myself to my feet. If I looked like Jonah Hex the next day, I'd know why.

Through the tall grass, the Airstream sat twenty feet in front of me. To my right, four of Díaz's men approached cautiously. The sun had completely set, but ambient light from the car headlights helped me make out their silhouettes. The gunfire and a small explosion allowed me to move without worrying about being heard.

I whispered into the walkie. "Gris, four men east of the Airstream. Can you see them?"

"I can just make them out. Where are you?"

"In the sawgrass against the fence."

"Fight from there so I don't accidentally shoot you. I can see figures, but I can't differentiate them."

One of Díaz's men fell to the ground. Only one of the other men seemed to notice.

"Was that you?" I asked.

"Was what me?"

Another man fell to the ground. This time I saw the arrow. I had no idea when Mr. Morales became Woody Strode in *The Professionals*, but it suited him.

The two men still on their feet opened fire on the Airstream. Rapid-fire UZIs or some other movie villain weapons. The sound of the guns competed with the pings and ricochets of the bullets piercing the thin metal. The aluminum couldn't have given much resistance, the bullets flying straight through.

I fired my pistol from behind the tall plants. Aiming for the body, I hit one of the men in the thigh. I'd never been that good a shot, but I was still going to blame the darkness.

The other guy whipped around toward me, firing the whole time. I dropped to the ground, eating dirt and cutting my face more. The pampas grass above me got mowed by the barrage.

"Fuck!" I screamed about ten times. And then it was quiet—well, not quiet because of all the other gunfire, but the one guy had stopped firing.

When I finally got the balls to look, I watched Tomás slide himself out from underneath the Airstream. Dirt mixed with the blood on his face to create a strange camouflage.

"Thanks, Jimmy," Tomás said, "but me and my abuelito had it covered."

"Where's Mr. Morales?"

"Up here," Mr. Morales said, waving from the top of the Airstream. He was flat on his belly.

"You two, both of you," I said. "Need to get on the other side of the wall. They're coming at us hard."

"These punks are nothing," Mr. Morales said. "Biggest danger for me is breaking my hip when I try to get down."

"Fernando Palomera is dead," I said. "Díaz isn't after Juan anymore. He's trying to kill all of us. Get inside."

"He's been trying to kill me for weeks," Tomás said. "I'm done hiding."

"Seriously, how do I get down from here?" Mr. Morales said. "I don't remember how I got up here."

I smelled smoke. Flames rose from somewhere near the front of the house.

"Angie and Juan," I said.

"Go," Mr. Morales said. "My grandson and me. We will protect each other. And we'll take care of these punks. Now find me a ladder, nietecito."

It was hard to miss an SUV on fire when it was parked halfway into your living room. Black smoke billowed from the back windows, quickly filling the room. The fire had spread into one corner of the living room. Plaster might not burn, but the curtains, wall, bookcase, and lounger in the corner fueled flames that rose to the ceiling.

Bobby stood at the side of the SUV, one hand shielding his face from the flames. A bandana covered his mouth and nose.

"Where did the fire come from?" I asked.

"Molotov cocktails," Bobby said. "They went old school."

"We got to get this fucking thing out of here!" I shouted.

"No shit," Bobby said.

With the fire mostly in the back of the car where the Molotov cocktail must have landed, Bobby reached inside and started the engine. He leaned back out, coughing and blinking the smoke out of his eyes.

"Fuck me!" he shouted. "Find me something heavy."

I grabbed the heaviest thing in the room, my hardcover copy of William T. Vollmann's 1,300-page masturbpiece *Imperial*. I handed the overwritten opus to Bobby. I had no plans to finish reading the last 950 pages anyway.

Bobby jammed the brick-shaped tome onto the gas pedal and threw the SUV in reverse. The engine roared, and the tires spun, not quite catching any ground. Bobby came around to the front. We pushed, rocking it back and forth until the burning SUV got free and backed wildly toward the other cars in the driveway. It crashed against the closest vehicle.

"Water," I said. "Fire extinguisher. Something. I got to put this out. My fucking house is on fire."

"Plan B, bro," Bobby said. "The fucking house is fucked."

"But it's my house."

"Sorry, man. We can't stay. All of us got to get the fuck out of here."

"Did we have a plan B?"

"I'll come up with one," he said. "Get your family."

I watched the fire burn out of control. The only good thing was that the giant opening the SUV had made was now impassable due to the flames. The fiery lining on the shit cloud.

I got on the walkie. "Gris, Buck Buck, Snout. The house is on fire. It's out of control. Meet up in the backyard."

"Fuck!" Bobby yelled.

"What? What is it?"

"My mixtape. It ain't playing no more. Fuckers must have fucked it up."

"You can play it for me later," I said. "I'll get Angie and Juan. You try to concoct a foolproof plan by the time I get out back."

"Will do, but no guarantee that it won't involve explosives," Bobby said. "In fact, I can almost guarantee it will involve explosives."

"At this point, I don't care," I said. "Let's blow the assholes up."

At the basement door. Shave and a haircut. Angie opened it. Juan stood a few steps down, holding her hand. He cried uncontrollably, his face red and wet. He looked lost.

"I smelled smoke," Angie said. "How bad is it?"

I shook my head. I didn't have the heart to say that the house was most likely going to burn down. "Wrap some wet towels over your face until we're outside."

"What's the plan?"

But I barely heard her. I concentrated on Juan's scared face. He blinked the tears from his eyes, staring at me with fear and confusion.

"Do you trust me, Juan?" I asked him.

He nodded.

"You do everything that Mom and I tell you to do, and things are going to be fine."

He nodded again, maybe believing half of that. I'd take what I could get.

"What are we doing?" Angie asked. "Where are we going?"

"Bobby's working on it."

"I'm trusting you," she said. "Let's get out of here."

We hurried to the back door.

"I would've thought Bobby coming up with the plan would have raised some objections," I said.

"I'm so far out of my element," she said. "You guys are better at stupid plans than me."

Bobby and Griselda were already in the backyard by the time we got there. The sound of gunfire had died down, a few shots here and there, not the full-out war from before. With us in the backyard, I suppose there was less to shoot at. The smell of smoke filled the air, but it was easier to breathe outside. We held handkerchiefs, towels, and pillowcases over our mouths, eyes watering.

"Wait for me at the back wall," I said to Angie. "It should be easier to breathe. Stay low. You got your gun?"

She nodded.

"I'll go with you," Griselda said. "You don't have to do this alone."

I dropped to a knee, holding Juan's shoulders. "Stay with Mom, okay? She's got you."

He nodded, eyes watering not just from the smoke. How much could an eight-year-old endure? How bad was this screwing him up?

Juan took Angie's hand. Griselda followed. They walked through the smoke to the far end of the backyard, sitting on the ground with their backs against the wall. Angie whispered in Juan's ear. He smiled a little bit, nodding, but his body still shook from crying.

On the roof, Buck Buck and Snout pivoted like human tank turrets in their blinds, looking for targets. They made robot sounds with their mouths to match their movement. Buck Buck fired a shot. He turned to Snout and said, "That's five."

"Hey!" I shouted up to them.

They both turned to me, smiling and waving. They looked like they were headed out on a transatlantic cruise, not in the middle of a gun battle.

"Hey, Jimmy. How you doing?" Snout asked. "We been shooting up a storm."

"I told you guys to get down. The house is on fire."

"You can't end on a tie!" Snout shouted back.

"Don't worry, boss," Buck Buck said. "We ain't killed no one. Legs and arms mostly."

"What's it look like out there?" I asked.

"Mostly dark," Buck Buck said, "but from what I can see, getting shot took the fight out of a lot of them. They're scattered. Some got in their cars and split. The ones still fighting, they mean to earn their paycheck."

"You guys kicked some serious ass today," Bobby said.

"Get your asses down from there!" I shouted. "Bobby's got a plan B."

"Cover me, brother," Buck Buck said.

Snout fired into the yard, still making robot sounds as he turned. Buck Buck climbed out of his blind and slid down the terra cotta tile to the edge of the roof. From there he dropped himself down. He was surprisingly graceful for a big, dumb guy.

"Your turn, Snouter," Buck Buck said. "Make it snappy."

Snout stood to follow. It was probably my imagination or a retroactive memory, but the shot that hit Snout sounded louder than the others. The sight of Snout's body buckling in the middle and the look of surprise on his face made me cringe. Not pain, but insult.

"Oh, fuck," Bobby said.

Snout swayed and fell over the top of the blind. He slid down the terra cotta tiles on his side, a half dozen of the tiles coming with him. Bobby and I ran to catch him, the tiles raining down on us. They thumped against my head and shoulders. Bobby and I managed to break Snout's fall but didn't quite catch him. We all hit the ground awkwardly, Snout on top of us.

"Teddy!" Buck Buck yelled, running to join us. For a second, I didn't know who he was referring to.

"Careful," I said to Bobby as he braced Snout's neck and turned him on his back.

"It hurts," Snout said, confused.

Shot in the gut. His shirt was already soaked in blood.

"No, no, no!" Buck Buck screamed. He pushed me to the side and shook his brother's shoulders. Bobby put a hand on his shoulder, but Buck Buck knocked it away. Buck Buck cried openly, pulling Snout to him. "Teddy."

"Quit shaking me, dumbass," Snout said. "That hurts more."

"Angie!" I screamed, waving her over. She glanced at Juan. Griselda said something to her.

Angie ran to Snout and immediately used the towel she had been breathing through to put pressure on the wound.

Buck Buck turned to me. "I don't understand, Jimmy. What's happening? Why would someone shoot Teddy?"

TWENTY-THREE

With the house my grandfather built burning out of control behind me, I walked out the back gate and onto the four-foot swath between the wall and the canal. Across the canal was a dirt ditch bank and then the field of sweet corn behind it. With most of us behind the house, the gunfire had died down. I didn't see any of Díaz's men out back. I waved everyone to follow.

Bobby and Buck Buck carried Snout as carefully as they could, Angie maintaining pressure on the wound. Griselda followed, carrying Juan and yelling into her phone. Juan cried freely, but as painful as it was, there was nothing I could do but watch.

"I don't care," Griselda said into her phone. "I don't care. I got a man shot here. If you don't get an ambulance out here now, I will come over there and fuck you up, Ted. I will fuck you up." She listened and hung up. "They're sending someone now, but you live in the middle of nowhere. At least twenty minutes."

"Where are we going?" Angie asked. "We can't move Snout much more. I need to get him stable, stop the bleeding."

"The cornfield is the only cover," I said. "Not exactly the cleanest place. Might be the filthiest, but you should be safe."

"Doesn't matter," Angie said. "Let's just get there."

"I'm fine," Snout mumbled. "I want to keep shooting at people."

"You'll shoot more people soon," Buck Buck said.

I dug in the dirt near the wall, locating the two-by-six boards we had hidden. I grabbed one. Griselda set Juan down and lifted the other one. We stood them straight up and let them fall to the other side, creating a span across the canal.

"Gris?" Angie said. "Do you have a tampon?"

The men all looked at each other, the timing weird and awkward.

Griselda reached in her front pocket and tossed Angie a small bullet-shaped object. Angie caught it, took it out of its wrapper, and jammed it in Snout's bullet wound. Snout screamed.

"Goddamn," Snout said. "You could have warned me."

"You're a big girl," Angie said. "Be careful carrying him over. It's going to be awkward."

Bobby backed up onto the boards. As he put his foot down, Buck Buck froze and gasped.

Rufus had poked his head from the cornfield. We all jumped. In the darkness, his monster head looked demonic, eyes glowing. The big dog emerged from the stalks.

"Dang," Buck Buck said. "Scared the poo out of me."

Joaquin followed behind Rufus, as nonchalant as ever. He walked to the canal edge, leaned down, and stabilized the other end of the board. Bobby walked backward over the board.

As they slowly crossed, the boards sagged in the middle from the weight of three men. Buck Buck swayed for a moment but righted himself.

"He's slipping," Buck Buck said. "My fingers are slipping."

"It's not far," Bobby said. "You drop him, he dies."

"No pressure, brother," Snout said.

Rufus barked. I turned in time to see a man settling into a crouch against the wall behind us, drawing down a rifle in our direction. I got my body between him and Juan and turned to shoot, but before I could, Tomás appeared from nowhere and tackled the man.

"Keep moving!" I shouted at Bobby and Buck Buck. They picked up their steps across the boards.

"I got them," Griselda said, pushing me and taking my place in front of Juan and Angie. "Help him."

I ran to help Tomás, but he didn't need it. By the time I got there, the guy on the ground was motionless and Tomás held a bloody rock. He tossed it to the side, looked at me, and walked back toward the front yard.

"Where's Mr. Morales?" I asked. "Where's your grandfather?"

He didn't answer.

When I got back to the makeshift bridge, Bobby and Buck Buck had made it across the canal. They carefully carried Snout into the cornfield, disappearing into the nearest row.

Angie carried Juan over the boards and joined them. She turned before disappearing. Juan gave a halfhearted wave, but he was clearly in shock. Angie mouthed, "I fucking love you."

"I fucking love you, too," I said.

Joaquin guided them into the cornfield. Rufus scanned the area one last time, nose sniffing the air. He followed Angie and Juan.

Griselda and I waited back-to-back, ready to defend against any new threat. Half a minute later, Buck Buck and Bobby walked out of the cornfield. Buck Buck took a step onto the board to cross, but Bobby put a hand on his shoulder.

"Stay with Snout," Bobby said. "Stay with your brother."

"I can't stand when Snout gets hurt," Buck Buck said. "I get so scared."

"You need to look after Angie and Juan, too," I said. "Protect them for me."

Buck Buck nodded and returned to the cornfield. At the edge of the stalks, he turned back.

"Hurt them," he said.

"Oh, you fucking A bet we will," Bobby said.

"Snout's going to want the play-by-play later."

"We won't leave out a thing," I said.

Buck Buck blew a snot rocket out of one nostril and disappeared into the field.

Bobby loaded more shells into his shotgun as he crossed back over the canal to join me and Griselda. He racked a shell into the chamber. "You ready for this, baby?"

"I'm ready," Griselda said.

"I was asking Jimmy," Bobby said, winking and smiling.

I hated leaving Angie and Juan, but it was time to finish this shit. They were in good hands. Joaquin, Rufus, and Buck Buck wouldn't let anything happen to them. I trusted them completely.

It was just as hard to leave Snout. I didn't know a lot about gunshot wounds, but he did not look good. His blood still covered my clothes. I had fought side by side with the Buckleys so many times, been in so much danger, and yet we had always treated ourselves as invulnerable. We had gotten hurt plenty, but never anything that a stiff drink didn't cure.

This fight was for everything. A real fight with real consequences. And it was time to end it for tonight and forever. Snout wasn't the comedy relief in my life. He was family, and Díaz was about to learn what we did for family in the Imperial Valley.

Bobby, Griselda, and I walked through the black smoke toward the front of the house. We all wielded shotguns. Ash, blood, and dirt stained our skin and torn clothes, a postapocalyptic trio straight out of a B-movie trailer. If Bobby's mixtape had still been playing, this was when "Rock You" by Helix or some equally anthemy hair metal song would have kicked in. The Blue Angels might as well have flown over our heads at that moment. You could put eagles on our shoulders. We were America incarnate, ready to kick some fucking ass.

The house was now an inferno, the front half lost in flames. The light of the fire illuminated the entire scene. It looked like a battlefield, which I suppose it was. We walked past a couple of Díaz's men on the ground. No threat, moaning or cradling wounds or too exhausted to move. Others remained completely motionless. I didn't check any pulses, but there was going to be a body count when this was over. The score would be tallied at the end of the game.

We walked around the side of the house, heading toward the front yard. With the Airstream just ahead of us, I stopped and pointed for Bobby and Griselda to spread out. Bullet holes had punctured the trailer on all sides, the small windows shattered.

I pointed to the side door with Bobby and Griselda on either side of me. Keeping my back to the trailer and my shotgun at the ready, I poked my head in and out of the open door. It took me a second to process what I had seen. When I had, I rushed into the trailer.

Mr. Morales lay faceup on the small bed. His eyes were closed. Leave it to Mr. Morales to take a nap in the middle of a firefight. The plexiglass on the floor crunched under my feet as I approached.

"Mr. Morales?" I said, giving him a shake. "Nestor?"

I shook him harder. No response. I took his pulse.

Bobby and Griselda were at the door.

"What is it?" Bobby asked. "Is he—?"

I nodded. "Yeah. Mr. Morales is dead."

"What? Shot?"

I gave a quick examination of his clothes. No blood. No signs of trauma. Even his facial expression lacked any sign of pain or surprise.

"It doesn't look like it," I said. "I don't know."

"Fuck," Bobby said, walking away.

I sat on the edge of the small bed, staring at Mr. Morales. He couldn't be dead.

"You can mourn later," Griselda said. "We've got to go."

"Give me a minute," I said.

"We've got a fight to finish," she said.

"One fucking minute," I said, snapping at her.

She nodded and left me with Mr. Morales.

It wasn't until I realized that he was dead that I knew how much I had taken Mr. Morales for granted. Reliably across the street, he had been a constant in my life and the lives of everyone I cared about. Mr. Morales had acted as a grandfather to both me and Juan. I didn't know what life was going to be like without him as a part of it. I dreaded telling Juan. It would crush him.

A lot of the fight had drained out of me. For everything I had done, for all my intentions, Snout was laid out in a cornfield shot in the belly, and Mr. Morales was dead in a bullet-riddled Airstream. A big part of me just wanted to say fuck it. Walk in the other direction. Give up.

But that wasn't going to happen. I never fought because I wanted to. I fought because I had to. And this fight wasn't over yet.

I shook out a blanket and covered Mr. Morales's torso and face. It seemed like a thing that people did in that kind of situation.

"I'm going to miss you, old man," I said, and left to rejoin the battle.

Bobby marched toward the front yard, the butt of his shotgun at his shoulder, looking for a target. Griselda chased behind him. I lagged behind both of them, eventually catching up to Griselda.

"Sorry about snapping at you," I said.

"We're in the middle of a gunfight," Griselda said. "I think I can handle a harsh tone."

As Bobby neared the corner of the house, one of Díaz's men popped out from the other side of the wall.

"Look out!" I shouted.

The man fired his rifle and missed. Bobby returned fire, but the man had ducked back out of view. Griselda and I lifted our weapons and waited for him to emerge again, never losing stride. A second later, another shot fired and the man fell forward from behind the wall.

Bobby instinctively shot at the movement, striking the falling man. He performed an awkward spin before he hit the ground.

"Don't shoot," Tomás said, walking out with a hand in our direction, the barrel of his shotgun still smoking. He stood over the man on the ground and gave him a kick with the tip of his foot.

Bobby walked next to them, his eyes never leaving the direction of the front yard. "I didn't think you had any real fight in you, Morales. Thought you only gave orders, stayed behind the lines. But you're a little bit of a badass."

Tomás had already walked away a few steps by the time I caught up to them.

"Tommy," I said. "Wait up."

He stopped and turned.

"I found Mr. Morales," I said. "I'm sorry. What happened?"

"He came down from the trailer. Said he needed a rest. I left, and when I came back, he was in the trailer, dead. I don't know what killed him. Doesn't matter. Fuck the why."

"Damn, man," Bobby said. "I loved that fucking guy."

"Me, too," Tomás said. He walked back toward the front yard in search of more bloodshed.

The SUV that had battered into the house was now a black shell, smoking but no longer on fire. Two other cars burned. The remaining cars in the driveway and yard appeared abandoned. Doors flung open. A couple of Díaz's men lay scattered around the front yard.

"It's a hellscape," I said, not wanting to waste the opportunity to use the word "hellscape" literally rather than figuratively.

"If Díaz is gone," Tomás said, "we're going to have to do this all over again. He's the one that matters."

Tomás walked with purpose toward the middle of the yard.

"I'm calling you out, Díaz!" Tomás shouted. "You want to take Mexicali, step up and take it from me. Your rep won't mean shit if people learn you punked out."

From behind a car, Porfirio Díaz stood and fired a shot in Tomás's direction. He missed. Tomás broke toward the nearest tree, getting his back up against it.

Díaz climbed in the car, started it up, and attempted to maneuver out of the driveway. The SUV smoldered in front of him. Tomás approached from the side. Díaz was boxed in by the other cars behind him.

Díaz went in the only direction possible, driving over the front yard. He attempted to barrel through the enormous hedge that separated the yard from the street. I didn't know what kind of plant that hedge was, but I did know that I had never trimmed the thing in the five years that I had been back in the Imperial Valley. Even Joaquin, who was tireless and liked a challenge, had avoided the job. The hedge was essentially a giant, thick-limbed spider terrarium that gave people allergies by looking at it. Just the thought of that hedge made my arms itchy.

Díaz's car made it halfway into the hedge before the plant's density absorbed it. Caught in the roots and branches, appropriately like a spider in a web—seriously, that thing was filled with black widows and other nasties—the back end fishtailed but made no progress.

Tomás marched forward like a T-1000, guns drawn. It didn't look like he cared whether or not he won this battle, just so long as it was over that night.

Griselda, Bobby, and I followed twenty yards behind Tomás, our guns all aimed at Díaz's car.

"That guy should've thought about running earlier," Bobby said.

"I don't think he considered the possibility of losing this fight," I said. "It didn't sink in until too late."

Díaz's car got free of the hedge just as Tomás placed a hand on the trunk and pumped a round through the back window. The car fishtailed onto the road, kicking up branches and dust. Tomás covered his eyes with his hand, blinded by the dust. Blocked by cars on the road to the south, Díaz headed north.

Griselda, Bobby, and I caught up to Tomás. He rubbed his watery eyes, blinking out the dirt.

About a half mile away, headlights approached from the north, filling both lanes. A whole mess of cars. At least a dozen.

The lead car's red-and-blue light bar indicated it was law enforcement or an ambulance. The cavalry had finally arrived. I guessed it was Ceja Carneros. I might finally be able to forgive him for that time he knocked out my tooth.

The four of us walked abreast of each other, like the poster for a Western movie. With the cars coming right at him, Porfirio Díaz stopped and attempted to make a U-turn on the narrow road. I could have told him the shoulder had become a mess from water and gopher holes, but he didn't ask. The soft dirt swallowed his tires, spinning and sinking him deeper in the silty quicksand.

Tomás, Griselda, Bobby, and I lifted our shotguns in unison, almost in range of his car. I held my finger on the trigger. We were fifty yards away.

Díaz managed to get the car out of the soft dirt. Back on the road, he headed in our direction on a collision course. The car accelerated.

"Not yet," Tomás said.

The car gained speed, the glare of the headlights blinding me as they approached.

I felt the shotgun shake in my hands. It was probably the weight of the thing, not my terror. Probably.

"Aim low," Tomás said. "Now."

We all fired simultaneously at the speeding car. The sound of the shotguns drowned out the sound of his front tires exploding. The car swerved left and right. Twenty yards in front of us, the car drove straight into the empty concrete ditch across the street. After the loud crash, the horn honked. A head on the steering wheel.

Tomás walked forward a few steps and turned to the three of us. "Let me take care of him."

"No way," Griselda said. "He's under arrest."

"I'm not going to kill him," Tomás said. "I can't. If he's alive, I have leverage. I can maybe work out a deal with the cartel. For me, but more importantly for Jimmy and his family. In an American jail, he's still dangerous. In my hands, I can control the situation."

"He could be dead right now," Griselda said.

"If he's dead, you can arrest him," Tomás said.

I turned to Griselda. "If it's the best way to keep Juan and Angie safe, we have to trust Tommy."

"I don't trust him," she said. "That's the thing."

"My grandfather died fighting the pendejo," Tomás said. "I want to kill him. I should kill him. But I can't. It's not the right thing to do. At least, not yet."

I looked up. The approaching headlights were only a quarter mile away.

"Blame me for everything that happened," Tomás said. "Any bodies, put them on me. Drug war gone bad. Whatever story you need me to tell. Jimmy and everybody else, they're bystanders. Make me the villain. Put me on the most wanted list."

"I trust him," I said to Griselda. "There are plenty of people to arrest. We need to get Snout to a doctor. If there's a chance he can end this, we need to take it."

The car horn stopped blaring. Tomás turned and ran toward the car without waiting for permission.

"Fuck," Gris said. "Okay."

"Thanks, Gris," I said.

Bobby gave her a quick kiss. "It was the right thing to do, baby."

Bobby and I fast-walked to catch up to Tomás. The trunk of the car pointed almost straight in the air. Circling around, we found the front door wide open. The car was empty. I looked up and down the ditch. Nothing.

"He's headed into the wheat," Bobby said.

"Wheat Field War?" I asked.

"I haven't thought of that in years," Bobby said. "Fuck yeah."

"Like when we were kids," Tomás said. He pointed at Bobby. "You're John Riggins. I'm Earl Campbell. Jimmy, that makes you Franco Harris."

"I'm surprised you remember," I said.

"I don't forget good things," Tomás said. "You remember how it works."

"Like yesterday," Bobby said. "I'll Riggo the shit out of this guy."

"He's leverage," Tomás said, flipping his shotgun around and holding it by the barrel. "We need him alive." He swung it in the air, feeling the weight of his new bludgeon.

Bobby did the same. We looked at each other as if there was more to say, but there wasn't. Bobby and Tomás walked into the wheat field.

I checked on Griselda. She stood in the middle of the road and flagged down the approaching cars. I recognized many of the vehicles. Friends and acquaintances, people from town that had come to the country to help, because help was needed. A couple lowriders, a lot of pickup trucks, a taco truck, and one Baja bug. Ceja's patrol car led the way.

Griselda flagged him down. When Ceja got out of the car, I gave him a wave and took off toward the field. He gave me a puzzled look, but that was his resting expression.

I headed around the perimeter. I shouldn't have been smiling, but it had been a while since I'd been in an official Wheat Field War.

When you're a kid on a farm, boredom is the mother of invention. I had often lit things on fire or exploded other things for the fuck of it. That's bored-alone stuff, though. When friends came to visit and all the dirty jokes had been told, an invented game of violence was a great way to kill an evening.

Wheat Field War was created when I found a box of long wooden dowels in my pop's woodshop. They probably had some other use, but at three feet long and a quarter inch in diameter, they made perfect swords. They beat the shit out of wrapping paper tubes, that's for sure. Wheat Field War was born. There weren't any rules, per se. Two teams chased each other through the wheat at night, smacking each other with the dowels at every opportunity. It was ball-shrinkingly terrifying to be in any field at night. Country dark and full of skittering sounds. Ten times worse when someone jumped out of a row and welted your arm with a sharp smack of wood. Half the times I had pissed myself in my life had been during a Wheat Field War.

I couldn't remember why the Wheat Field War maneuvers were named after our favorite running backs. Each name represented a different pattern or approach to the battle. Riggins, like its namesake, was straight ahead, row by row. Earl Campbell moved forward in a crisscross pattern. And Franco Harris circled around the other side and moved across back rows. By combining all three patterns, the three of us could cover a lot of ground, making it difficult to hide.

The wheat wasn't nearly as high as the corn in the field across the way, so it was easier to catch movement. The dark made detection difficult, but to be completely out of view, you'd have to duck low. You can get lost in corn, but not wheat. Needlepoint that on a pillow.

Díaz had made a critical error when he fled into the field, although he could not have known how experienced the three of us were at fighting in a wheat field. In his defense, it was a very specific skill that few people shared.

Tomás and Bobby ran their patterns in the wheat field. Bobby cawed like a crow every thirty seconds. Mind game or signal, I had no idea what he was trying to communicate, but I knew it was him. We didn't have crows in the desert.

I booked around to the other side. When Franco Harrising, the key was to make sure no one exited out the back. I needed to keep Díaz from getting out of the field. Or catch him when he did.

Even though I had quit smoking, I still wasn't much of a runner. The short sprint to the dirt road on the other side of the field made me queasy. My heart beat in my head like a Philthy Animal drum solo. I promise-lied to myself for the thousandth time that this would be the year that I got in shape.

With the ditch bank slightly elevated, I had a decent view of the top of the wheat field. If I got on my toes, I could see even farther. A bigger moon would have been helpful, but the stars and ambient light from my burning home gave me some light to work with. With no wind, I figured I should be able to spot any movement. We had never used flashlights when we had played as kids, but I wished I had one at that moment.

It wasn't the most dignified move, but I hopped along the dirt road, eyes peeled for Díaz. I alternated the hopping with walking on tiptoes like a damn ballerina. I never took my eyes off the field. I listened for any sounds, eventually hearing a faint crunch of wheat.

Right in front of me, I caught movement. The wheat shifted unnaturally. Not a gust or an animal, but displaced to the side in a way that could have only been something moving forward. I followed Tomás's lead and held my shotgun by the barrel. I moved toward the perimeter, planted my feet, and waited for Díaz to emerge.

The moment I saw an arm, I leapt.

I missed braining Bobby with the shotgun by about a quarter inch, hitting him in the shoulder. He punched me in the throat, so even Steven. My forward momentum knocked us both to the ground. Rolling off Bobby, I gagged and coughed, unable to catch my breath.

"I guess we're a bit rusty at this," Bobby said. "You okay?"

Obviously not, because I couldn't speak. I shook my head.

Then I saw Díaz. I pointed and gasped not-words in his direction. He had emerged from the field fifteen yards up the road. Bobby's back was to him. Díaz held his pistol at his side.

Díaz spotted us just as Bobby turned. Neither Bobby nor I had time to draw our weapons. Díaz smiled and aimed his gun in our direction, walking to us slowly.

"Fucking farmers," he said.

"The Fucking Farmers was the name of my short-lived punk-abilly band," Bobby said.

"You—"

Díaz never got a chance to finish that thought. A rock flew out from the field and hit him just above the ear. He stumbled to the side, his legs buckling. The pistol fired when he hit the ground.

Díaz tried to stand, his feet wobbly underneath him, but Tomás was out of the field and on the bigger man. He yanked Díaz's gun from his hand and tossed it into the field. Tomás spit in Díaz's face and then proceeded to hit his shoulder over and over again. Right in the spot where Mr. Morales had struck him with an arrow. Tomás's hand was soon red with the downed man's blood. Díaz passed out from the pain, woke up from the pain, and then passed out again. Tomás never stopped hitting the man's arrow wound. It was brutal.

Finally, Tomás stood and caught his breath. He patted down Porfirio Díaz to check for any additional weapons.

Bobby and I walked to them. The three of us stood over Díaz. As an unconscious pile of muscles and wounds, the man looked weaker, less intimidating. All bullies' fate. How quickly power could be taken away. Sometimes all it took was a well-thrown rock.

With Díaz defeated, my thoughts turned to Angie and Juan. They were all that mattered. All that ever mattered. I ran down the dirt road back toward the house. That's where I needed to be.

"I'm trusting you, Tommy," I said over my shoulder. "End this."

TWENTY-FOUR

The cemetery parking lot was full of mud-covered pickups, cars, and a couple tractors. More vehicles lined Evan Hewes Highway almost to the prison. Half the Imperial Valley had come to pay their respects to the late Nestor Morales. Hundreds of people whose lives Mr. Morales had had an impact on and, if I overheard correctly, a few that just wanted to make sure that he was dead.

It was one of those rare days in the Imperial Valley where the weather hit its sweet spot. Floating around eighty degrees with scattered clouds and a slight breeze. Cold beer and swimming-in-the-canal weather. There would be a crowd at Mossy Slides or down at the Highline. A new generation of kids shooting the tubes or waterskiing in the canal, being pulled by a pickup on the bank.

I walked with Angie and Juan slowly through the cemetery, shaking hands and saying hello to the people I knew. Father Joe took me aside and asked me to say a few words. I told him that I didn't think I could get out any words and there were plenty of people that knew Mr. Morales longer and better than me.

"Nonsense, Jim," Father Joe said. "You'll do fine."

Tomás Morales was noticeably absent among Mr. Morales's relatives. Considering that he was wanted for questioning by every law enforcement agency in the United States, Tomás couldn't exactly act as a pallbearer. He had become the scapegoat for all the violence. The most believable part of our lie.

The final tally of the "Showdown at Rancho Veeder"—we still hadn't settled on a good name for the incident—ended at six dead, fourteen wounded, and twenty-two arrested. The police reports constructed by Griselda and Ceja were pure fiction worthy of Elmore Leonard. The story had been reported as a gang confrontation that started at Morales Bar between factions of Tomás's men and Díaz's men. The violence had bled over onto my property, ending in the destruction of my house and the deaths and injuries of many men.

I didn't know if the story would hold water, but the truth was equally ridiculous, which was to our advantage. The real test would be whether or not the insurance company bought it.

As soon as Tomás had subdued Porfirio Díaz, I returned to the house to be with my family. By the time I got there, Griselda was already in the process of getting medical attention for Snout, the ambulance having arrived soon after Ceja.

Seeing Angie and Juan walk out of that cornfield with Rufus by their side put a smile on my face that I didn't know I had left in me. Juan looked scared and confused, but it was over. He was safe, and we were together.

The three of us stood on the ditch bank and held each other. We barely noticed the clusterfuck of police, firemen, sheriffs, paramedics, curious onlookers, and future convicts that filled my property. The flames from the house rose to the height of the big pine. Smoke filled the air.

When Bobby eventually joined us, he gave me the full story. He and Tomás had dragged Díaz to Morales Bar and loaded his semiconscious body into Mr. Morales's car. Tomás drove away that easily. I waited for more details, but other than a brief message, that was it. It wasn't much of a story.

"Tell Jimmy," Tomás had told Bobby, "I'll do everything I can to keep him and his family free of the cartel. It's what my abuelito would have wanted, and it's taken me until he was dead to finally listen to the old man."

I had to trust Tomás. I had no other choice. I was putting my faith in a childhood friend turned crime lord. What could possibly go wrong with that plan?

Away from the gathering crowd at the cemetery, Angie, Juan, and I stopped at the gravesites of my parents and Yolanda Palomera. Juan put a bouquet of flowers on his mother's grave. I put flowers on my mother's grave and a paperback copy of *Fat City* on Pop's. I always brought him books that I thought he'd like. He wasn't a flowers type of guy.

It was coming on the fifth anniversary of my return to the Imperial Valley. The five years had seemed simultaneously like a week and an eternity. I had a clear memory of driving past the Salton Sea preparing to spend time with Pop during his last days. At the time, I had no plans to stay. Now I had a wife and son and roots. And no plans to leave.

I dropped to a knee next to Juan, putting my arm around him. Angie stood behind us with her hand on my shoulder. I brushed some dust off Pop's headstone.

"I'm doing my best, Pop," I said.

"You can't do more than that," Juan said.

Returning to the funeral, we found Bobby and Griselda at Mr. Morales's gravesite. Rows and rows of folding chairs surrounded the coffin and open grave. Bobby had saved seats for us behind the immediate family. We all hugged. I already had tears in my eyes.

Bobby gave me an elbow. I turned to see Joaquin pushing Snout in his tricked-out wheelchair with flames painted on the sides. Buck Buck cleared out a space for him, chucking a chair to the side. They both waved in our direction.

The first few days had been touch and go when they finally got Snout to the hospital, but they don't make living things tougher than the Snouter. The gunshot had torn through him and damaged some organs, but the doctors seemed to have figured that out. It was the damage to his neck and spine from the fall off the roof that put him in the wheelchair. It wasn't clear if that situation was temporary or permanent. Like everything, Snout took it in stride. No hard feelings.

With the house no longer livable, I had no work for Joaquin. We moved the damaged Airstream to Buck Buck and Snout's property. It wouldn't take long for Joaquin to spruce it back up. There wasn't nothing a little Bondo, baling wire, and spit couldn't fix. His new job was as temporary nurse and assistant to Snout. Snout was even teaching him Boggle, which was hilarious to watch. Snout's teaching method appeared to be mostly yelling in two languages at a smiling deaf man.

Rufus stayed with us. We brought him over to the Buckleys' with Joaquin, but two days later he was back. He was Juan's dog now—if he was anyone's. The two were inseparable. There had even been a brief argument before the funeral about Rufus attending. Juan and I thought he should be there. Angie nixed the idea. I wouldn't have been surprised if he had shown up on his own.

With the fighting done, Angie and I focused our attention on Juan. He had been shaken up by the whole escapade, and Mr. Morales's death still hit him hard. He had lost his mother so young, it didn't resonate as much. Mr. Morales's death was the first real loss he was fully processing. We made an appointment with a good counselor in San Diego. Once a week, Angie or I would drive him up there so that he could talk about his feelings. I didn't know how much good it would do, but between doing something and doing nothing, I only knew one choice. I prayed every night that I hadn't screwed him up.

The funeral began. After four of Mr. Morales's nieces sang a beautiful rendition of "Tragos Amargos," Father Joe gave him his official send-off. I had always liked Father Joe's sermons and his ability to combine personal anecdotes with religion. He hadn't just lost a member of his church. He had also lost a good friend. He led everyone in a prayer and on the word "Amen" he looked straight at me. I nodded. If Father Joe thought I should say something, I would.

"And now Nestor's friend and neighbor, James Veeder, would like to say a few words."

Angie gave me a kiss. I stood and walked to the podium, still unsure of what I was going to say. The microphone kicked feedback, I jumped, and everyone laughed. That helped to break the tension.

"Mr. Morales—I can't get myself to call him Nestor—was a constant in my life," I began. "Always there. Growing up across the street, I was often at his bar more than at home. The free sodas he gave me might have been a factor, but I know it was more than that. He accepted me as family, and I never thought of him as anything but.

"That doesn't mean that I didn't take him for granted. I'm ashamed to say that I did. Ashamed that it took me so long to see that most people don't have a person as selfless and loyal as Mr. Morales. Someone that's always watching out for them.

"Mr. Morales loved me. He loved my wife. And he loved my son. And we loved him.

"It's a long story, but I recently went down to Mexico looking for my son's grandfather. I didn't need to. He was already right here in the Imperial Valley. Right across the street.

"I'm going to miss the hell out of him. Just as I'm sure everyone here will. That's all I got. Thank you all for coming out."

The wake was, of course, at Morales Bar. Pop had met Yolanda there, which led to Juan's birth. I had met Yolanda there as well, which led to her death. Tomás and I played as children outside the bar, which set everything else in motion. For good or bad, Morales Bar was a focal point for the big events in my life.

When Mr. Morales's will had been found, it was revealed that he had left the bar to Juan. My eight-year-old son was now a publican.

To oversee the rebuild on the house, we had moved into Mr. Morales's place in the back. Mr. Morales took a lot of pride in never closing his bar. Angie and I made the decision to keep the business alive. Morales Bar would remain open for all your alcoholic needs. Angie took a leave of absence from her nursing job and embraced her role as bartender, and it was fun to be doing it together. Bobby helped out. We paid him in beer. I didn't plan on making any changes, except in the jukebox. It needed considerably more Tony Joe White and Jerry Reed on it.

Laws be damned, I let Juan serve the drinks at the wake. It was his bar, and he loved interacting with the customers. When he finally had to cut off Ceja, it was a showstopper. If you haven't seen an eight-year-old bartender tell an eight-year-old (mentally) police officer that he's had too much to drink, you're missing out on some classic comedy.

There was nothing somber about the evening. It was truly a celebration of a man we all loved and respected. A man who had impacted all our lives.

A few hours and five beers into the wake, I saw a familiar figure at the back door of Morales Bar. Not someone I had ever expected to see again. Little Piwi filled the doorframe. I hadn't seen him since Mexico. He nodded me over. I grabbed an empty bottle off the bar, pretended to drink it, and followed him outside. A bottle wasn't much of a weapon, but I wanted something in my hand.

Tomás stood in the shadows of the abandoned cockfight pit. Mr. Morales hadn't used it in years, but it still had that cockfight pit smell.

"Thanks for giving my abuelito a righteous goodbye," Tomás said.

"The funeral was something," I said.

"You didn't see me, but I was there," he said. "He was the man we should all be."

"I'm starting to realize that."

Neither of us said anything for a moment.

"I see Little Piwi's back," I said, turning to Little Piwi, who stood guard near the back door of the bar.

"No hard feelings. We're both professionals."

"What are your plans?" I asked.

"You're looking at the newest employee of a certain Mexican drug cartel," he said. "I convinced them that Porfirio Díaz was not the man for the job. If he couldn't handle a couple local farmers, how was he expected to maintain a city of a million people? They came to the conclusion that a local should manage their business interests in Mexicali."

"You work for them now?"

"It was the only resolution," he said. "I'm doing the same job in a different way. When threatened by a hungry animal, you feed it or it eats you."

"And Díaz?"

"He will not bother you. Or anyone."

"Then it's done?" I said. "It's over."

"For you, yes," Tomás said. "Your family is safe."

"Thanks, Tommy."

"Take care of the bar. It's his legacy and was once my home as well."

Tomás waved over Little Piwi. I shook Tomás's hand, and the two of them walked down the dirt road that ran along the canal into the darkness.

Returning to the bar, I almost bumped into Griselda standing by the back door. She watched Tomás walk away.

"He wanted to pay his respects," I said. "Say goodbye."

"Who?" She smiled. "I didn't see anyone."

We went back in the bar, found Bobby and Angie, and the four of us drank until Juan cut us all off.

At the end of the night with Juan and Angie both asleep, I found myself walking through the remains of my former house. The floor plan was still visible, but the house was irreparable. Little could be salvaged from the devastation.

I kicked at the ashes and debris, thinking that maybe some relic would appear. Maybe I thought I would find some totem from the past and everything would all of a sudden make sense. A photograph or family heirloom that would give me some sense of closure, a coda to the life of the house. Mostly I found unrecognizable, misshapen, burnt things that held no significance. Melty plastic blobs. A charred lamp that hadn't worked since I was in high school. A half-burnt book. The husk of our charred sofa.

They were only possessions. Most replaceable, all unnecessary. The most important things in my life were asleep across the road. This had been my house, but my home was more than a building.

I couldn't have known it at the time, but the moment I had returned to the Imperial Valley, I was home.

Bobby stumbled across the street and through what used to be my living room. He held a beer in each hand.

"I got to take off," Bobby said. "Wanted to say goodbye. Great wake. You did right by Mr. Morales."

"Where are you going?" I asked.

"I'm irrigating tonight and tomorrow. Have to change the water."

"You sure you need more beer to do that?"

"I figure if I keep drinking, I can drink my way all the way back to sober. That's like science, right?"

We both stood for a moment, looking at the remains of my house and the fields that surrounded it.

"You need a hand?" I asked.

"Hell yeah," he said. "Grab your mud boots, a shovel, and anything that would be fun to blow up. I've got some leftover M-100s and a few bad ideas."

Yeah, I was definitely home.

BOBBY MAVES' FIGHTIN' SONGS FOR FIGHTIN'

1. "Modern Day Cowboy"—Tesla
2. "Hair of the Dog"—Nazareth
3. "Pure Rock Fury"—Clutch
4. "The Hammer"—Motörhead
5. "Round Up the Horses"—Orange Goblin
6. "P.F.F."—Hank Williams III
7. "The Trooper"—Iron Maiden
8. "I'm Shipping up to Boston"—Dropkick Murphys
9. "Rock You"—Helix
10. "Cajun Hell"—Exodus

11. “How Heavy This Axe”—The Sword

12. “Battery”—Metallica

13. “Fundamental”—Puya

14. “King of the Road”—Fu Manchu

15. “Ol’ Unfaithful”—Alabama Thunderpussy

16. “The Legend of Pat Brown”—The Vandals

17. “Where Eagles Dare”—The Misfits

18. “Cruisin’ for a Bruisin’”—The Reverend Horton Heat

19. “Powertrip”—Monster Magnet

20. “Jerk-Off”—Tool

ACKNOWLEDGMENTS

Huge thanks to:

The entire team at Thomas & Mercer. For the last five years (and five books), I have had the pleasure of working with an incredibly smart and enthusiastic group of booklovers. It's a good feeling to trust your publisher and be trusted by them. A special shout-out to the incomparable Jacque Ben-Zekry, one of my favorite people on the planet.

My developmental editor, David Downing. We've worked together on four books now, and it takes a lot of pressure off me in the writing process knowing that he's going to be keeping me honest after the drafts are done.

Bart Lessard, my friend and the author of the novels Rakehell and Dead Men's Teeth. He's the only person I trust to read my works in progress. That's a big deal. There's nobody I'd rather have a drink with and talk writing and story. And for the word, "masturbpiece."

Every single person that calls Holtville, California, their home. It's just a dot on the map to the rest of the world, but those of us that know it, know how special it is. I'm proud of where I'm from. These books wouldn't exist without the uniqueness that makes my hometown great. Go Vikings!

My family and friends. The support that everyone has given to me and my work for the last two decades has been amazing. Especially my mom, my biggest fan.

The crime fiction community, including the authors, readers, booksellers, convention organizers, reviewers, and everyone in between. Discovering this second family was one of the great perks of publishing my first book. I have never met a more supportive and inclusive group of people.

My incredible wife, Roxanne. I don't know how I got so lucky to spend my life with such a smart, talented, funny, curious, and beautiful woman, but I'm glad I won that bet.

Imperial Valley was written at Beulahland and Rocking Frog Cafe in Portland, Oregon.

ABOUT THE AUTHOR

Painting by Roxanne Patruznick

Johnny Shaw was born and raised on the Calexico/Mexicali border, the setting for his award-winning Jimmy Veeder Fiasco series, which includes the novels *Dove Season* and *Plaster City*. He is also the author of the Anthony Award–winning adventure novel *Big Maria* and the urban-crime novel *Floodgate*. His shorter work has appeared in *Thuglit*, *Crime Factory*, *Blood & Tacos*, *Shotgun Honey*, *Plots with Guns*, and numerous anthologies. Johnny lives in Portland, Oregon, with his wife, artist Roxanne Patruznick.